Published by Pink Tree Publishing Limited in 2023

All characters and events in this publication, other than those clearly in the public domain, are fictitious and any resemblance to real persons, living or dead, is purely coincidental.

Copyright © Pink Tree Publishing Limited.

The moral right of the author has been asserted.

All rights reserved. This book or any portion thereof may not be reproduced or used in any manner whatsoever without the express written permission of the publisher except for the use of brief quotations in a book review.

For questions and comments about this book, please contact pinktreepublishing@gmail.com

www.pinktreepublishing.com
www.agathafrost.com

V 1.2

WANT TO BE KEPT UP TO DATE WITH AGATHA FROST RELEASES? *SIGN UP THE FREE NEWSLETTER!*

www.AgathaFrost.com

You can also follow **Agatha Frost** across social media. Search 'Agatha Frost' on:

Facebook
Twitter
Goodreads
Instagram

ALSO BY AGATHA FROST

Peridale Cafe

30. Mince Pies and Madness

29. Pumpkins and Peril

28. Eton Mess and Enemies

27. Banana Bread and Betrayal

26. Carrot Cake and Concern

25. Marshmallows and Memories

24. Popcorn and Panic

23. Raspberry Lemonade and Ruin

22. Scones and Scandal

21. Profiteroles and Poison

20. Cocktails and Cowardice

19. Brownies and Bloodshed

18. Cheesecake and Confusion

17. Vegetables and Vengeance

16. Red Velvet and Revenge

15. Wedding Cake and Woes

14. Champagne and Catastrophes

13. Ice Cream and Incidents

12. Blueberry Muffins and Misfortune

11. Cupcakes and Casualties

10. Gingerbread and Ghosts

9. Birthday Cake and Bodies

8. Fruit Cake and Fear

7. Macarons and Mayhem

6. Espresso and Evil

5. Shortbread and Sorrow

4. Chocolate Cake and Chaos

3. Doughnuts and Deception

2. Lemonade and Lies

1. Pancakes and Corpses

<u>Claire's Candles</u>

1. Vanilla Bean Vengeance

2. Black Cherry Betrayal

3. Coconut Milk Casualty

4. Rose Petal Revenge

5. Fresh Linen Fraud

6. Toffee Apple Torment

7. Candy Cane Conspiracies

8. Wildflower Worries

9. Frosted Plum Fears

Other

The Agatha Frost Winter Anthology

Peridale Cafe Book 1-10

Peridale Cafe Book 11-20

Claire's Candles Book 1-3

1

Sweet spices filled the air of Julia's Café as she transferred her latest batch of mince pies from their cooling rack. Cinnamon and nutmeg blended with hints of citrus zest atop the inviting scent of brown sugar and dark caramel. Under the stark kitchen lighting, the golden crusts glistened with a melt-in-the-mouth richness. They were as buttery as Michael Bublé's voice, crooning Christmas hits on the radio atop the fridge.

Though her hands worked with expert precision to stack the tiny pies on the serving plate, Julia's mind raced, never further from baking. She had poured extra care into preparing these festive delicacies, wanting every detail perfect. But it would take more than Christmas pies to lift spirits tonight.

Beyond the kitchen, muffled voices mingled in the enclosed yard outside, replacing the café's usual buzz. The front was closed and cleaned, ready for the morning.

But Julia hadn't stayed late to bake mince pies.

Tonight was different.

Tonight, Julia and her fellow villagers had a mission.

The creak of the back door announced Jessie's arrival from the yard, letting in the frenzied whispers of the crowd before she rested the door in the frame. Julia's daughter wasted no time and plucked a still-cooling mince pie from the rack, juggling the hot pastry before it could burn her fingers.

"I didn't think you could top them, but these taste even better than last year's batch," Jessie said after a steaming bite. "New recipe?"

Julia shook her head, dusting icing sugar over the stacked spiral. "My mum's usual recipe. Maybe a little extra nutmeg?"

"Well, they're delicious," Jessie said, scanning the hundreds of trays lining the counters as she leaned under to dig out a box of toilet rolls. "People will have no problem gobbling them down tomorrow."

As Jessie counted the toilet rolls crammed inside the box with a scanning finger, Julia bit her lip, her mind as far from tomorrow's mince pie-eating competition as it had been from the baking. "Are you sure tonight is a good idea?"

"It was *your* idea," Jessie reminded her.

"After a drink at Richie's."

"I think it's brilliant."

"It could make things worse."

"Isn't that what we want?"

"Worse for *us*." Julia sighed, closing her mother's handwritten recipe book, not that she'd needed it; she knew the standards by heart. "I was *half*-joking."

"Yeah, well... sometimes the best ideas come from a joke over a cocktail. It's harmless fun, Mum." She shrugged, licking sticky cinnamon crumbs from her lips. "Nobody gets hurt, just... inconvenienced. And face it—compared to what James Jacobson is trying to do to us, it's *nothing*."

The distant rumble of machinery punctuated her words, and Julia knew her daughter was right. She inhaled, steadying her nerves as the roaring engines rolled closer. She hated head-on confrontation unless she had a good reason, and James *had* given them many reasons since announcing his development plans.

Their concerned phone calls had fallen on deaf ears. Worried letters to the council had gone unanswered, and protesting emails might as well have been lost in cyberspace. And their placards, posters, and petitions had been as useful as a mountain of junk mail piling up on the doormat of a vacated house.

James Jacobson had left them little choice.

"Before it's too late," Jessie said, nodding at the back door, the toilet rolls crammed under her arm. "They start digging tomorrow, and before we know it, half of Peridale will be bulldozed to make way for the Howarth Estate."

Taking a deep breath, she scooped up the plate and nodded for Jessie to open the door. "You're right. Before it's too late."

Out in the icy yard, all eyes turned to Julia, and she was glad to see some smiles pricking up frost-bitten cheeks as flared nostrils inhaled the result of her evening's baking.

No matter what happened tonight, it had become Julia's mission to keep spirits high in their fight against James. Distracted or not, she could make a few hundred mince pies blindfolded, with one arm tied behind her back. She stepped out of the kitchen and let eager hands grab for their pre-fight provisions.

The turnout in the café's modest yard astonished her. So many familiar faces mingled in the shadows, their breath frosting the air. Julia's husband, Barker, stood by the door to his PI office under the café, steady as always. Her gran and step-grandfather, Dot and Percy, crowded around the cracked open gate with Ethel, their former foe turned friend. They peered out at the field together like an octogenarian totem pole.

"Even better than last year's," Barker said after a bite.

"I already said that. Get your own line," Jessie teased, eliciting titters from the tense group. "More nutmeg seems to have—"

"You're *never* going to believe the size of the digger!" Dot exclaimed.

"*Two* diggers," Percy added. "Are they wanting to reach the Earth's core?"

"They'll have that field of fine grass chewed up in *seconds*," Ethel muttered. "Look at *him*, strutting about like a circus ringleader. I've never seen a man with a face I'd like to slap more than James Jacobson's!"

"We'll keep our hands to ourselves," Detective Inspector Laura Moyes instructed above the noise, letting out a puff of vape smoke as her girlfriend—and Julia's oldest school friend—Roxy, plucked two mince pies from the diminishing stock. "I won't hesitate to make arrests if I need to. But you're right, he does have that kind of face."

"Always grinning," Amy Clark, the church organist, whispered, pulling her pale pink cardigan tight. "Gives me the chills."

"Smirking, more like," Shilpa muttered. "And that man can't take 'no' for an answer. He's made a dozen offers to buy my post office for his road access, but I still won't—"

"Quiet!" Dot waved a gloved hand. "Listen…"

The machinery groaned to a halt closer to the back wall of the yard than Julia liked. Doors slammed, and moments later, heavy footsteps padded down the cobbled alley alongside the café.

"Tomorrow, a new age begins for Peridale!" bellowed the unmistakable voice of James Jacobson. He slapped his palm against the café wall as he passed, the thump making Julia flinch. "Nothing can stand in our way."

Raucous laughter echoed off aged stone, curdling the peppermint and liquorice tea sitting in Julia's empty stomach; she hadn't been able to eat a mince pie yet. She met Barker's firm gaze, drawing strength from his calm demeanour. James and his associates carried on, their posh accents striking a jarring note in the tense air.

"Once we get the path cleared, we'll start on the village green," one builder said. "How big do you want this roundabout to be, boss?"

Gritting her teeth, Julia fought to contain her outrage. How dare they discuss steamrolling Peridale as if it were decided? She sensed the crowd looking at her, waiting for a response.

"I turned away all accommodation requests from James' builders," Evelyn assured them all, clutching her crystal necklaces. "The tea leaves promise fate *is* on our side."

But they needed more than fate to combat James' ruthless ambition. They needed direct action. Julia hardened her worries with a bite of the nutmeg-heavy mince pie before accepting a roll of toilet paper from Jessie; it *was* better than last year's batch, but maybe a little too much sugar.

If James insisted on threatening their home, they would show him this village would not surrender without a fight. Unfurling the first unsullied white sheet, Julia licked the crumbs from her lips.

"Julia?" Dot whispered. "Ready when you are."

Without hesitation, Julia gave the nod, and Dot pushed open the creaky gate into the night.

Villagers poured into the moonlit field behind the café, brandishing their toilet rolls. In moments, the dormant machinery disappeared under swirling white streams, but Julia hung back to study the gigantic sign with the computer-generated renders of the new sprawl of homes that would soon jut from the edge of the grass.

The sign read: 'Coming Soon! The Howarth Estate

- An abandoned 1800s plan of local visionary, Duncan Howarth, reborn in the modern age, for a modern Peridale. Phase One coming next year. Enquire to secure your plot now!'

Two hundred houses to shadow their small rural community. Two hundred houses out of most locals' price ranges. Two hundred new stony-faced newcomers with deep pockets who'd erase the village she loved. A brand-new roundabout occupied the space where the village green sat, with a road leading to the pearly gates of the new estate—right through where Julia's Café stood.

Years of memories in the café flashed before her eyes. It had seen divorces, deaths, births, new family, found family, long-lost family, all over a slice of cake and a cup of tea. Julia's family, Julia's friends, their stories as deeply rooted as the grass and trees James would start digging up in the morning.

Julia charged into the crowd, tossing the defiant white streams of paper over the diggers. Peridale was their home, and they wouldn't let James Jacobson rebuild it in his own image.

Not without a fight.

2

The winter chill nipped at Julia's fingers as she arranged silver bells across the café's frosted bay window while the church choir welcomed the first morning of the Christmas markets. Their belted rendition of 'O Come, All Ye Faithful' rose into the misty morning air in steaming trails above the village green. All around them, stallholders unpacked their wares, transforming the green into the annual festive haven.

Behind Julia, Jessie smiled at her phone in one hand while draping tinsel around the picture frames with the other, the distracted picture of young love. Near the revolving display cabinet, Sue took her time selecting baubles for the small tree, her brows pinched in a different kind of distraction.

Despite the yuletide buzz swelling through their small community, an anxious twist left over from last night's antics lingered in Julia. She gave the silvery bells one final adjustment before turning to the source of the latest knot in the rope: five hundred pounds in shiny purple twenties laid out across the café's counter. Jessie caught her eye as she tucked the last corner of tinsel behind the framed sketch of the café as The Shepard's Rest pub from centuries ago.

"Figured out where that money came from yet, super sleuth?" Jessie asked.

"The envelope was waiting on the doormat when I came in this morning," Julia recited again, folding her arms across her crimson Christmas jumper dotted with gingerbread men. "Aside from the 'For the cause' scribbled on the front, there are no other clues. And I don't recognise the handwriting."

"Me neither," Sue muttered.

"I don't think I do either." Jessie tilted her head at the envelope as she tugged rustling tinsel from the 'Christmas Decs' box dug from the store cupboard. "Well, that narrows it down. Could be anyone."

"A *rich* anyone," Sue pointed out.

Julia nodded to herself, a small smile playing on her lips as she eyed the anonymous donation. It wasn't so much the amount that mattered—though each penny was a soldier in their campaign—but the solidarity it represented against James Jacobson's Howarth Estate plans. That sense of unity had been a hard-won battle, sparked by the scandal she'd helped drag into the light: the corruption of James and the now-disgraced Greg Morgan, the MP who'd resigned from behind bars.

Yet, as the initial fury settled into a simmer in the streets of Peridale, villagers lulled themselves into a false sense of victory. Julia knew better. With Greg awaiting trial and the villagers' guard down, James' plans were far from thwarted. She could almost hear the echo of bulldozers in the distance, a stark reminder that their fight was far from over.

"It'll pay for more flyers at least," Jessie said, draping a length of red tinsel around Julia's neck. "I could ask Veronica about an ad in *The Peridale Post* too? That'll get us a full-page spread. We need to keep momentum up over Christmas, or people will get distracted by all the mince pies and carols, and come the new year—"

"Bye-bye Peridale's soul," Sue interrupted with a sigh.

And bye-bye to Julia's Café if James continued to twist arms to get his elusive road access approved. The echo of his pat on the outside wall shuddered down the alley and prickled across Julia's shoulders.

"Great idea, Jessie," Julia said instead, joining Sue

in the bauble selection; they'd opted for the blue and silver set this year. "Any ideas what we could do with the donation, Sue?"

But Sue's distant stare was fixed on the cash, her fingers frozen in mid-air with a bauble inches from the nearest plastic branch. Julia sensed the turmoil churning beneath her younger sister's placid expression; she'd confessed weeks ago about accepting an immense 'mortgage' loan from James in the spring, one that had trapped her family financially even as it kept them afloat. Sue had sobbed over the shame of taking his money, of how trusting James had been a mistake that now had them barely covering the repayments of their crumbling new-build house. And Julia felt helpless.

"Maybe our Christmas money fairy will visit you next?" Julia whispered, giving Sue's shoulder a gentle nudge.

Sue blinked, snapping from her thoughts as she managed a thin smile. "That would solve a few things. Pearl and Dottie's room has a crack running from floor to ceiling, and the radiators are on the wobble again. Motorised valves have gone. They were only new when our house was built last year, but the plumber said they were fitted wrong."

"And we'll be having more of the same on *that* field if James gets his way," Jessie said, jerking her head towards the back wall as she gathered the shiny notes into a pile. "What if this is from him?"

"From James?" Julia asked, scepticism wrinkling her nose. "Why would James fund protests against himself?"

Jessie shrugged. "To mess with us? He's not against sneaky games. Proved that with how far he went to win that planning committee last month." She squinted at the envelope again before shaking her dark hair. "Was just a thought."

Julia examined the cash again, doubt churning her gut. She'd ripped up a blank cheque from James to snatch the café so he could knock it down for his road, so the last thing she wanted was his dirty money muddying the waters. The manipulative tactic would never have crossed Julia's mind, but now that her daughter had said it... had this gift come with invisible strings attached?

"Wherever it's from, we'll put it to good use," Julia declared, scooping the money into the donation box for their campaign. She wouldn't let James sabotage the spirit fuelling their efforts, no matter his ploys. "The man might claim to be a local, but he doesn't know how *we* think. Not really. We're never going to beat James at *his* game. He needs to beat *us* at *ours*. If he wants to fund that, *let him*."

"Nothing comes for free," Sue said, her eyes clouding again.

"James hasn't gone back on his agreements yet, has he?" Julia asked gently. "With your loan from him? Or co-owning the library?"

Sue shook her head. "But it's only a matter of time, isn't it?"

Julia ached to take away her younger sister's burden, but no easy solution for Sue's dilemma existed if James held financial power over her. She could only hope to topple his greedy ambitions before her sister's family faced repercussions for allying against him.

"His fight isn't with you and Neil," Julia assured her. "We'll figure a way out of this, I promise." Even as she offered hollow reassurances, Julia struggled to see a neat solution to their predicament. "There's always a way."

Sue didn't look convinced either. Jessie rolled her eyes at Julia's optimism from the other side of the counter as she framed the beaded curtain with tinsel.

"His fight is with the *whole* of Peridale," Jessie muttered, forcing the stapler into the wall with a whack. "And he'll buy up the whole village given half a chance."

"There's always a way," Julia repeated, taking the

star from Sue's frozen hand to wriggle it onto the peak of the tree. "*Always.*"

The next hour flew by as the market stalls, packed with hand-crafted decorations, fresh wreaths, roasted nuts, and mulled wine, brought in the customers. Regulars and tourists flooded the café, shaking off the chill with red-cheeked smiles.

Working like the well-oiled machine the trio had become, they sent out a flurry of sweet gingerbread lattes topped with swirled cream dusted with gingerbread crumbs, steaming mugs of marshmallows bobbing in cinnamon-spiced hot chocolate, mountains of mince pies, and their new bestselling turkey, cranberry, and stuffing sandwiches with mini pigs in blankets on the side. The new drinks had been Julia's idea, the sandwich Jessie's, and Sue had costed everything up to give them the best profit margins Julia had seen in all her Christmases working at the café.

If the field behind the café weren't a constant lingering presence in Julia's mind, the morning would have been as perfect as they came in the café.

But it was difficult to ignore.

For every grinning tourist, unaware of the peril Peridale faced, there was double the number of antsy locals, and Julia only had to let her gaze linger on Sue for more than a few seconds to see how subdued she was under her polite smile.

Before Julia could lose herself in cooking up a solution to her sister's dilemma, their gran, Dot, burst into the café, with Percy and Ethel in tow. Their two dogs, Lady and Bruce, trotted at their feet, in matching fluffy jumpers. Dot and Percy had dragged their usual fur coats out of the wardrobe, and their new friend—and shadow—Ethel had a fur to match.

"Who invited the yetis?" Jessie whispered, already reaching for a large teapot while Julia grabbed the cups to put on a tray, suppressing a laugh.

"*Fresh flyers!*" Dot's voice cut through the din as the elderly trio split up and weaved through the tables to distribute the new material; their fur coats rubbed against everyone too slow to move out of the way. "It's *imperative* that you read *every* word, folks."

"Imperative," Percy echoed.

"Important *also* works," Ethel added, casting a glance at Dot. "But yes, make sure to read *every* word. Both sides. Took twice as long to print them."

"You stood there and watched Percy and I do all the work as usual, Ethel," Dot said. "But every word. *Both* sides."

"I did *just* say that, Dorothy."

"And *I* already advised they should read *every* word."

Jessie leaned in and said, "There's an echo in here. And to think, this is them on the *same* side for once. I think I preferred it when they were at each other's—" She straightened up. "Snazzy coat, Dot! Mince pie, or are you saving room for the eating contest later?"

"I shan't be taking part in such a grotesque display of gluttony," Dot said, tugging her fur coat together before she dropped the latest stack of flyers onto the counter. "Sue, you'll want to have a word with your Neil. He's just told us this is the last batch we'll be getting from the library for free, despite the printer being a *public* resource open to *all* villagers."

Sue paused behind the counter, on her way to the kitchen with a tray stacked with cups balanced against her hip. "You've printed hundreds this week alone, Gran. The budget for paper and ink has gone through the roof."

"Oh, pish posh!" Dot wafted a hand. "James Jacobscrooge likely has more loose coins in his coat pockets than the library spends on paper in a year!"

"*Jacobscrooge?*" Jessie mouthed to Julia as she put the pot on the tray. Julia could only shrug. "That'll never catch on."

"Well, Dorothy, I *did* point out," Ethel said,

clearing her throat as she joined Dot at the counter, "that it wouldn't make much sense for a weasel like Jacobscrooge to fund our campaign from his own pockets, would it?"

"Maybe he didn't leave the donation, after all," Jessie suggested.

"What donation?" Dot asked.

Scanning the café, Julia retrieved the donation box from the counter and pried the lid off to show Dot and Ethel the notes bursting over the edges.

"Anonymous donation 'for the cause,'" Julia whispered, tugging out a chunk of the money. "Which means paying for our own paper and ink from now on."

"Who sent it?" Dot asked.

"You know 'imperative' but you don't know 'anonymous?'" Ethel huffed, folding her arms over the thick fur. "Sometimes, I wonder if you snacked on lead paint chips as a child, Dorothy."

"I'm sure *you* did. Would explain your hair." Dot cast a sharp glance at Ethel's short lilac curls while she pushed up her own grey ones. "And of course I know what it means. But *you* know, and *I* know, and *everyone* in Peridale knows that if there's a mystery to solve, Julia *will* solve it."

"Sorry, Gran." Julia secured the lid. "No clues so far."

"Bah humbug, I say," Ethel grumbled. "This money smells fishier than Dot's socks. Who has that sort of money lying around to throw at us?"

"This from the woman with breath strong enough to pull in ships to a harbour." Dot tucked the money inside her jacket after a quick flick through. "And let's be grateful that there is someone out there. We might have to upgrade our operation and go to a real print shop. The library isn't feeling so welcoming these days, what with all of James' propaganda."

"Posters and roller-banners all over the place!" Percy announced, joining them after finishing his table canvassing. "There's even a dedicated computer for registering interest in the Howarth Estate houses."

Julia pictured the creep of corporate posters and digital interfaces corrupting the cosy library's nooks and crannies. It was only last summer they'd fought so hard to stop the public library falling into James' clutches. His co-ownership was the compromise that had steadied the ship, but it sounded as though the flag had swapped since her most recent visits when researching her café's history.

"As I said, Sue, you'll want to have a word with that husband of yours," Dot warned as Sue carried their tray to the table nearest the counter where Ethel and Percy had settled. "He needs to pick a side."

"Neil *is* on our side. Believe me, he's no happier

about the posters than you. But he's only the manager." Her averted eyes revealed her worries about Neil facing repercussions. "James holds the strings."

"Even Pinocchio cut his strings eventually, dear," Dot said.

Before Julia could wade in to defend her sister, the rev of a sports car engine drew her attention outside. Her pulse spiked as James' sleek silver vehicle glided down the cobbled-road and screeched to a silencing halt outside Richie's Bar. For a moment, the busy market stood still to stare in his direction. The locals were glaring, the tourists gawking. And the man himself, James Jacobson, emerged wearing a sharp suit, dark sunglasses, and an obnoxious grin, surveying the Christmas market as though there was nothing there.

Julia's grip tightened around the donation tin as a team of builders hurried from the side of the café towards James. Whatever they said to him caused his smile to drop, his sunglasses to rip off, and his stare to go straight between the café and the post office. He set off at a jog as Julia pushed through the beaded curtain into the gleaming kitchen.

"I'll take the rubbish out," she announced, scooping the half-empty bag from the bin.

No one attempted to stop her as she snuck out the back door into the yard's crisp cold. Bypassing the vestibule leading to Barker's basement office, she traversed the slippery flagstones towards the back gate. Clutching the bag, she paused to admire the toilet paper-draped sign with its hidden digital renderings. The mummified diggers were a work of art too.

James stood, flabbergasted, surveying his vandalised machinery. Around him, a dozen builders swarmed, tearing off chunks of frozen toilet paper with loud cracks and crinkles. Julia watched, a swell of satisfaction rising within her as his scanning gaze landed on her. She lobbed the rubbish bag into the bin as a scowl dragged down his handsome chiselled features. He raised a hand, beckoning her over with a wave.

But Julia would do no such thing.

"Might want to grab your winter coat, James," she called. "Frosts this time of year can be brutal."

Before he could respond, she pivoted and marched back inside, head held high. Let him stew outside in the cold. She had a café to run and a village to save. The drive to keep fighting surged through her veins as she resumed her place behind the counter, ready for whatever the day sent her way. Yet, as she grabbed a teapot for Evelyn's usual, an uneasy whisper in the back of her mind hinted that the morning's triumphs might pale before the trials yet to come.

3

Jessie meandered through the market on her lunch break, dodging children chasing each other with snowballs mushed together from the melting piles clinging to the edges of the road. She welcomed the normality away from Dot screaming "Just one more pie, Percy!" at the chaotic mince pie eating contest.

She passed a stall selling mulled wine where a familiar figure stood examining a delicate glass bird ornament, turning it to catch the afternoon light.

She smiled to herself, taking in Dante Clarke's stylish camel-coloured wool jacket and navy-blue scarf knotted at his throat. Even on his days off from the *Riverswick Chronicle*, the reporter was always dressed as if he'd stepped out of a catalogue.

Catching her gaze, his dark eyes sparkled as he raised a steaming paper cup, held in gloved fingers, in a casual greeting.

"Lunchtime tipple?" Dante tilted the cup towards a vat of mulled wine simmering over a small fire, his voice smooth and teasing. "I warn you, it's dangerously strong this year."

Jessie considered it, stepping closer. "I'd love to, but maybe later? Promised Veronica I'd stop by her stall." She touched his arm, her fingers lingering. "But I'll be back, so don't wander off."

"Don't take too long, yeah?" He slipped an arm around her waist, and she caught her breath as he flashed that wide grin that made her middle feel funny. "I've missed you."

"We went to the cinema two days ago."

"Exactly." Leaning in for a kiss, he added, "Practically a lifetime."

"This shouldn't take long. Still on for tomorrow?"

"Meeting your parents *officially*?" He inhaled, scratching at his short, knotted hair with gloved fingertips. "Your dad's an ex-detective, right?"

"He won't interrogate you." She paused, and added, "Much. We could rearrange if you're too scared?"

"As if." He winked, loosening his hold of her. "Go on. Sooner you're done with Veronica, sooner I can warm you up with some mulled wine. Your nose is as red as Rudolf's." He kissed the tip of her nose and stepped back, leaning on the bar of the mulled wine shop. His elbow slipped off the polished wood, and he spilt wine into the frosty grass. "You didn't see that."

"See what?"

As Jessie turned to leave, Dante caught her hand, his fingers encircling hers. She paused as their eyes locked, pulse quickening at his touch. For a second, the chatter of the market faded, the charged space between them alive with unspoken words. Jessie softened, slowly sliding her hand from his lingering grasp.

"Five minutes," she said.

Dante's smile crinkled the corners of his eyes. "I'm counting down the seconds."

Head low, Jessie grinned to herself as she weaved through the villagers bundled against the winter chill, as nervous for Dante meeting her parents as he was, but she wasn't going to let him know that. She still couldn't believe she was dating someone, let alone someone as handsome, intelligent, and funny as Dante. Nearing *The Peridale Post*'s debut stall at the market, she couldn't believe she could hear the raised voice of her editor over the festive hum, either.

Veronica Hilt, Jessie's other part-time boss when she wasn't working at the café, grappled with a woman grasping for a stack of flyers. Behind oversized red glasses, Veronica's piercing stare seared into her challenger, who had faint laugh lines creasing her polite yet insistent smile. The woman's tailored emerald blazer and jangling badge attached to a lanyard lent an air of authority; Jessie had spotted her weaving through the stalls with a clipboard a few times that morning.

The flyers, she recognised in an instant. They included a picture of the recent 'Get to know your local MP, Greg Morgan' front page, detailing his arrest, along with a picture Jessie had taken of him being dragged out of Wellington Heights in handcuffs only a few weeks ago. The tongue-in-cheek headline had caused a small stir when it had gone to print, and then, like most things in Peridale, people mostly moved on. The woman fighting for the flyers, however, seemed far from moving on.

"There were *no* rules about what we could or could not have on our stalls," Veronica grunted through gritted teeth, her grip unrelenting. "I read the terms and conditions inside and out, Martha."

"I don't care what *you* think, Veronica," Martha, the woman in the emerald blazer, muttered in return. "I won't have you spreading lies about Greg at *my* market."

"You only organise the market, Martha," came

Evelyn's airy voice, the mystic B&B owner, who had a crystal ball and tarot card stall next to *The Post*'s. "This market is for the people of Peridale, something you clearly won't understand if you're on a man like Greg Morgan's side."

Evelyn returned to her crystal ball while Martha and Veronica grappled with the flyers once more. Jessie edged forward, prepared to leap in, but with a sharp tug, Martha stumbled backward and toppled into a muddy puddle on the green. Her winning flyers fluttered around her like fresh snow. She looked around the market as shoppers slowed to watch the kerfuffle, a scarlet hue blooming across her cheeks. Chest rising from a shallow breath under the weight of the silent stares, she tried to shake the mud—as stubborn as her embarrassment—from her hands.

Despite their altercation, Veronica stepped around the stall to offer a helping hand, but Martha pushed Veronica on her way up, causing her to fall back into the stall. Her large glasses tumbled off in the process. Jessie, incensed by Martha's aggression, rushed to steady her editor.

"That was uncalled for!" Jessie cried at the woman she didn't know. "She was trying to help you up."

"I don't want *her* help," Martha said, staring down at the flyers soaking up the muddy puddles. "She's done enough damage to our family."

Examining Martha's ID badge, Jessie noticed 'Event Organiser' etched below 'Martha Morgan'. *Morgan*? Greg's surname and Veronica's maiden name. Couldn't be a coincidence, and she had said they were family. Did Greg have a slightly younger wife Jessie's research hadn't uncovered? Or maybe a fourth sibling Veronica hadn't told her about?

"You've always seen the worst in Greg. You're jealous of his successes," Martha continued, and Veronica's response came as a mocking snort, but Martha persisted, "Greg's arrest was all a scapegoat to distract from James Jacobson and his schemes. *He's* the real crook here. Greggory has nothing to do with any of it."

"Is that what your precious Greggory told you?" Veronica muttered under her breath. "I'm not going to argue with you about which awful man is worse, Martha."

"Because you *know* I'm right."

"Is that what I think?" Veronica couldn't hold back her laugh as she scratched at her spiky grey hair. "You have a problem with my stall? I want it in writing. I paid my pitch fee like everyone else. Until then, run along, Martha. I'm sure someone is committing a minor market infraction somewhere."

"You're a witch, Veronica. A *rotten* witch, and you always have been!"

Veronica composed herself with a measured shake of her head. Stooping to retrieve her glasses, her hand stopped mid-air as Martha crushed them underfoot with a booted stomp. Muttering about knowing 'the real Greggory', the market organiser stormed off into the crowd.

"*The Tower!*" Evelyn declared at her stall as she turned over a tarot card with a knowing nod, her voice carrying over the crowd's murmur. "Ruin, downfall... James and Greg, *both* ensnared by fate's trap. Their downfall *is* inevitable."

A hushed interlude ensued as Veronica settled herself behind the 'SAVE PERIDALE'S SOUL sponsored by *The Peridale Post*' banner fronting the stall. The market's rhythm fluttered as the silent onlookers traced the organiser's every move with amused and bemused stares, but they soon moved on.

"Martha's your family?" Jessie asked Veronica. "Another sister?"

Her chin recoiled into her neck at the suggestion. "No."

"You have an older brother," Jessie offered, almost nervous about bringing Sebastian up. "You don't talk about him either."

Veronica dug in her coat pocket to pull out a second pair of glasses, these plain black, but no less giant. From another pocket, she produced a satsuma and started peeling it with one hand while she pushed on the spare frames with the other. "Because Sebastian has been dead for years. Martha is our youngest cousin. She grew up over the hill from us. She worships Greg and always has."

"Why?"

"Not important," Veronica said, staring off towards the distant rolling fields. "There's a fresh batch in that bag there. One to anyone who'll take them on your way back to the café."

She took the flyers, but Jessie still had questions after the unexpected altercation.

"If you want to talk about anything, I'm—"

"I know." Veronica cut her off with a forced smile. "You're a sweet, sensitive girl, Jessie, and I know your generation likes to talk and Tweet through every thought and emotion, but I don't need to focus on things that aren't important right now." Adding fresh flyers to the stall, she said, "What's important is spreading the word about Greg and James before a giant housing estate pops up on the other side of your mum's café. Everything else is white noise, and Martha talks nothing but white noise."

"But why would Martha be so convinced of Greg's innocence?" Jessie pressed, unable to help herself.

Veronica's posture stiffened, her focus anchored on the newspaper's headline while she avoided Jessie's inquiring gaze. Her lip quivered as she summoned a frail smile, but it was erased by the sound of a balloon popping like a gunshot in the distance. She glanced around, her whole body tensed as if she were expecting someone to emerge from the crowd.

"You're worried Six is still out there, aren't you?" Jessie kept her voice soft. "Carrying out Greg's last order to have you..." She couldn't finish the sentence. "Six hasn't been seen since Greg was arrested, and he's the last member of the Cotswold Crew gang who isn't behind bars, so I don't think he'd—"

"I'm *fine*, honestly. And a stupid system if you ask me. Numbers for names? No wonder the rest of that gang are behind bars. *Flyers*."

Jessie gave Veronica's shoulder a final squeeze before moving into the crowd, resolved to focus on her duties. She worried about Six being out there too, her own run-ins with the thug still making her jump at every noise outside her flat after dark, but like with Dante, she wanted to keep a brave face to not worry anyone.

With everything that had been going on these last few months, she was tired. Looking down at the headline, she'd hoped putting Greg behind bars would have ended the worrying, but it had only started a new chapter.

Flyers in hand, Jessie knitted through the villagers,

pausing every few steps to press pages into gloved hands. Most accepted the information, while some waved her off, not wanting to face the controversy embroiling their village.

At the vegetable stall selling parsnips, Brussels sprouts, and marked-down pumpkins left over from Halloween, Denise Coleman was all too happy to take a flyer.

"This Jacobson fella won't stop making me offers to buy my farm," she said with a shake of her head. "And I've heard he's trying to buy Howarth Forest too, and the Farley's farm. He'll tear it all down as soon as he gets the chance. *And* my Polly saw James' builder sniffing around her school. Think he's trying to close us in with a ring of fancy houses until we all leave?"

That was exactly what Jessie thought James was planning, but before she could open her mouth to respond, screeching tires drowned her out.

James' sleek sports car swung into reverse outside Richie's Bar. He mounted the curb and came to an abrupt stop, tossing puffs of leaves in its wake. With tyres spinning, James executed a clumsy three-point turn, his back bumper clipping a nearby stall on the way before he raced away in a blur. A cardboard box tumbled off the edge, sending glass baubles crashing to the cobbles in an explosion of red and gold shards.

Martha threw her hands up as she raced to the

edge of the green, screaming for James to come back and pay for the damage, but he was already roaring past The Plough pub up the street. Jessie shook her head, doubting if they could ever pierce James' impenetrable ego.

"I think you're right," Jessie replied to Denise.

"Can't believe he grew up at Fern Moore. Makes you wonder where it all went wrong," she said, holding her hand out for a cut. "Gimme some of those flyers. I'll make sure every one of my customers gets one."

"And mine," said Malcolm Johnson at the Christmas wreath stall next to hers. "Sooner that swine leaves us alone, the better."

Handing over the flyers as the growling engine faded into the distance, Jessie glanced at her watch, remembering her promise to join Dante at the mulled wine stall. She hurried back with her last few flyers, but he'd moved on, leaving his cup behind half-finished. A text message waited on her phone.

> **DANTE**
>
> Sorry, had to run. Chronicle needed someone to cover the riveting story of an Oakwood Nursing home resident building a giant model train set in their room (think they rang the paper themselves???) I'll see you tomorrow night? Excited and nervous. Nervcited? Call me a wordsmith ;) P.s. I owe you a cup of mulled wine.

Jessie bit back a smile as she typed out her reply.

> **JESSIE**
>
> I'll hold you to that, wordsmith. And don't worry, I'll tell Mum and Dad to go easy on you. Only two or three rounds of interrogation. And I'm nervcited too ;) Enjoy the trains.

Handing out the last of the flyers to the people between the edge of the green and the café, Jessie returned to the warmth with only a few minutes left of her break.

Inside, spectators leaned forward, hands cupped around mouths bellowing encouragement. Percy sat red-faced at a table in the middle, pie crumbs resting on his potbellied penguin jumper while Amy remained cool as she nibbled the flaky crust edge like a delicate squirrel. They were the last two remaining still scoffing down pies, with the other eight who'd started the contest slumped in their chairs, looking worse for wear. Julia hovered by, grinning with her thumb positioned over the button of the stopwatch.

"*C'mon, Percy!*" Dot cried, beating her fist down on the table. "You can win this. Amy is slowing down!"

"I think I might burst, dear."

"Don't be a quitter!"

"I think I'm going to…"

As Percy buried his head into the bucket between the two tables, Jessie returned to the counter to finish the turkey and stuffing sandwich she'd abandoned to go and see how Veronica was getting on.

Peering past Dot as she tried to spur Percy on, Jessie noticed Martha weaving in and out of the stalls, keeping a watchful eye over things. Given everything they'd printed about Greg in *The Post*—cousin or not—how could Martha believe his innocence? Jessie hoped there weren't more people like her out there.

"And that's *time!*" Julia called, clicking the stopwatch. "I think we have our winner. Congratulations, Amy!"

"She must have cheated," Dot cried in an instant. "Look at her, she's a waif! Check her sleeves."

"I think she won fair and square, Dorothy," Ethel replied, flicking through the latest issue of *The Post* in the corner. Its headline read: 'Howarth Estate Groundworks to Start Despite Protesting Locals.'

"Percy shouldn't have had two helpings of eggs and soldiers this morning."

While Julia handed Amy the small trophy they'd bought for the occasion online, the café's cosy chaos soothed Jessie's frayed nerves after her stressful break. Once the mince pie contest crowd cleared and the afternoon continued as usual, she took her plate to the kitchen to join her mum washing up at the sink.

"So," Jessie started, brushing her leftover crusts into the bin. "Please tell me you've come up with a brilliant new plan to stop James ploughing ahead?"

Julia tucked a stray chocolatey curl behind her ear as she lifted her head, her smile tight. "The toilet rolls *were* my plan. We need something big and bold that will show James that he can't intimidate us into compliance, but..." Flicking the soapy suds from her fingers, she exhaled through flared nostrils. "I'm flying blind."

The back door rattled open, and Sue edged in sideways, balancing a heavy milk crate.

"We'd better come up with something quick if we have any hope of stopping this mess going ahead," Sue said, plopping the crate on the stainless steel island. "It's only a matter of time before they get started. They've finished unwrapping their diggers."

"What do we do, Mum?"

Inhaling a deep breath, Julia tossed up her hands. "We hope for a miracle."

After all of Jessie's hard work uncovering the lies and corruption that had led them to this point, Jessie couldn't believe their last hope was to wait for a Christmas miracle.

∽

A few feet below in the windowless basement office, Barker drummed his fingertips on the smooth mahogany surface of his desk, staring at the blank document open on his laptop. The soft jazz spinning on the vinyl player did little to encourage his creativity as he willed the right words to flow.

His latest mystery novel, *The Body in the Time Capsule*, was selling better than he'd expected, but that only added pressure to ensure this third instalment was just as compelling. He'd wanted to put his research into Duncan Howarth to good use, crafting a murder mystery set in the mid-1800s about an industrialist trying to steamroll a charming village.

Yet, every sentence he typed found itself highlighted and deleted. The freedom of being independent of a publisher should have made writing easier, but it wasn't so simple cracking his own whip.

Sighing, Barker ran a hand through his greying

dark hair. His concentration kept slipping, attention snatched away by the faintest sounds drifting from the busy café above. He pictured Sue or Julia staggering between tables, struggling to keep loaded trays aloft. Raucous laughter pricked up his ears, the cackle belonging to Dot or Ethel. They were morphing into the same person lately. From the lack of cheering, the mince pie competition had come to an end, and the lunch rush was in full swing by the clinking of cutlery on plates as chairs scraped against the floorboards.

Five minutes passed without further disruptions, allowing Barker to type out a new opening paragraph. Just as he reached for the delete key, an ear-splitting mechanical roar shattered the quiet. His shoulders tensed as the deafening noise reverberated through the floor and quivered the desk.

"What the…?" Barker muttered, blinking into the hazy light.

His heart sank as he pushed out his chair.

Last night's antics would never have stopped things for good, but he'd been so lost trying to craft the perfect words all morning, he'd forgotten what day it was. Frustrated, he closed his laptop, resigning from his writing efforts for the afternoon. He looked up as two-year-old Olivia awoke from her nap with a startled frown creasing her forehead.

"Noisy, Dada," she said as she pointed to the door.

Barker agreed before pulling on her winter coat and boots. With Olivia held tight on his hip, he dragged the needle off the vinyl record and made his way upstairs.

In the yard of the café, Julia, Sue, and Jessie were watching from the gate while Dot, Percy, and Ethel were scrambling to set up a protest with their megaphones on the edge of the field. The diggers, now free of their wrappings, edged closer, filling the countryside air with the heavy stench of diesel. Julia clutched his hand as the digger reared its head, and without a moment of hesitation, crunched up its first mouthful of earth.

Clinging tight to her hand, he sensed his wife's waning warmth. She'd been such a driving force since she'd read the pleading letter at the ill-fated planning committee meeting, sent to them through the centuries from Duncan Howarth. Each day, he sensed her inching away, a subtle retreat like the last whispers of sunlight on a cold winter's evening.

"Does this mean we've lost?" Jessie asked in a small voice. "For real *lost*? There's no going back from this. It's started..."

Barker searched for the right words, but like with the opening of his new book, he drew an almighty blank.

The diggers were never supposed to get this far.

Once a city detective, he couldn't believe he cared so much about protecting their rural way of life, but that's why he'd moved to Peridale. Even with all the noise, life in Peridale was mostly quiet.

Not perfect, but peaceful.

Olivia began to fuss in his arms as the digger churned up clumps of grass and soil, the damage irreversible. He stroked her dark hair—thicker and curlier, more like her mother's every day—as he glanced at Julia fighting back tears. He put his arm around her, wishing he could ease the pain.

But perhaps some fights weren't meant to be won.

The digger continued its relentless march forward as the geriatric trio screamed into their megaphones, their cries drowned out by the growl of progress. Defeat pressed down as the clawed mouth spat soil into the back of a waiting skip, the mound growing at a terrifying speed.

Before the chomping teeth went back for another bite, one of the builders on the ground yelled for the driver to stop, waving both hands above his head as the lingering builders moved in.

"You've hit something!" he cried. "Might be a pipe?"

"There are no pipes," another called. "It's just an old empty sheep pasture."

The driver of the digger jumped out as the dozen

or so builders in high-visibility jackets and helmets closed in around their discovery. They exchanged fraught looks as the megaphones grew quiet. Even with the lively hum of the Christmas market on the other side of the café, Peridale seemed to hold its breath.

"What's going on?" Dot's bellowing voice demanded, but they only continued to whisper amongst themselves, some standing, some crouched, all staring at the disrupted patch of soil that had halted their work.

"What do you think has happened?" Sue asked.

"Maybe it is a pipe?" Julia suggested.

"Whatever it is, I'm glad they've stopped," Jessie said.

Barker was glad too, even if a gut instinct told him they shouldn't be.

A car screeched to a halt on the other side of the café, where the jovial chatter of the Christmas market was at odds with the strained atmosphere of the field. James Jacobson charged down the alley, his phone at his ear.

"We *demand* to know what's going on!" Dot called in his face as he burst through their protest. "You can't ignore us forever."

"Oh, yeah? Watch me," James said before collaring one of the builders. "You there,

Carmichael? Why aren't you digging? I told you to get started."

"It's McCormack, sir," the young builder replied. "And we've found something. You might want to see this."

"Some old pottery?"

The builder shook his head and waited until James was close enough to whisper something in his ear.

"*Bones*?" James cried, on the verge of a laugh. "What kind of bones? It's probably just an old sheep. No need to grind to a halt. You have a schedule to keep."

But the builder shook his head, and though he didn't say the word out loud, the shapes he made with his lips were clear enough for Barker to read them; the same word uttered countless times at crime scenes during his former career as a detective.

"Did he just say…" Julia whispered.

"*Human*," Barker said, pulling Olivia tight. "Something tells me they won't be digging much more today."

4

A hush fell over the café as Detective Inspector Laura Moyes stepped inside later that afternoon. The creaking door seemed louder than usual in the abrupt silence. Gossipy chatter, filling the room only seconds before, faded into tense expectation as all eyes fixed on the inspector.

Moyes stood tall in the doorway, hands clasped behind her back. For once, not even the faint scent of her vape device trailed her, though the young officer Julia recognised as Police Constable Jake Puglisi followed her in, mirroring the DI's grim expression.

Julia's plastered 'keeping up appearances for the sake of the customers' smile froze, hovering behind the counter, teabags suspended over a boiled teapot waiting to be served.

Barker, cradling young Olivia in the crook of his arm, straightened in his seat by the window. His half-eaten festive turkey sandwich sat forgotten. Dot and Ethel leaned forward over the next table, staring at the DI over their teacups. Percy set down his fork, a piece of mince pie hovering halfway to his mouth, despite having stuffed himself into second place at the contest earlier. Jessie perched on the adjacent chair, looking up from her laptop. Moyes met Julia's gaze, eyebrows knitted with shared concern, and Julia sensed Jessie's next article was about to take a turn for the worse.

Outside, the cheerful sounds of the market carried on, oblivious to the atmosphere within. Even the choir continued their glorious warbling as villagers browsed the displays, the news of the unearthed discovery in the field not spreading despite the crowds.

"Well, Detective?" Dot was the first to break the silence. "What did they find? Bones?"

"Yes." Moyes paused as if gathering herself. She reached into her pocket as she glanced at the 'NO SMOKING' sign. "I regret to announce the bones found earlier by the builders have been identified as *human* remains."

"I *knew* it!" Evelyn gasped, clutching her turban. "I saw *bones* as clear as a full moon on a cloudless night in the tea leaves this morning, but I didn't want to believe it."

"I'm sure," Dot said, pursing her lips. "Detective, they must have been down there a while if they're... just bones?"

"*Just* bones," Moyes confirmed. "Given the completed state of decomposition, forensics estimate they've likely been there for several decades in a shallow grave."

Gasps echoed through the room, and Julia's was one of them. Turning, she looked through the beaded curtain to the back door, seeing the field in her mind's eye. The teabags fell from her grip, landing on the tray next to the teapot with a soft thud before she clutched the counter. Sue's hand buffed across her back in wide circles as Julia stole another glance through the beads. So much had happened back there, and there'd been a body buried deep underground for decades?

"The remains are likely those of an adult male," Moyes continued after a moment. "So, we're looking for someone who disappeared a very long time ago. We're checking the records for missing persons, but until we have a concrete year, I'm going to need all of your help more than ever. If anyone knows anything, now is the time to speak up."

Moyes' eager eyes swept across the bewildered faces as Julia's thoughts spun. The DI had first arrived in Peridale as a cold case expert over a year ago during the time capsule case. She'd stuck around to become their new detective, but given her shellshocked expression, even she didn't seem to be taking this in her stride.

"At least narrow it down for us," Ethel called over the creeping chatter. "Decades? *Which* decade?"

"I suspect the 1960s," Evelyn said, wafting a hand. "Just a feeling."

"Anything that's not a cryptic 'feeling' from the tea leaves?" Dot demanded.

"The coins, Detective?" PC Puglisi whispered, though the café had fallen quiet enough that everyone heard. "Halfpennies, they said?"

"Yes, thank you, Constable. They had slipped my mind." The inspector exhaled through her nose, casting a sharp glance at him. "Several out of circulation halfpenny coins, extremely aged, were recovered in the soil around the body. Since there's no way to know yet if they were buried with him, I saw no need to confuse matters by highlighting that extraneous detail."

Puglisi wilted under her stern gaze. "Right, yes. Sorry to interrupt."

But the information had already sparked a flurry of excited whispers throughout the café. Coins. Halfpennies. That tiny, intrigue-laden detail seemed to spark connections, firing in many minds at once, but nothing for Julia. She wasn't sure she'd ever seen a halfpenny.

"Halfpennies, you say?" Dot called, tapping a finger to her chin. "Well, that *does* narrow it down, Detective. Pre-decimalisation or post?"

"I'm sorry?"

"Post," Puglisi offered, before adding, "My grandad collects coins."

"That narrows it down to the 1970s." Dot gave a firm nod, clearly pleased with her deduction. "Doesn't it, Percy?"

"Quite right, my love," Percy agreed, dabbing his mouth with a napkin. "The currency shake-up was so difficult to get used to. They introduced it in 1971, if I recall correctly?"

"Okay," Moyes nodded, batting Puglisi with the back of her hand, prompting him to start writing. "So, we're looking for someone who went missing at least after 1971?"

"I can do you one better," Ethel said after a slurp of her tea. "They only kept the halfpenny around to get us used to the switchover. It was out of circulation by the mid-80s. Argued against that, myself. Drove up inflation like you wouldn't believe."

"Are you sure?" Dot asked. "I could have sworn I

had halfpennies rattling around in my purse for decades."

"1984," Jessie declared from behind her laptop, which caused some raised eyebrows from the elders. "Memories are great, but search engines exist, too."

Jessie's confirmation set the café ablaze with gossip again, and Barker caught Julia's eye, breaking into a comforting half-smile. After hours of nonstop guesswork about the bones since their discovery on James' field, the speculation could now focus on more concrete clues.

Moyes cleared her throat, regaining the attention of the debating elders and chattering room. "If the coins are related to our ill-fated friend, I'm looking for any information about an adult man who went missing between 1971 and 1984." Nobody came forward with the man she was looking for. "Anything?"

Julia's mind whirred, grappling with memories that held little use; after all, she was born in 1979. Moyes sighed, her weariness showing through once more. She lifted her hands in an appeal to the silent crowd.

"*Nothing?*" She raised her eyebrows. "A man who went mysteriously missing in those years and was never seen again in Peridale?"

Her question dropped like a stone into a pond,

casting ripples outward through purse-lipped frowns, down-turned mouths, and distant, seeking stares. A few shook their heads. Most stared past Moyes into the middle distance, sifting through the years. But no bolt of recognition came.

"I can *feel* that he's very lost," Evelyn offered, to which many groaned. "I'd like to lay some crystals at the site where he was found."

"Once the field is released," Moyes said, nodding for Puglisi to open the door. "If anything comes up, you all know where to find me. Until then, I have an investigation to start."

Julia continued making the abandoned pot of tea as the weight of Moyes' revelations sank in. The day should have been filled with festive cheer to distract from the construction's start, not chilled by thoughts of a secret burial on their back doorstep.

"The digging has stopped," Julia said to Barker when he joined her in the kitchen for a quiet moment with Olivia, "but this wasn't how I wanted it to happen."

"We haven't had much choice throughout this," he reminded her as he handed Olivia over for a cuddle. "Whoever this man is, maybe he's looking down on us and helping with the fight."

"Maybe," Julia agreed.

If this unknown villager had waited forgotten all

these years beneath their collective feet, he deserved the truth being brought into the light.

Justice, no matter how long delayed.

But as she held Olivia close, like with stopping James Jacobson and his Howarth Estate plans, Julia wasn't sure if she was the one who could make such a thing happen.

~

In Veronica's cottage later that night, Jessie and her editor worked at opposite ends of the table in an unusual silence. Teetering towers of books stacked by messy piles of newspapers filled the dining room, banishing the show-home perfection left behind by the previous owners, Johnny and Leah.

As comfortable as Veronica seemed in her new home these days, she shrank more into the clutter with every passing hour. She'd barely uttered a word since asking if Jessie wanted milk in her coffee.

"Any Shakespeare quotes to sum up today's madness?"

Her editor glanced over her black frames with minimal interest. "What?"

"You've *always* got a Shakespeare quote for every occasion."

"Oh, right." She pushed up her glasses with a shrug. "Nothing is coming to mind."

Though often annoyed by the quotes, Jessie longed for the normalcy of some Shakespearean mumbo-jumbo followed by the specific act and scene of the play it had been plucked from.

"'Ye nasty developer's diggers do stand still thanks to ye olde bones dug upeth on thy field...eth...'" Jessie's attempt barely raised a smile. "It's halted James' plans for now, at least. Gives us more time to protest. Might even help the council revoke the planning permission?" Veronica offered a single nod, but nothing more. Sighing, Jessie enquired, "Any luck with the front page layout?"

Veronica shrugged, lingering on her screen. "Just slotting in the pictures you sent."

She turned her screen with a weary flourish towards Jessie. The mock-up glowed with the photograph Jessie had captured on her phone: the watchful gazes of forensic officers behind police tape, churning through the soil for more clues.

"I wonder if we'll ever find out who he was?"

"No doubt some defined chapter of this man's story is yet to unfold." She lifted her glasses to pinch her nose before letting them snap back into place. "Whoever he was, let's hope he's at peace after all these years."

Veronica turned the screen back and rubbed her palms down her lined cheeks. Behind her fingers, she seemed to wrestle with concerns from beyond their quiet evening of work. Jessie pondered what might be troubling her editor. Could it still be Martha's grilling at the market?

"It does still mean a delay for James," Jessie repeated. "That's got to be a win, right?"

Across the table, Veronica offered only a non-committal hum. She usually exuded crazed energy from dawn until midnight, fuelled by pots of coffee. Such an unrelenting pursuit couldn't be healthy—especially at her post-retirement age—but Veronica had been intent on exposing her corrupt brother since taking the reins of *The Peridale Post*. This was the first time Jessie had seen her so defeated.

"You *can* talk to me, you know?"

Veronica gave no response, though she nodded as if making an internal decision. Then she met Jessie's gaze. Behind her glasses, her eyes turned to steel. "Exhaustion forgets decorum as darkness looms."

"Shakespeare?"

"*Veronica*." She offered a smile. "Maybe you should go home? It's been a long day for both of us."

"Only if you promise to get an early night?"

Another flat smile. "Need to get this front page to print before midnight. Our Cotswold Media Group overlords will be pleased it's not 'yet another' Greg, James, or Howarth Estate headline. They've asked me to 'pull back' from spotlighting my imprisoned brother. There have been *complaints*."

"Complaints from Greg and James, surely?"

"Newspaper readers, according to the stern email I received this morning."

The source of Veronica's mood?

"Suppose this is a bad time to ask if my mum can pay for a full-page protest ad?" she said. "What will you do?"

"Continue as we have. I won't be silenced from delivering the truth about what's happening in this village. It's my duty."

"*Our* duty."

She rubbed the back of her neck, her frustrations rising on Veronica's behalf. The interference of suits in charge, dictating from their distant offices, reminded her all too much of the council who'd decided the fate of the field. Outsiders claiming authority because a piece of paper deemed them important, ignoring those with actual boots on the ground.

"As long as we stick to the facts, they can't stop you, right?"

"Oh, they can *try*, but I won't be muzzled. 'Though this be madness, yet there is method in it.'" Veronica moved closer to her screen, and Jessie was relieved to hear something Shakespearean. "Hamlet, Act Two, Scene Two. Let people complain. I will keep printing the stories until James stops benefiting from my brother's council string-pulling. Now, if you're not in a hurry, shall we go over what you've written?"

They reviewed Jessie's completed write-up of the police announcement together. Veronica suggested tightening certain sections and adding an appeal for any readers with information on missing persons to come forward. By the time Jessie uploaded the updated version to the paper's shared drive, her lids were heavy. The old clock's hands neared midnight as Jessie closed her laptop with a yawn, stretching her aching shoulders.

"Whatever it is, you can talk to me. I thought we trusted each other?"

"Jessika," Veronica said, peering over her glasses with the sternness of that English tutor she'd first met last year. "You might be the *only* person I trust right now. Go and get some sleep, and I promise I'll do the same."

With a last lingering glance at Veronica's hunched form in the dim glow of the screen, Jessie pulled her jacket tighter and stepped out into the night. Passing under a streetlamp, she couldn't resist checking her phone despite the late hour. A few unread messages awaited her, including one from Dante asking if the 'meet the parents' event was still on for the next day. She replied uncertainly as she let herself into their cottage.

The familiar comfort of home greeted her. Peering into the nursery, formerly Jessie's bedroom, she saw Olivia fast asleep in her cot, bathed in the glow of a swirling starry nightlight. She shrugged off her jacket and left it on the coat rack before heading into the sitting room, expecting to find her mum and dad deep in an investigation of the mystery bones.

Instead, she found them dozing on the sofa, Barker's arm around Julia's shoulders, keeping her tucked against his chest. *Breakfast at Tiffany's*, one of Julia's favourite films, neared its end on the screen. The pair parted, and Julia patted the space between them without a word.

Jessie settled in, accepting the remains of Barker's mulled wine as she wriggled her toes in front of the crackling fire. Mowgli, the smoky grey Maine Coon, blinked up at her from the armchair before curling back to sleep. Moments like these made her feel like she had never left, never more at ease or safe than when she was at home with…

Jessie jerked awake, her breath catching in her chest beneath a heavy blanket. The mug of mulled wine sat atop a coaster on the table where her feet had been, the embers of the fire dying out. She lurched upright in the empty sitting room, her heart pounding as she strained to listen in the darkness.

Something had woken her.

A noise.

A scream?

Perhaps it had been a dream.

Silence.

Was the spiced wine playing tricks?

About to settle back into the cushions, she noticed the faint glow of flashing blue lights at the edges of the curtains. Heart pounding, she untangled herself from the blanket. At the window, she twitched the curtain edge. A police car sat outside Veronica's cottage across the lane, the hypnotic pulse of its lights swirling in the middle of the night silence. She raced into the hallway, slipping into the first footwear she found before running into the cold night.

She hurried across the lane in Barker's oversized slippers, the lights staining everything in shades of icy blue. A wave of dread rose as she scrambled along the garden path.

This couldn't be happening.

Not after the day they'd had.

She spied movement through the cottage window—two bulky silhouettes she didn't recognise moving around inside. Had Six found Veronica? On closer inspection, they were police officers. Were they overseeing a second body discovery?

Jessie barely knocked before bursting inside. Relief washed over her at seeing Veronica clutching the kitchen sink at the end of the hall. She didn't turn at the sound of the door, giving no indication she even registered Jessie's panting presence.

PC Puglisi stepped out of the dining room, the policeman's formal hat atop his head somewhat warping his cheeky-chap appearance. His eyes shone with a sympathy that raised the hairs on Jessie's arms.

"Sorry to disturb you so late." He glanced at Veronica's rigid form. "We've just delivered some upsetting news to Miss Hilt regarding a deceased family member."

Jessie's mouth dried, her thoughts tumbling from adrenaline and dread. A family member? Surely he didn't mean...

"Has something happened to Greg in prison?"

Even uttering his name left a sour taste. The notion of political cronies exacting backroom vengeance in prison twisted Jessie's stomach almost as much as Greg's weaselly face.

"Greg remains in custody." Puglisi removed his hat, turning it nervously in his hands. "We have informed Veronica that the remains found in the field earlier today have been positively identified as those of her other brother. Records indicate he went missing in 1979."

Jessie struggled to process his solemn words. 1979? So, not Greg, which left only one possibility. She stared at Puglisi, a slow realisation dawning through her exhausted thoughts.

"Sebastian?" she whispered his name, and Puglisi nodded.

At the sink, a visible shudder ran through Veronica's frame. Discarding the oversized slippers, Jessie crossed the cold kitchen tiles, and she wrapped her trembling fingers around Veronica's shoulders.

"I'll give you a moment," Puglisi called. "We can discuss this further tomorrow, Miss Hilt, once the shock has worn off."

After the front door latch clicked shut, Veronica released a long breath that misted the window above the sink. Jessie gave her shoulders a bolstering squeeze, the officer's revelations swirling in her mind as she sought words of comfort. But what could she say? How could there be any words?

All Jessie knew about Sebastian was that he was Veronica and Greg's older brother, and Veronica had told her he had died. But if he had gone missing in 1979, how could she have been certain?

"I'm so sorry." Jessie leaned in, speaking softly in Veronica's ear. "I... I'm here."

Veronica's head dipped lower, her silver hair glowing in the moonlight streaming through the foggy window. She peeled her white-knuckled hands from the sink's edge to pat Jessie's hands.

"Oh, my best student." Veronica's voice cracked, choked by tears. She made no move to wipe them, even as they dripped from her jaw. "My best friend. Of course, you're here. I... I..."

Jessie's own vision blurred. "I'm here."

A violent sob wracked Veronica's frame, her resistance crumbling as she turned into Jessie's embrace. Tutor, editor, friend... Jessie had never seen her like this, and it frightened her.

"I've waited for this moment for forty years," she whispered. "*Forty* years."

"I don't know what happened," Jessie reassured her, still holding tight. "But whatever it is, we'll find the answers. I promise."

"Oh, I already have the answers. I know who killed Sebastian, and I always have."

5

After a slow Sunday at home, Monday morning dawned grey and dreary, matching the bleak mood that had settled over Peridale since the identity of the human remains had been revealed.

Julia leaned on the back gate of her café yard, clutching a steaming mug of hot chocolate, watching the police activity unfolding on the field. DI Laura Moyes directed her team in sweeping grids across the churned soil, metal detectors and probing sticks in hand. They would stop, confer, mark spots with little red flags stabbed into the dirt, and carry on with their searches. From how often Moyes was stopping to vape, they weren't having much success.

Julia shifted her weight from one foot to the other, conflicted emotions warring within. On the one hand, she was glad for any delays to James Jacobson's ruthless development schemes, but why did it have to be like this?

A tragedy tangled together across forty years—the mysterious, unsolved fate of Veronica's missing brother—a mystery pre-dating Julia, and mostly lost in the villagers' consciousness.

And trapped in the middle was Veronica herself, Julia's neighbour, who kept very much to herself. She respected the dedication Veronica showed to exposing deceit in the newspaper since Julia's old school friend, Johnny, moved away. And she'd been a fantastic mentor to Jessie. But Julia found Veronica to be rather withdrawn and isolated, consumed body and soul by her work, never much time for anything other than a quick wave over the wall or a rushed coffee.

Still, hearing Jessie's recollection of how distraught she'd been two nights ago had rattled Julia. She'd started Sunday morning by taking Veronica a cottage pie and a Victoria sponge cake, along with an offer that she'd help any way she could. Veronica had seemed to appreciate the support, but she'd repeated what she'd told Jessie.

"Thank you, but this won't be a long case," she'd said in her pyjamas on her doorstep, her eyes red raw. "I know what happened to Sebastian, and now I'll finally be able to prove it."

Lost in her thoughts, Julia didn't notice her father, Brian, until he startled her, appearing out of nowhere at her side.

"Oh, it's like you knew I was coming to find you!" He held up a delicate silver necklace dangling with aquamarine stones shaped like little hearts. "Here, have a little look at this, will you? For Katie? For Christmas. Reckoned the blue would bring out her eyes. What do you think?"

Julia nodded. The necklace was lovely, but her gaze kept drifting back to the police milling about the field. Her father followed her stare.

"What have I missed? Been away antique hunting all weekend over in Cambridgeshire."

"They found a body when they started digging," she explained. "Bones. They think they're from a man who went missing in 1979. Sebastian Morgan?"

"Sebastian?" His bottom lip puckered out as he thought about the name. "Hmm. Can't say the name is jumping out. That was the year you were born. No wonder you look so glum." He tucked the necklace into his jacket pocket and planted a whiskery kiss on her cheek. "Chin up, my sunshine." He sang a line of 'You Are My Sunshine' to her. "I used to sing that to you when you were a little girl. Always put a smile on your face."

Julia did smile as she leaned into her father's

comforting embrace. For a moment, with her face pressed against the worn leather of his jacket, she could almost believe she was a few years old again.

"Really *that* bad?" He squeezed her tight, then held her at arm's length. "Will you be alright here if I get back to the shop? Left Vicky from the coffee van watching the place. Not sure if I trust her with a latte, let alone my antiques."

"I'll be fine, Dad. Feel better already."

"The magic touch," he said with a wink. "So, the necklace?"

She pushed forward a smile. "I'm sure Katie will love it."

"You always were my sunny girl. Chin up, love."

With one last worried glance at the police tape fluttering around the field, her father went on his way back to his antique shop on Mulberry Lane.

On the field, DI Moyes sent vapour curling skyward, but Julia suspected the secrets to this puzzle lay closer to home than forensic science could deduce. She turned away from the gate and headed back inside to a scene almost as dramatic as the field.

Despite being Monday, villagers clamoured for insight at every table following the development of an identity. Word had spread through the usual gossip channels, although Julia had kept her lips sealed, per Jessie's request.

Still, that hadn't stopped scalding rivers of speculation flooding the village. And at the centre, soaking up all the attention and peddling her version of events, was Ethel. The purple-rinsed gossip held court from the middle table with Dot and Percy, customers hanging on her every exaggerated word.

"Oh, *yes*, I knew Sebastian *very* well," Ethel declared, a tinge of melancholy to her dramatic tone. "He was homeless. Lived in a tent in that alley next to the café."

"Was Alistair Black's toy shop back then," Dot cut in. "I *did* know Sebastian too, if you'd let me—"

"I was always taking him soup and bread," Ethel steamrolled on, unwilling to relinquish the limelight. "Blankets for when it got nippy. He was a secretive fellow. Never would say why he was living like that. But we had some nice talks over the meals I brought him, the dear soul."

"You blathering nonstop while he tried to eat, no doubt," Dot muttered into her tea, and Ethel shot her a daggered glare. "I *actually* knew him, Ethel. If you'd just let me—"

"I think *I* knew him best out of anyone," Ethel continued with a faraway look, hugging her teacup. "Was probably his *only* friend at the end. Yes, I'm sure I was. I should be the one talking about him to television reporters if they come asking questions—"

"Maybe let someone else who actually remembers Sebastian say their piece?" Dot slammed her cup down, sloshing tea onto the saucer. "Since you clearly don't know a fig about why he was camping, you can't have known him as well as you're claiming."

Sensing an imminent explosion from her gran, Julia handed out complimentary mince pies to distract the room. She pressed two into Ethel's hands as a sugar-glazed peace offering and gave her gran an imploring 'please spill' look while Ethel had her mouth full.

Dot dabbed her lips with a serviette, chin lifted. "Well, I do happen to recall exactly *why* Sebastian Morgan was camping out there in 1979. And before you spray more fantasies, Ethel, dear, he definitely *wasn't* homeless."

Ethel froze mid-bite, eyes narrowing to slits.

"Strange for a young chap to be sleeping rough by choice," Percy pointed out, taking three free mince pies onto his plate. "Especially if the weather was anything like this."

"It was around Christmastime," Dot confirmed with a nod, squinting off into her memories. "There was snow, and Sebastian pitched his tent there as a protest. Ah yes, it's all coming back now. He was demonstrating against... now who was it trying to develop that field first?"

Julia's breath caught. She leaned in closer. "The field James Jacobson is building on? Duncan Howarth, you mean?"

"Duncan would have been dead over a hundred years by that point," Percy pointed out. "But now that you've mentioned it, my dear, I remember a commotion about something being built there before. Nasty business him disappearing like that. I can't believe I didn't think of Sebastian when the DI was talking about the halfpennies. I sat next to him on the bus sometimes. Friendly chap. I helped with the search party."

"We *all* did," Ethel mumbled through her mince pie.

Dot looked off at Julia with a sad smile and said, "Well, I say *I* knew him. I only knew of Sebastian through *your* mother, Julia."

"My mother?" Julia whispered, the words jamming in her throat as faraway memories of her mother flooded back. Pearl had died when Julia was twelve. "How?"

She refilled Dot's teapot and did something she rarely did while working—she pulled up a chair at the table, needing to hear whatever fragmented recollections remained of her mum.

Ethel brushed crumbs off her cardigan, smiling over the last tasty bites of mince pie. "Well, if you *finally* have some *real* wisdom to impart, let's have it, Dorothy."

Dot grumbled as she picked up her fresh steaming teacup and added a splash of milk for the first fortifying sip. "Right... 1979. Was a *long* time ago. But let me think back and see what I can remember..."

6

1979

*D*orothy pulled her coat tighter against the chill as she left Alistair Black's shop. Wooden toys knocked together in her wicker shopping basket as she trudged through the snowy market on the village green. She paused, checking her silver wristwatch. Late. Heaving an annoyed groan, she quickened her pace through the snow. She didn't know why she'd agreed to help in the first place.

Her son's antique stall came into view, half-buried behind the carousel. She'd told Brian he'd picked the worst pitch, but it had cost the least, and the deluded lad had convinced himself he could sell snow to snowmen. He paced in front of his ramshackle collection of 'treasures', checking his watch.

"*Mother!*" he announced, holding out his hands

with a cheeky grin. "I bought you that gorgeous 1920s art deco watch for your birthday so you could get better at timekeeping."

"I think it's faulty." She shook the watch at her ear. "Always running ten minutes behind."

"Which explains why you're *twenty* minutes late how...?" He grabbed her wrist and peered down his nose at the ugly thing. "Perfect working order. In fact, it might even be a couple of minutes ahead. You just wanted to stay inside twitching at the curtains... like always..."

"I did a little shopping, *actually*. For Julia's Christmas presents. I told you... now that I'm a grandmother, things are going to change."

"I suppose that's better than sitting at home waiting for the world to come and find you."

"Wind your neck in, lad. I'm here, aren't I?" She pulled a handful of carefully wrapped mince pies from her basket, offering them up as an olive branch. "From your Pearl's latest batch. She left them on the kitchen counter with a note to bring you some. Never been the biggest fan, but she's getting rather good at baking, if I do say so myself."

"She's always been an excellent baker," Brian interjected. "You're always so critical of her. *Everyone* and *everything*, for that matter."

"I most certainly am not!"

"You told her that her chocolate cake was dry."

"It *was* dry."

"She made it for your birthday."

"A *dry* birthday cake." She pursed her lips as she arranged his disorderly display. "Are you really that upset at me for being late, Brian? I made it, didn't I? And on time is still technically late as the old adage goes. So by that measure..."

She trailed off under Brian's arched brow stare, fussing with an ornate mirror to avoid his judgmental gaze. His recent obsession with old tat and appearances irritated her to no end, but she bit her tongue.

"Mother, you do realise it's nearly Christmas, not a funeral?" He gestured at her black dress beneath an equally dark wool coat, looking her up and down as though surveying a particularly worrisome outbreak of the plague. "It's all very Queen Victoria. Look around, Mum, it's the 1970s, not the 1870s. A little colour wouldn't go amiss. And how about some bell bottoms? Everyone is wearing them." After a breath, he said, "And you know Dad's been gone five years now. High time you re-joined the world and stopped moping about. Things are on the up."

"If you say so, dear."

"I'm going to make us our fortune."

"Hmm."

"I *am*!"

"*Hmmm.*"

Since her son had decided dealing in antiques made him posh, Brian had grown increasingly pompous. His father, Albert, would have dropped dead for a second time if he could see his son's open-collared shirt and gold medallion necklace.

"I'm too old for all that rubbish," she said. "And besides, your father liked me in black. He—"

"What do you think about this for Pearl for Christmas?" Brian asked, showing her a pearl bracelet. "Cost a small fortune."

"You know she doesn't care about flashy stuff."

"Almost a compliment from you, Mother." He winked. "I just want to treat her right. Be the best husband for her. The best dad for little Julia. It's not too late for you to find someone, you know. Forty-five isn't the end of the world. Don't let going grey hold you back."

"Really, Brian, wind your neck in! The idea of remarrying holds little appeal for me. But by all means, do enlighten me as to how I should be conducting my love life. I'm sure my twenty-seven-year-old son holds *all* the answers."

Brian frowned, correctly interpreting her tart tone as the conversation ender as she'd meant it to be. With a resigned sigh, he turned his scrutiny on the passers-by instead, jumping in front of anyone who'd make eye contact to try to ferry them to his stall. When he wasn't looking for potential customers, he kept glancing off across the green with a narrowed stare.

Dorothy followed his gaze to where Pearl stood chatting on the other side of the carousel, with young Julia nestled in her arms. Pearl's cheeks glowed crimson from the cold, snowflakes clinging like glitter to her dark curls. Her companion, a wild-looking young man handing out leaflets beside a small mountain of duffle bags, had a mane of tawny hair like an aging John Lennon. Some people never knew when to grow up.

"Honestly, your wife has the most *questionable* taste in friends," she muttered. "She'll talk to anyone about anything."

"That's one of the reasons I love her, Mother. At least she has friends."

"I have friends!"

"Who?"

"Mabel Crump."

"You and Mabel haven't spoken since Halloween!"

"And I shan't speak to her until the new year, when I'm sure she'll apologise for putting that plastic spider in my cup of tea." She narrowed her stare on

Pearl. "Always picking up waifs and strays. Such a do-gooder. Aren't you worried?"

"About what?"

"Well, she's hanging off his every word."

The two of them stared off as Pearl laughed at something the raggedy man said. He gestured wildly at the falling snow like it was the most wonderful thing he'd ever seen, nearly upsetting the donation tin at his feet.

"No law against being friendly, Mother. You should give it a go." But Brian's gaze only narrowed. "He's that chap who's been living in that tent. Protesting something being built, I heard."

"In *Peridale*?" She laughed, shaking her head. "And pigs might fly! It'll be a lot of hot air. Anything not to get a job, I say."

"You might be onto something there, Mother. Can't all be entrepreneurs like me."

"Maggie Thatcher has been our Prime Minister for *five* minutes and she's already got into your head. She'll be out after her first term, you watch." Shoes crunching over the snow as she stepped forward, Dorothy found her ears straining. "You know, I might take Julia off Pearl's hands for ten minutes. Give her a little rest."

Dot left Brian to his 'entrepreneurial' devices and slogged across the village green and lingered near the toy shop she'd been in not ten minutes ago. She glanced into her basket again at the little wooden dolls, sure Julia would love them on Christmas morning.

"Come to your granny," she said, scooping Julia from Pearl. "Oh, look at that little red nose. You'll catch a cold stood around chatting the afternoon away."

The man looked like he hadn't seen a proper bath or haircut in months, let alone a simple comb. Still, Dot strained to eavesdrop on his impassioned diatribe, morbid curiosity getting the better of her. Behind the window in the toy shop, an enchanting Christmas carousel, a miniature of the one on the green, spun in time to tinkling music. Julia gazed wide-eyed at the flashing lights, entranced by the colourful movement.

"It's just *awful*, Sebastian," Pearl said, sounding on the verge of tears. "These plans can't go through."

"They won't, if I have anything to say about it!" Sebastian declared, wild strands of hair flying as he shook his head like a shaggy dog. "That Vincent Wellington won't get his way—I'll fight till my end if I must. And there are records, over a hundred years old. The council is denying they exist, but I have contacts. That land behind the toy shop *is* protected. There are contingencies that men like Mr

Wellington would rather the rest of us never find out about."

Dorothy scoffed under her breath. What a load of old tripe! Everyone knew the Wellingtons did what they pleased in Peridale, but their pockets weren't as deep as everyone thought. They'd fired half their household staff, and Vincent had that new mysterious baby that turned up out of thin air.

Behind Sebastian, vehicles rumbled from the vacant field where the old market hall had burnt down a decade ago. How did this man think anything would change in Peridale? It had taken the council ten years to get around to clearing the old bricks.

"Wellington wants to buy that land cheap and build a model village named after himself," Sebastian said, sounding rather unhinged. "Egomaniacs, the lot of them. My family farm borders the field that borders *that* field, and if I don't take a stand here and now, there's no telling how much more countryside his kind will swallow up. We're living in a new age, and *everything* has a price tag. It'll be the air we breathe next."

Again, she found herself rolling her eyes at his dramatics. If Wellington had wanted to develop the land, he'd have done it already. This Sebastian clearly spent too much time listening to Lennon and that strange wailing Yoko.

"Total *codswallop!*" she proclaimed when Pearl pulled herself away from the crackpot when he returned to handing out flyers, being ignored by all but a few. "Do you honestly believe Vincent Wellington has designs to pave over the countryside?"

Pearl took Julia back into her arms. "Vincent hasn't exactly denied the rumours when people have asked. And didn't you read the article in *The Peridale Post* last month where he said he hoped to 'cement his legacy' in the village? He must have meant *something* by that."

"You can't believe everything you read in the paper, and Vincent isn't as rich as he wants people to think. You know he only has one cleaner at that manor? *One!*"

Pearl sighed, jiggling happy baby Julia as the toy carousel flashed through its mesmerising rotation. "I just want my daughter to grow up in the same village I did, Dorothy. That's all."

"Well, I suppose I can't argue with that." She gave Pearl's arm an affectionate squeeze, guiding her away from the sputtering mechanical beasts. "But try not to worry yourself, eh? You don't need to be hanging around someone like Sebastian. You're married now, Pearl. You have a baby to look after. Focus on that."

Pearl sighed, shaking her head as she carried Julia off to Brian's stall. He seemed to have convinced someone to part with their money for an old plate, but Dorothy wasn't in a rush to get to be put to work; not if her payment was more pieces of jewellery that she only wore to stop Brian asking where they were.

She continued shopping, pausing at a stall selling books filled with empty pages. As she flicked through one with a red and white gingham cover, a Land Rover roared down the street, pulling up outside the post office, silencing the market.

Vincent Wellington climbed out, followed by a group of two men and a woman, all in suits. One had a thick moustache, the other bald, and the woman had a tall beehive. Doors slammed, and in turn, they stepped over Sebastian's tent, ignoring his protests.

The whole matter would blow over soon.

Dorothy was sure of it.

Nothing ever changed in Peridale.

And even if it did, a man like Sebastian Morgan wasn't going to be the one to stop it.

"Are you coming back, Mother?" Brian called from the stall. "Things to do..."

7

Jessie dragged her laptop closer at the counter of Richie's as she scrolled through articles about Sebastian Morgan's disappearance. According to a 1979 piece in *The Peridale Post*'s archives, he was born in 1949, making him only thirty when he was last seen on December 24th, 1979. One article referred to him as 'homeless' before he went missing. Another follow-up stated the police were still searching for him, and then nothing.

Two whole articles.

No further updates.

Having been homeless herself after a turbulent upbringing as a foster kid, Jessie knew how people could slip through the cracks. To have people not care. Nobody had cared about her until she'd stumbled into Peridale as a teenager and found a family; she'd picked the right café to steal cakes from.

But to fall off the face of the planet without a trace?

The poor guy.

The second—and final—article included a quote from Greg Morgan, twenty at the time, stating he believed Sebastian had left Peridale 'to start a new life and was likely fine and well'. But Greg wished his brother would 'contact the family to stop them worrying.' There was no mention of Veronica beyond stating Sebastian had a sister.

Richie interrupted Jessie's research by sliding an espresso martini across the counter, his sweet aftershave catching her nose and transporting her to a tropical bar by a beach. "On the house. You look like you need it."

Jessie offered a weary smile, easing the laptop halfway shut. She hadn't slept much. Veronica, silent for most of the night, had occupied Jessie's attention until she fell asleep on the sofa. Much like her parents had done, Jessie removed the mug of cold coffee from Veronica's grip and covered her with a blanket. The little sleep Jessie had managed had been upright in an armchair.

"Work research," Jessie said, keeping it vague. "But thanks, I appreciate—"

The bar's door swung open and Richie's father, James, walked in, followed by a team of builders. She closed her laptop and stuffed it into her bag.

"On second thoughts, that's my cue to leave."

"You don't have to go on his account," Richie said, looking around the quiet bar. "But I get it. You wouldn't be the only one boycotting this place these days. Don't think it'd be worth opening the doors if not for the market, and even that's quiet today."

"Mondays in Peridale for you." She left off that Dot had insisted they all boycott the bar, and any other businesses owned by a Jacobson. "And I'll be back. As long as the drinks are on the house and you're as charming as ever."

Richie laughed. "If only the local guys appreciated my charms and free drinks as much as you, maybe I wouldn't be so single."

"The man of your dreams is around the corner, I'm sure." She swung her bag over her shoulder and took one swig of the martini. "Especially if you make all the drinks as good as this one."

"I put a little extra effort in for my mates," he said with a wink. "Don't be a stranger."

Without looking in James' direction as he settled into a booth with the builders, laughing as though it was 'just another day' in the village, Jessie made her way to the door.

"*Journalist girl?*" James called after her as she gripped the handle. "Tell Mummy I'll be visiting her in the café soon. I have some business I'd like to discuss."

"Save yourself the trip," she muttered, not looking back.

The cheek of that man. How was it his son was so unaffected by the unfortunate roots of his family tree? What was that old saying about not judging the son by his father's sins? Veronica would know, but she hadn't answered her 'good morning' text message yet.

Hurrying past the waning market as the stallholders stood around uninterested—though Martha still marched about with a clipboard like it was a military ship that needed a firm hand—Jessie hopped across the road to the packed café. Had to be the busiest place in the village, which meant the gossips were cooking up Sebastian stories as delicious as Julia's baking. But they weren't talking about Sebastian at all.

1980s politics was the afternoon's hot topic, and Jessie couldn't have cared less. She made herself a coffee—minus the martini—and her mum filled her in about what she'd missed of Dot's story before she'd ventured off onto a 'Thatcher, Thatcher, Milk Snatcher' tangent.

"He lived in a tent out there in winter?" Jessie confirmed, nodding at the wall. "Protesting who?"

"Vincent Wellington, apparently."

"Katie's dad?" Jessie arched a brow. "He died when you found out you were pregnant with Olivia."

"But he was very much *alive* in 1979."

With her coffee, Jessie settled into the corner to comb the archives for more about Sebastian's past. A new name meant a new thread to pull, and it wasn't long before she spun gold. Another 1979 article caught her eye, this time from summer, with the headline: 'A New Dawn For Peridale?'

Beneath the bold text, Vincent Wellington—a man Jessie could only remember as being frail in his nineties, unable to talk after one too many strokes—stood proud in front of Wellington Manor. Long before Jacobson turned it into luxury apartments. He had a full head of icy blond hair, a stern expression, and a tailored suit. He held a tiny baby in his arms—Katie or that brother of hers, she assumed—and was flanked by three people. Two men, one bald and one with a moustache, and a woman with a gigantic beehive that towered over the men, despite her short stature.

"Sorry to interrupt," Jessie called, spinning the laptop. "But does anyone recognise these people?"

Dot, Percy, and Ethel all leaned in, squinting at the screen. Recognition dawned on Dot's face first.

"That's *them!*" Dot announced with a wagging finger. "That's who I saw getting out of the Land Rover with Vincent that day. I'd recognise that beehive anywhere. Oh, what's her name? She was some rich woman. Last of her line of an old family who used to rival the Wellingtons." She clicked her fingers, scrunching her eyes. "What *was* her name?"

"Glenda?" Percy suggested.

"No, it was Glenys," Ethel said. "I'm *certain* of it. Glenys Martin."

"Gwen Dean," Jessie corrected from the article. "She refers to herself here as a 'tycoon looking to brighten Peridale's future.' The bald bloke is Arnold Jessop, a builder and architect, and the man with the moustache is Harold..." She glanced up with a dry smile. "Harold *Morgan*."

"*Another* Morgan?" Dot groaned. "A relation to Sebastian, surely?"

"He *must* be," Ethel insisted, almost spilling her tea in her eagerness to lean over and stamp her finger on Jessie's table. "Keep digging. Have a look on that *FaceTweet* or *TicTac*, or whatever it is everyone's on. See if he's any relation."

Jessie opened a new search window. She could ask Veronica who this new relation was, but given her reluctance to talk about Martha Morgan, she didn't want to annoy her with more family questions. Not so soon.

"Maybe if we solve what happened to Sebastian," Dot mused loudly over the bubbling whispering, "it can help us stop what's happening here and now. He seemed so *sure* there were 'contingencies' that would stop Vincent Wellington building on that field."

"There can't be, given our current predicament with Jacobscrooge," Ethel said. "Stay on *track*, Dorothy."

"I *am* on track, Ethel. Vincent didn't get to build his new model village, did he?"

"Your point being?"

"What my Dorothy is trying to say," Percy spoke up, his mouth full of mince pie, "is that if there were contingencies in place to prevent further building after the market hall burned down, perhaps Sebastian found them?"

"I've just had an idea!" Ethel announced, half-rising from her seat. "If Sebastian discovered what those contingencies were, maybe that's why he was murdered?"

"That's what *I* was trying to say!" Dot snapped. "Oh, Ethel White, I could throw my shoe at you sometimes. But yes, if we find those contingencies, maybe we can stop what's happening here and now. We're on borrowed time, but..."

Dot's words floated away with the rattle of the bell as the door opened, and Veronica stepped inside. Even bundled up in a scarf and hat, she was recognisable enough from her glasses for the rest of the café to fade to silence.

"Aren't we all on borrowed time?" Veronica said, dragging her scarf under her chin.

The crowd murmured awkward condolences for Veronica's loss, which she either didn't hear or chose to ignore. Jessie closed the laptop and her editor managed a smile when she found her in the crowd.

"We are *terribly* sorry," Dot said, attempting to usher Veronica to her table. "Why don't you sit down and tell us everything you know about what happened back then? We were *just* talking about it." She paused, adding, "Not in a gossipy way, mind you. Just using our collective memories to piece together some puzzle parts. I knew your brother rather well. Lovely man. Cared about a worthy cause... and such lovely, long hair."

"I knew him too," Ethel announced. "You can share my tea, dear. Barely touched it."

"Veronica isn't here to answer questions," Jessie called, standing between Veronica and the troublesome trio. "Why don't I take you into the kitchen for coffee—"

"I'm not here for coffee either. Is your dad in? I have an appointment in his office, but I didn't want to go around the back in case I saw—"

"Oh, you *poor* thing!" Dot cried, pulling out the chair next to her with a pat. "My tea is much fresher than Ethel's, and stronger."

With a nod from Julia as she parted the beads, Veronica set off across the café, and Jessie followed behind. In the kitchen, before Veronica left through the back door, Jessie plucked a satsuma from the fruit bowl and dropped it into her editor's pocket.

"I can come down with you if—"

"I need to do this on my own," Veronica whispered, patting Jessie's cheek with a smile. "We'll talk later."

~

Shadows danced along the pipes and stone walls from the multi-coloured lights Julia had strung across the ceiling in the basement. She must have let herself in like a Christmas fairy at some point since decorating the café. The lights winked red, green, and yellow, contrasting with Veronica Hilt's anxious pacing and the jolly festive jazz drifting from the speakers.

"Maybe I should turn the music off?" Barker reached for the remote control.

"Leave it on. Please. Sebastian loved Christmas. He..." Her voice caught. "He'd always get so excited when it snowed."

Barker nodded, allowing the music to continue. He knew where the conversation was headed, but he needed to let it unfold at Veronica's speed. She'd been in his office for five minutes and hadn't stopped pacing.

"I was *supposed* to be home that Christmas," Veronica continued, almost to herself. "Graduated university earlier that year. Had my first official teaching job and wanted to impress the headmaster. Young. Keen. *Far* too keen. The drama teacher had a nervous breakdown when his wife left him, and I got stuck with directing the nativity play. Didn't know how to say no back then. Young... keen... and I despised every second of it. If I had *just* come home..."

She sank into the chair across the desk, eyes glistening behind her black frames as she stared up at the ceiling.

"You think you could have prevented what happened to Sebastian if you'd been there," Barker stated.

Pursed lips held back tears. She took a deep breath before continuing, "On the phone, I mentioned having a theory about Sebastian's disappearance. Something I've suspected for a very long time but could never prove. And it's not just a theory. I *know* it to be true."

Barker leaned forward, elbows on the desk. "You said you had evidence worth sharing? I told you I'm here to listen."

"I've tried before, you know. In the past, I mean. Tried telling people what I believed happened. But I learned quite quickly that no one wanted to hear it. They gave me *those* looks reserved for 'hysterical' women." She spat the words with venom. "Maybe times have changed. I haven't said anything yet, and you're looking at me like you might believe me."

"No reason not to."

"Bet you saw a lot of that in the police?" She chewed at her lip, skirting around the question. "Tons of men in suits not taking women seriously?"

He nodded. "More than I'd like to admit."

"Sebastian's disappearance derailed my life," Veronica continued. "I almost lost my first teaching job when I missed the first few weeks of term in the new year. They were understanding at first, so I poured all my energy into trying to find him. Chasing every thread. Hitting every dead end. People said I was losing the plot. It's like they forgot I was looking for a person. My *brother*. Felt like Sebastian had never even existed. Come the spring of 1980, the headmaster gave me the ultimatum. Return to the classroom or quit." Eyes clenched, she shook her head as though the wound of the decision had never healed. "What was I supposed to do? I never decided to stop trying to find Sebastian, but... that's what time does to you. I was only twenty-five." She held up her wrinkled hands with a sigh. "*Forty* years..."

She paused, weighing her next words. He dimmed the volume a couple of notches, clasped his hands, and leaned further across the desk.

"To understand what happened, you'll need the full picture," she said. "Of my family, I mean. Of the tensions between my brothers and me after our parents died. My father died that year, 1979. His liver gave out in February. Mum's heart the year before. They worked themselves to death. Almost worked us to death in the process." Glancing down, she looked into the corner of her eye, as though towards the field, but her head couldn't quite turn. "Grew up on a small dairy farm a few fields over on the other side of the hill. Always something to be doing on a farm, and if you weren't doing it right, a belt or a cane would set you straight. It bonded us when we were younger. Sebastian was the eldest. He got away first. Greg *hated* that. I hated that, to be honest, but I loved Sebastian." A warm smile lit up her twisted features. "Sweet, kind, caring... Greg used to be, but he changed when he hit his teens. Saw himself as different. *Better.* When I moved to university, I think Greg saw it as a betrayal. Sebastian encouraged me, but Greg barely said two words to me after I told him I was leaving. He still had a few more years on the farm, and he looked at us like we left him to it." Her brows furrowed. "I suppose we did, really, but I couldn't stay there. They wouldn't even let me read books." She glanced at the storybooks he'd been reading to Olivia, still scattered on the rug. "Can you imagine that? Not letting a child read?"

Barker couldn't, but from Jessie's stories and the things he'd seen during his time in the police, he knew there were many people who would treat their children in ways that would make any well-adjusted person's toes curl.

"Sebastian was last seen on Christmas Eve at Vincent Wellington's annual party at the manor," she revealed. "Half of the village saw him there, and then poof! *Gone.* I came back a few days after Christmas when I didn't hear from him. Nobody told me. Had to find out from some woman in the street. Police insisted Seb must've run off to join some hippie commune, but that wasn't my brother. He had a passion for nature—for preserving the land, but after our father died and left the farm to Seb in the will, that became his focus. But Greg?" She snorted. "He thought Seb was soft. Naïve. Greg had his eye on bigger things... on rising in politics and lining his pockets along the way. Started pressuring Seb to sell the farm the second our father died. Thought he deserved to cash in on his cut.

"And you think..."

"That Greg killed Sebastian?" She nodded without hesitation. "With no evidence of foul play, the local police at the time didn't act on my suspicions. When enough time passed for the lawyers to sign on the dotted line, the farm passed to Greg. He sold it in a heartbeat to our uncle. Paid for him to live in the lap of luxury in Cambridge while he got his politics degree. He bought a flashy car, flashy suits, and Greg Morgan never looked back. *You* put the pieces together, Barker."

Barker flinched at the force of her words. Greg's capacity for anything, from corrupting committees to hiring gangs, was no secret. But jumping to murder, especially that of his own brother, was a big leap, even for Greg.

He was aware of the statistics: most murders are committed by those close to the victim, with family and friends often topping suspect lists. Yet, the idea of Greg, in his twenties, resorting to such drastic measures to acquire a farm, seemed less immediately acceptable to Barker than it did to Veronica.

"Any evidence beyond a hunch?" he asked gently.

"Don't think I haven't tried. Greg's *always* been careful, even as a young man. He was a big shoplifter when we were kids. *Poor* kids, I might add. And he did used to steal me books, but he'd steal all sorts. Things he didn't even need. Once stole an empty pram left outside a shop because 'it was there for the taking,' and sold it on. He didn't get his slippery reputation from his politics alone. I trust my instincts about him, but I'm no hysterical fool. The law requires more than instinct."

Barker nodded. He knew that bitter truth all too well from his own career chasing justice. For all the cases he'd closed back in his official days, as many had slipped through his fingers due to a lack of evidence, firm hunches or not. Sometimes those cases still rattled around in his brain on late nights tossing and turning, so he could only imagine what Veronica had been going through for four decades.

"There is *one* thing," Veronica said after the Christmas jazz was allowed to claim the silence again. "You'd think if Sebastian deserted the farm it would pass to the next eldest sibling, which is me. Except, my father was very old-fashioned. He was lucky to have the farm to own to pass on. Should have gone to my uncle, his older brother... but I think grandad trusted my father most to keep the farm as it was. My father thought women had their place, and it wasn't owning farms. Made sure to put that in his will. Greg was there when the will was read. He'd have known the farm would have gone straight to him the moment Seb was out of the picture. I confronted Greg once. Asked him outright if he'd played a part in Sebastian's fate."

"And what did he say for himself?"

"He smiled at me. This slow, cold smile that didn't reach his eyes. And he said, 'Dear sister, I'd brush up on libel laws before making wild accusations, if I were you.'" She barked a sharp, metallic laugh. "Those words have never left me. That was the last time I spoke to him as a sibling. To me, that's as good as a confession."

A shiver ran down Barker's spine. He could almost hear Greg's smooth menace dripping from those words as if he were at one of his press conferences.

"He *didn't* deny it," Veronica continued. "It might have been better if he did. I could have lived all these years thinking he might be innocent, but it's like he *wanted* me to know what he did." She left the chair to pace again, wringing her hands. "It was a little easier when he was hidden away in the council and I didn't have to see him every day, but he had to go and get himself elected as our MP, didn't he? All his wildest dreams come true, and my worst nightmare."

"But look what he did with those dreams," Barker said, nodding at the stack of *Post* issues by the filing cabinet. "Went straight to bribery, corruption, and being James' puppet. I know it's no consolation, but Greg *is* behind bars."

"You're right." The pacing stopped. "It isn't a consolation. He could still wriggle out of the trial. I've heard rumours he might be released on bail. He can't get away with this again. Not now that Sebastian's body has been found."

Veronica's chest heaved as years of built-up frustration seemed to pour out of her. Sebastian's fate, Greg's corruption, the erosion of Peridale's rural culture—all blending into a toxic cocktail she was helpless to untangle alone. Barker rose from his desk, moving around to grip Veronica's hands, grounding her crackling energy.

"This is really difficult for me to say," she said, her gaze wandering to the door for the first time, and to the field on the other side, no doubt. "I can't do this alone. I need your help. I've read the archives. You were a good detective in this village, even if your wife did keep beating you to the chase, but Julia's hands are full fighting James. Jessie says you're a good PI. The best, in fact. If you can link Greg's rise in power to

Sebastian's demise, expose the dark roots of his corruption once and for all... we could finally bring Greg down, and hopefully James with him, from association alone."

Moved by her vulnerability, Barker started to reply as Veronica pulled away. She dragged an envelope stuffed with money from her pocket and thrust it into his hands.

"I don't expect something for nothing."

The thickness of the envelope silenced Barker for a moment. This case would require a dedication stretching far beyond money. It would consume hours, days... digging through a past he'd barely been alive for, sifting for truth. Unearthing secrets many powerful people wanted left buried. Perhaps the trickiest case of his career.

"I will help you," he replied, putting the money back in her pocket. "As a PI, but as your neighbour first." He was moved by the surprise in her eyes. "As your friend. What you've done for Jessie this past year... this whole village..."

"Barker, I don't need charity, I need—"

"The *truth*, I know. I'll do my best for you, Veronica. I promise."

Relief washed over her as she dug into her pocket. She pulled the envelope out again, but it returned when Barker stepped back, holding up a hand.

"Well, then," she said after clearing her throat, patting him on the shoulder, "let's hope you're as good as Jessie says you are, eh?"

"'I have a spirit to do anything that appears not foul in the truth of my spirit.'"

A smile washed across her face. "Measure for Measure. Act Three, Scene One. Yes, I do believe you are determined, my good man, and filled with spirit. For the first time in forty years, I feel hope this might come to an end."

With a promise to keep in close contact throughout his investigation, Barker showed Veronica to the door, and her steps seemed lighter as she left through the back gate.

After grabbing a fresh coffee from the café and filling Jessie in on what her editor had shared, Barker sank into his office chair. The heft of what he'd just agreed to settled across him. Pursuing this mystery would demand vast energy and concentration. He opened his laptop to the first page of his new book. He'd been pulling words like teeth when Veronica had called ahead, but his hopes of making a start before Christmas had left with her.

There was always next year.

As he pulled up a new search window to start his digging, a fresh spark of hope flickered deep within. If Barker could prove her theory that Greg's political career had been sown from the seeds of his brother's death, it might offer the key to stopping Greg Morgan and James Jacobson.

And their dreaded Howarth Estate love child, once and for all.

~

Julia dropped the unopened post onto the steel island in the kitchen after convincing her gran to continue speculating at her cottage. Across the island, Olivia babbled in her highchair, chubby fists smearing mashed potatoes over her cheeks. If one of them had to be cheerful, Julia was glad it was Olivia.

She pulled the stack of unopened post from that morning towards her. Bills, advertisements... and a thick cream envelope that made her fingers tremble. Fancy white cardstock with gilded edges. She ripped it open with a butter knife, almost expecting another donation, but she extracted a glossy invitation decorated with holly and candlesticks.

"'The esteemed Mr James Jacobson requests the honour of your presence at the Inaugural Peridale Winter Gala,'" she read aloud. "'An evening of fine dining, entertainment and dancing in celebration of our charming village and its bright future.'" Arching a brow at Olivia, she said, "Bright future, my foot."

Julia crumpled the invite and lobbed it into the bin. Unlike his Halloween invitation, it wouldn't make its way onto the cork notice board. At least she wouldn't have to dream up an excuse not to attend his farce.

Rifling through the rest of the post, she discovered another envelope that gave her pause. Plain white, no address, no stamp, the now-familiar 'For the cause' scribbled on the front. She pulled out another neat pile of notes. Her breath caught as she thumbed through—six hundred pounds this time.

"A donation or a bribe?" Julia mused to Olivia. Since Jessie had said it, these mysterious donations reeked of Jacobson's fingerprints. "What to do, eh?"

After cleaning up Olivia's dinner, Julia tucked her into her pram, ready to take her home once she'd finished with the café. She pushed through the beads and added the money to the rest. More flyers, though she wasn't sure they were doing much outside of adding to the village's litter.

In the glow of the twinkling lights and the display cabinets filled with the day's minimal leftovers, Julia set to work sweeping the hardwood floors with slow movements. She leaned on the broom handle near the long wall with the tinsel-framed photographs. From a sketch of the rowdy The Shepherd's Rest tavern in the 1700s, to the 1800s tearoom, the 1900s toy shop, and to Julia's grinning face on opening day less than a decade ago.

Recently separated.

Childless.

Fearless.

And ready to conquer the world in her pink apron.

Lingering on that image, her throat tightened. She wished she could rekindle that naïve confidence. Outside, fine snow swirled under the streetlamps lining the village green. Julia gazed at the falling flakes, imagining her mother standing out there decades earlier, cradling infant Julia outside the old toy shop, rallying villagers against looming bulldozers with Sebastian Morgan.

Through the snow, a hand rose to wave at her.

James Jacobson lingered under the streetlamp outside Richie's, breath foggy in the chill.

"Evening, Julia," he called, his tone deceptively pleasant and loud enough to reach her in the café. "Enjoy your little pause button, won't you? Won't be long 'til the diggers resume their work. I'll drop by to see you soon."

Julia bristled, her hands clenching the broom. The back door opened, shattering the heavy atmosphere. She tore herself from the window as Jessie and Barker walked in, stamping fresh snow off their boots.

"Reinforcements from the chippy," Jessie

announced, lifting two greasy bags oozing the scent of salt and vinegar. "Nothing gets the mind working like chips."

Barker gave Julia's arm a supportive squeeze; she must have looked as shocked as she felt at James calling to her through the snow.

"Veronica's hired me," he revealed. "She's convinced that Greg killed Sebastian, and even if our former MP isn't the culprit, Jessie has filled me in on Vincent Wellington and his building pals. The suspect pool widens."

"And there's more," Jessie said, biting a chip in half. "I dug deeper into Harold Morgan. You know Martha Morgan?"

"Not that I can think of," Julia admitted.

"Christmas market organiser for the council? You will have seen her around. Green blazer. Clipboard. Sort of face that always looks like it's about to tell you you're wrong."

"Actually, now that you mention it…"

"Well, she's beating the 'Greg is innocent' drum louder than anyone right now, and not only is she Greg's cousin, she's also Harold's daughter. Harold is Greg's uncle, and Greg sold their family farm to *him* before he ran off for his expensive education. Martha and Harold still live there to this day."

"That timing can't be coincidence," Barker

pondered, popping a piping hot chip into his mouth. "If Greg orchestrated his brother's disappearance to get the farm, he'd need to sell it to keep his hands clean, which keeps him in the frame, and adds the uncle."

"*And* Vincent Wellington," Jessie pointed out. "Even if he is dead, he'd have still wanted Sebastian out of the way back then. Might be worth talking to Katie to see if she knows anything."

"We need to find the other two as well," Barker said.

"Arnold, the architect, and Gwen, the gilded investor," Jessie added, pushing a tray of chips towards Julia. "Mum, what do you say? You're being unusually quiet."

Julia glanced back at the window, but James was long gone. She considered her thoughts as she chewed a mouthful of salty fried potatoes.

"We start fresh in the morning," Julia said, lifting into the breeze of a second wind. "Duncan Howarth wanted to develop that land in the 1840s, Wellington tried again in the '70s, and now Jacobson's picked up the torch. They keep trying to pave over us, but we won't be the ones to lie down and surrender. We can't."

Barker smiled, slipping a supportive hand around her waist. "And if we can prove Greg murdered his own brother, it destroys Jacobson's last shreds of his flimsy reputation. It will show everyone his true colours for getting into bed with Peridale's most corrupt."

"We have a *pause button* on the destruction," Julia echoed James' taunt with quiet defiance. "Let's use this delay wisely and expose the worms threatening our home before they return. But first, chips. These *are* really good."

"Brain food, I told you," Jessie said, craning her neck back to drop one in her mouth. "*The Post* runs on these things."

After a quick dinner and seeing Jessie and Barker out the back door into the swirling snow, Julia finished cleaning for the day. With the café sparkling for Sue's solo shift in the morning, she pulled Olivia's pram down the front step.

Locking the door, she looked off to St. Peter's Church across the green as snow swirled around its pointed spires. She pictured the little graveyard behind it, cast in the shadow of Howarth Forest, her mother's final resting place.

"I won't let you down, Mum," Julia whispered into the darkness. "For Olivia's future, and for Peridale's present."

8

Crisp snow crunched under Julia's boots as she walked across the green. Flakes clung to the garlands draped around the lampposts, softening Peridale's edges under winter's gentle veil. The church beckoned the start of another day with nine chimes.

The market was busy, as was the café, but nothing Sue couldn't handle. With Olivia spending the morning with Dot, Julia readied herself to investigate the case, knowing whom she would interview first—if she could find Gwen Dean. She spotted Jessie and Barker near the bratwurst stand, salted pretzels in hand. She caught their attention with a wave.

"Ready to get cracking on our suspect list?"

Jessie offered her the last bite of her pretzel. "As I'll ever be. Strengthening myself before surprising

Uncle Harold Morgan. Turns out he was the one to transform Veronica's old family farm into an ice cream shop, and it's just a short walk over the hill."

"Sounds like I got the easiest draw," Barker said, pulling on his wool gloves. "Found Arnold Jessop at Oakwood Nursing Home, and he was happy for me to visit. Tea and biscuits next to a blazing radiator? Almost feel guilty."

Julia laughed, but the moment of levity faded as Jessie nodded towards the end of the market. "Some aren't feeling so jolly this morning."

Veronica darted around in front of *The Peridale Post*'s stall, bundled in a heavy overcoat coat, black to match her large glasses. She had no qualms about blocking shoppers' paths to shove flyers at them. Most averted their eyes and veered away, reluctant to engage.

Just like Sebastian from Dot's recollection.

"She's kicked things up a notch, if possible," Jessie murmured, pulling her phone from deep within her pocket. She swiped away a text message notification that had three red hearts attached, her cheeks turning a similar shade, before showing them a mock-up headline. "I've told her she can't print this, but she isn't listening. She's crossing over into slander territory."

Julia squinted at the headline: 'Did Greg Morgan Murder His Brother in 1979?'

"And *that's* why detectives don't solve murders of those close to them," Barker said. "Best we can do for her is find out the truth. This has consumed decades of her life, so let's not let it consume any more."

"Do you think she's right?" Jessie asked, typing out a quick reply to the message that had darkened her cheeks. "That Greg is behind this? Also, let's do the whole 'meet the parents' thing with Dante when things have calmed down."

"But I was looking forward to interrogating your new boyfriend." He feigned a sigh of disappointment. "And if Greg did kill his brother, it's not going to be easy to prove, so let's get a move on. Julia, did you find Gwen?"

She nodded. "I think so, and if I've found the same Gwen Dean from that old article, how the mighty have fallen."

With a promise that they'd meet up at Dot's later for their next protest planning meeting, the trio split off. As Julia weaved through families queuing for the small carousel, a ripple of anticipation prickled down her spine.

Julia didn't warm much in her sputtering Ford Anglia. She shivered, driving out of the village under dull skies, the old car's wheezing heater coughing out gasps of warm-ish air. By the time she'd thawed a little, she was peering up at the grey clouds blending into the Fern Moore estate's utilitarian housing blocks. She pulled into the small car park opposite the wooden play park and slammed the creaky door.

Locking her car, she noticed James Jacobson emerging from Daphne's Café across the way. She might have suspected him of following her, given how often their paths crossed, if he hadn't arrived ahead of her. Head down, she grabbed the box of donations from her boot and hurried across the estate before he noticed her. Despite the cold, she'd been having a fine morning and wanted to keep it that way.

She arrived at the opening of the alley leading to Fern Moore's food bank, just as the owner, Hilda Hayward, did. Hilda's grandmotherly smile banished Julia's uneasy knot at seeing James. Hilda left the trolley she used to ferry donations and gave Julia a tight hug.

"Always a pleasure to see you, Julia!" Hilda beamed as she looked into the box of donations. "And even more donations? Your café is turning out to be one of our biggest contributors."

"All thanks to my customers."

"People always feel more generous this time of year, don't they?" Hilda dropped the box of tins and boxes into the trolley. "Every little helps, for the cause."

"For the cause," Julia echoed, and as she followed Hilda down the alley to the metal shutters of the food bank, she wondered if Hilda was the one behind the donations. She dismissed the idea as soon as it came. If Hilda had that kind of money to throw around, it would go to the food bank. Her best bet was still the richest man in Peridale.

"That swine has been showing up here more and more," Hilda said under her breath as she pulled up the shutters, following Julia's stare to James lingering outside the café. "Whacked the rent up for all those shops. Blamed it on inflation, but they'll be empty again before long. People 'round here can't afford the prices Daphne has been forced to bump up to. That Jacobscrooge is such a greedy devil."

Maybe the nickname would catch on, after all.

She followed Hilda under the shutter with the trolley, her cheeks burning from shame. "I'm so sorry I ever suggested to James to invest in this place. I foolishly thought he could be a force for good here. A guardian angel instead of a vulture bleeding it dry."

Hilda patted Julia's glove. "You meant well, dear. He is a charmer, but alas, I don't think there's a redeemable bone in his body. After that mess with poor Ronnie, I did try to warn you about what he had planned, but I hoped I'd heard wrong." She paused, and Julia remembered the warning all too well from a summer's day meeting in Daphne's when Julia had still thought of James as a friendly acquaintance. "I heard whispers about James having 'big plans' from my old contacts from my days working for the council. Greg was foul back then, too. He and James are well-suited—chinless charmers."

Julia's ears pricked up at the mention of Greg. "You knew Greg well?" Hilda shrugged, tilting her head from side to side. "Did you know his brother, Sebastian? Went missing in 1979?"

"I'm afraid not, dear," she said. "I knew Greg in his forties, and he was no better back then. Cheated his way through the ranks at the council. I did read about those bones in the paper. Terrible news."

From behind one of the shelves packed with cereal boxes, Billy Matthews, Jessie's ex-boyfriend, grinned at Julia around the edge of a box of frosted flakes.

"I thought I recognised that voice," he said. "How's it going, Mrs S?"

Julia managed a thin smile. "I've had better days, but I'm sure things are on the up. How are you, Billy? All settled in at your new job, it seems."

"Food bank beats the army any day, though some days I can't tell the difference between Hilda and my old drill sergeant." Hilda chuckled as she unloaded the beans and tinned tomatoes from Julia's customers. "How's Jessie doing? She still seeing that guy?"

She nodded, her smile polite.

"Awesome," he said, clearing his throat. "You here to lend a hand? We're boxing up the Christmas parcels. Not long until the *big* day!"

"Oh, don't stress me out, Billy," Hilda said with a sigh. "It comes around quicker every year. And these donations are from the café, so I'm sure Julia is just passing by. Make her a tea. Still like that peppermint stuff?"

"Yes, but no thank you. I *am* passing through, but there was something. I was hoping you'd know where I could find a Gwen Dean? I saw she commented a little thank you message on your post about offering heating grants for people's gas meters? Said it was keeping her warm, so I assumed she must be on the estate somewhere?"

Billy nodded. "Lived here as long as I've been alive. Still fancies herself as posh, despite being in the same circumstances as the rest of us. What's she done?"

"Nothing that I know of, yet. I'm helping Barker investigate the cold case of Sebastian Morgan's disappearance for Jessie's editor at the paper."

"Spray painted the mural in Veronica's office above

your step-mum's salon," Billy said. "Nice lady. Gwen's involved with her brother's death?"

"I'm looking to rule her out."

Hilda considered this, then nodded. "Well, if it's to solve poor Sebastian's fate, I trust your discretion. Gwen's flat is just around the corner. Fourteen on the ground floor, and you didn't hear that from me."

Thanking them for the tip and promising discretion, Julia left Hilda and Billy to their organising and walked around the corner. She rapped on Gwen's paint-chipped door, praying the woman would prove cooperative.

Gwen Dean, with a ratty grey-rooted beehive half the height from the old photograph, leaned on a cane with a handle carved into the shape of a swan. She peered through the door chain as she eyed Julia with a distrustful glare.

"Whatever you're selling, I don't want it," she barked, moving to push the door shut. "And if you're one of them missionaries, it's too late to save me, darlin'."

"I'm here about Sebastian Morgan," Julia interjected, ducking with a smile.

The name made Gwen pause, glassy eyes narrowing behind her cat-eye glasses. After a silent assessment, she withdrew the chain and shuffled aside to allow Julia entry.

Gwen's modest flat bore hints of her former grandeur in the threadbare antique rugs and peeling damask wallpaper. She shuffled to a high-backed ornate armchair that resembled a throne and pointed the gold tip of her cane at the well-worn sofa. An offer of tea didn't follow.

"Aren't you supposed to show me your badge, or have standards really gone all the way down the toilet?"

"Oh, I'm not with the police." Julia laughed to herself at the assumption, looking down at the snowman knitted into her festive jumper. Gwen did the same, her brow lifting into a sharp peak. "My husband is a private investigator. He's been hired by Sebastian's sister."

"Veronica?" she barked. "That lass runs the paper now, doesn't she?"

"She does. Do you know her?"

"No." Gwen's eyes narrowed. "So, what brings you to my door? I didn't know Sebastian any more than anyone else who saw the straggly man around the village."

"Did you know his brother? Greg?"

Gwen shifted in her seat, fingers tightening around the cane clenched between her legs. "Young lad was always buzzing around Vincent for a job. Promised he'd sell him his family's farm if Vincent named a fair price. He's in prison now, isn't he?" Her ruby-red lips thinned into a dry smile. "Doesn't surprise me. You can tell people are bad eggs young if you know what to look for. Would have sold his granny for bus fare if he thought he'd make money at the next stop." She sniffed, the smile turning into a purse. "So, why are you here wanting to talk to me?"

"You were an associate of Vincent Wellington," Julia stated. "It's no secret that Sebastian opposed Vincent's development plans. I was hoping you could help fill in some of the blanks."

Gwen waved a wrinkled hand, a ruby ring on her finger catching the light. "Oh, I left *that* life behind long ago. No use dwelling on the past."

"I did read an old article where you referred to yourself as a 'tycoon.' It sounds like you had quite the successful business career at one point?"

To her surprise, Gwen let out a cackle. "A tycoon? Is *that* what I said? Yes, I suppose I did fancy myself as one. The world was my oyster once, or so I thought." Her eyes glazed over as she slipped into the past. "Inherited a pretty penny from my father. Generations of Dean family money. But I lost it all in the end—terrible investments. There's no accounting for a spotty education, no matter how many fancy schools Daddy paid for."

Julia tilted her head curiously.

"I tried my best, but I let myself be led by the wrong people. Bad advice." Gwen snapped her fingers. "And then, it was gone. I couldn't be bothered to try getting it back." She gave a nonchalant shrug. "I'm happy enough now, all things considered. I have a few treasures for a rainy day, and a roof over my head. Another version of me is out there, living a very different life. A version that never believed Vincent. I still resent that man, even after he drew his last breath."

"Was he one of those... wrong people?" Julia probed.

She scowled. "The *worst*. I sunk most of Daddy's fortune into Vincent's dream of his perfect Wellington Village. Claimed that land was as good as his. He called it a 'sound investment.' Should have known it would never take off, but I was young and foolish." She practically spit the words. "But alas, I signed the cheques and watched my accounts slowly drain while he carried on just fine until his final days."

Julia knew Vincent did eventually lose his fortune too, but he'd lost his health before that, and the brunt of the fortune lost had been after his death. Still, he'd burdened Gwen in a similar way he'd burdened his only surviving heir, Katie, with bankruptcy.

"Most of my money went to that damn architect he hired," she muttered, stomping her cane on the frayed rug. "I never saw a single penny of my 'investment' ever again. Tried to spin some gold out of the little pot I had left when the whole thing folded, but I wasn't built for the fast-paced business landscape of the 1980s. Couldn't keep up with it all. Ah well, life goes on."

"It does," Julia agreed, smiling around the flat. "I don't know if you've heard, but there are new plans for an estate development on that same land…"

"Some weird tribute to that old Duncan Howarth fella?" She rolled her eyes at the ceiling before snatching up the remote control. "I heard. Bound to happen someday, wasn't it? Council almost sold it to Vincent in '79. Maybe I'd be wrapped up in diamonds and furs if he'd followed through, but he pulled out of the deal at the last moment and buried the plans."

Julia leaned forward as Gwen flicked through the muted channels on the small television in the corner, sensing their time was coming to an end. "Why did he withdraw after all that time and money spent?"

"After Sebastian disappeared, Vincent thought it would make him *look* too guilty—like he'd got rid of the boy to clear the way. He always cared too much about his image. But he never spent enough time out of that dusty old manor to realise everyone hated him regardless of how he acted—a rich, pompous hermit obsessed with legacy." She rolled her eyes, turning the volume up a few bars as a reporter announced 'more snow on the way across the Cotswolds' during the late morning news. "I'm just glad Vincent is dead and buried. Went to the funeral to make sure the old goat was really gone. Now there's a man I'll *never* shed a tear for."

As Gwen's attention waned, Julia decided to change tact. "Did you ever have any direct dealings with Sebastian Morgan?"

Gwen paused, shifting in her seat after placing the remote back on the armrest. "I saw him at the party at the manor on Christmas Eve like everyone else. But no, nothing else." She shook her head. "You'll want to talk to Harold for information—Sebastian's uncle. Harold was gung-ho for the development plans—had the most to gain out of us. Whereas I..." she said, gesturing around her tiny flat, "had the most to lose. Now, if you don't mind, I'm going to ask you to run along. Lovely to meet you, but *Bargain Hunt* is starting."

Julia took the hint and showed herself out as Gwen kept her eyes glued on the small TV. Stepping outside into the cold courtyard, Julia exhaled, processing the conversation.

Out of the corner of her eye, she spotted James striding across the concrete courtyard from the direction of the café. Dodging behind a graffitied pillar before he could intercept her, Julia hurried to her car. As she reversed out of the space, the wheels skidding slightly on the snow, she replayed the key pieces of information from Gwen.

The failed Wellington plans, the shifting motives, and Gwen's lost fortune. She wasn't certain she'd ruled Gwen out, but she wasn't sure if she was a suspect either.

However, as Gwen had said, she did have a lot to lose, and lost she had. Harold, on the other hand, judging by Jessie's research, had come out on top despite Wellington Village's unfulfilled destiny. As she drove back to the village, she wondered how Jessie was getting on.

9

Biting wind whipped through Jessie's dark, messy hair as she peered back at the diggers shrinking into the distance. She walked with Dante in the middle of the frozen field, clutching his gloved hand. In her mind's eye, she pictured paved roads and soaring houses sprouting up from the spongy mud. She caught Dante studying her, curiosity glinting in his dark eyes.

"Penny for your thoughts?" she asked, nudging his arm.

Dante's lips quirked into a half-grin. "Just wondering when I can take you on another date, that's all."

"We're on one now, aren't we?"

"On our way to interview a suspect for your dad's new case? Romantic."

"Alright, Mr Fussy, just trying to make the most of..." Her words trailed off as she noticed Dante watching her with uncharacteristic seriousness. Her pace slowed, forcing him to do the same. "Is it about you not meeting my parents? I wanted you to meet them, but with what happened, it didn't feel like the right time. And Veronica needed—"

"No, no." Dante blew out a slow breath, his gaze lowering to the frosty grass. "It's not about that. I'm ready when you're ready. It's other stuff. Unrelated. You're right, this is the best date I've ever been on."

Jessie laughed, but she could sense there was more.

"You can talk to me," she offered. "That's what people like us do, right?"

"People like us?" His smile spread. "You know, we haven't put a label on this yet. Are we..."

"Dating," Jessie interrupted. "So, date, what's that bee in your bonnet?"

Dante collected his thoughts as he slowed, though that might have been due to the field's slope rising into a gentle hill.

"It's work. I've been thinking of handing in my notice at *The Chronicle*. The dud stories they keep sending me off on aren't why I got into journalism, and now that Greg is behind bars, my secret side project has hit a dead end. Feels like I'm wasting the degree I won't finish paying off until I'm Veronica's age. I'm not sure where my future is going if I stay there. Love the old folks, but being sent to the nursing home twice a week is grating on me. It's never *real* news."

"Can't say I'd enjoy putting up with that," Jessie admitted. "Applied to other newspapers? Could always see if Veronica has the budget to take you on. *The Post* would be lucky to have you."

"Well..." he began, casting her an investigative look as if anticipating her response. "I was thinking of going off to explore the wider world before getting in too deep somewhere new. Always wanted to see more and might even start a little travel blog. Who knows where it'll go, right? Mum and Dad say I should do it now before I get 'too old' and regret it."

Jessie blinked against the brisk wind as it took a moment for his confession to sink in. Dante planning to leave? Now, so soon after they'd admitted this spark between them? Her stomach skidded like a crashing car.

"I've seen all those pictures on your *Insta* from your gap year, and—"

"Nine months," she interrupted. "Didn't make it to the year. Wanted to come back home."

"Right," he said as they crested the hill. "But all those backpacking adventures across Europe and Asia with your brother looked incredible. I wish I'd done *that* before uni. Wish I'd found myself, like you did. But it's not too late. So, what do you think?"

"Oh, I..." She pulled her hand away, tucking it into her coat. "I think you should do whatever your heart tells you. That's why I went out there. Might even bump into my brother. Alfie doesn't seem to want to come back any time soon."

"Just me?" He laughed. "I wasn't just talking about *me*, you banana. What do you think about *us* going travelling? Together?"

"Oh..." Her reaction wasn't much different, staring dead ahead as they made their way down the hill. "I think... I think that's the ice cream shop next to that old farmhouse."

Leaving Dante trailing behind, Jessie ambled ahead towards the old farmhouse nestled in the valley below. A renovated barn stood next to it, contrasting the crumbling stone. A queue shuffled through the barn doors from the direction of a car park. Behind the barn, tucked away from public view, a thickset older man sporting a bushy moustache tinkered under the propped-up bonnet of a rusty ice cream van. Older and heavier, but Uncle Harold Morgan still looked the same with that moustache.

"That him?" Dante confirmed, and Jessie nodded. "Well, here goes nothing."

"Should we..." She paused, her words straggling off. "Should we get on with it before he disappears?"

Dante nodded, and they charged towards the van, where Harold stood muttering at the engine. Up close, Jessie noted the neat wool of his jumper behind the open mechanics' jumpsuit, and a glinting gold watch he'd been careful not to get any oil on decorating his wrist.

As Harold slammed down the bonnet with a grunt of frustration, Jessie cleared her throat.

"Mr Morgan? My name is Jessika. From *The Peridale Post*?" She tilted her chin at Dante hovering by her shoulder as she flashed her ID badge. "And this is my... er... associate, Dante. We were hoping for a quick word about your nephew's remains being uncovered in the field over the hill?"

Suspicion sparked in Harold's hooded eyes. He scrubbed at his hands with a rag but didn't offer them a handshake. "What's it to you? The police have been round with their questions already."

Jessie squared her shoulders, affecting the casual authority she'd seen Barker summon at the drop of a hat. "We're compiling a retrospective on Sebastian. We want to give readers a *sense* of the man, not just the mystery victim. The more details we unearth around his life and connections, the better chance people will come forward with clues to help the police solve a decades-old case."

Harold grunted, his attention wandering back to the engine. Jessie suppressed a flare of impatience behind a smile.

"Don't you want answers about what happened to your nephew?" Dante asked, his tone firm, no smile present; she'd never seen him look so serious. "I think *you*, of anyone, would want to know the truth."

So, Jessie was the good cop.

Harold scowled, his breath fogging the icy air. "Fine. But here's not the place for dredging ancient history. Let's get inside before we all freeze stiff."

Jessie shot Dante an impressed raise of her brows as they followed Harold through the backdoor. His smile barely lifted, and guilt wrenched in her chest. He'd expected a different reaction to his travelling idea, and she'd expected him to say anything but that.

Harold ushered them into the swarming shop. This chilly Tuesday afternoon rivalled any peak summer Saturday in the café, even if the prices were double anything they had on the menu. The scents of waffle cones, melted chocolate, and hot coffee swirled as they walked past the busy counter. He led them to a corner booth with a 'RESERVED' sign and ushered them inside.

Without asking what they wanted to order, he returned soon after—leaving Jessie and Dante in an awkward silence—and placed three towering concoctions before them. Jessie noted the caramel and chocolate drizzle spilling over the heaping mounds of what smelled like vanilla and honeycomb ice cream.

"Our best seller. Death by Chocolate Delight," Harold proclaimed before scooping a large bite. Icy cream melted over his tongue, and he sighed. "Never understood the appeal, myself. Can't fathom why folk queue in snow for frozen desserts... but who am I to argue with my own success?"

Jessie exchanged a puzzled look with Dante as she sampled her bowl. The sweet explosion of flavours made her eyes widen in surprise. She savoured a second melting bite before turning the talk to business. It was good. Great, even, and she wished they served more ice cream in the café.

"So, this was the family dairy farm back in Sebastian's day, I understand?" Jessie kept her tone light despite the weight of their quest. "Before Greg sold it to you after your nephew's disappearance?"

Harold gave a careless shrug. "Aye, belonged to my dear departed brother's side of the clan. Truth be told, young Seb was a mite soft for the tough life of farmers —no real head for business. Not sure why he inherited, but my brother was a law unto himself." He stabbed his spoon into the ice cream, half-devoured despite his criticism. "Not like our Gregory. He made the wise choice of liquidating into my hands after..."

He trailed off, and Jessie leaned forward.

"Sebastian's timing proved convenient for you," Dante remarked. "Any comment on that?"

Harold's spoon clinked against his bowl. "It wasn't like that at the time. No one knew the poor lad had come to harm back then." He shifted against the squeaky vinyl booth. "We just assumed Seb had had enough of country life and fled to the big city, or joined a commune, or moved abroad."

"If he'd moved abroad, he'd have needed a passport," Dante continued, his tone flat. "There'd have been a record of it, and he wouldn't have been considered missing."

"Okay, so not abroad." Harold's eyes narrowed to slits. "*Of course* we all worried about him, but there's no use crying over spilt milk, as my old nan used to say. Seb was an odd one. Stood out. Nobody knew what he was going to do next, so it was easy to believe he'd wandered down a new path."

Jessie squeaked the vinyl too, uncomfortable with how fast the interview had descended into hostile territory. She gave Dante a subtle kick under the table, widening her smile.

"My research showed you were a mechanic before you opened this shop? Turned it into quite the little empire. Don't imagine a farm of this size would have been easy to buy on your wages?"

Beads of sweat materialised along Harold's forehead. He appeared to weigh his response before replying, "I got lucky. Vincent Wellington felt obliged to finance some projects after his grand plans went belly-up. My skills are with spanners, not ledgers and loans, but I knew how to run a shop. Cars... ice cream... doesn't really matter. Once you oil the machine, and know which parts need replacing when, it runs itself."

"So, Vincent funded your endeavours after you publicly advocated for his development scheme?" She paused for Harold to offer a cautious nod. "The very scheme your nephew stood in the way of? Seems to me like you came out of his downfall quite well off."

"I thought this was supposed to be a remembrance piece?" He scowled. "I was only the mouthpiece for Vincent's pitch, on account of me being a man of the land. Weren't *my* blueprints he was peddling. All I did was give Vincent's idea of rural development two thumbs up. It was just a bit of public relations. Any loan arrangements between us came later out of kindness, not coercion, and he got back every penny by the end."

Jessie noted his thickening rural accent with interest. A telltale sign of defensiveness? Before she could probe further, Harold's gaze sharpened.

"That whole mess was donkey's years ago and ought to stay buried, if you ask me. If you're set on blaming anyone for my nephew's death, have a word with Arnold Jessop. He was the architect with the grand plans, and it wasn't just for *that* field. He wanted *this* farm too, and the land between. Even Vincent had to rein him in. Arnold wanted Wellington Village to happen more than *any* of us." Harold rose, dabbing ice cream from his moustache with a monogrammed handkerchief. "Now, that ice cream van won't get up and running before spring by itself, so if there's nowt else...?"

Dante opened his mouth to object, but Jessie's warning look made him swallow back further questions. She didn't want to throw more fuel on the bridge they'd almost burned to ash.

"That could have gone better," she said as they squeezed their way back outside. "Didn't even get to ask much about Greg, and he's the prime suspect."

"Harold's hiding something," he said, tone still flat. "He wasn't being honest."

Jessie let the words linger, sensing a double meaning. She almost whacked him with the back of her hand, to ask what he was playing at, but they were standing several feet apart. Turning to the field, she thought about setting off to Peridale without a second look back, but she glimpsed a familiar figure loitering near a green estate car.

Her breath caught in surprise to see the all-too-familiar figure of Six leaning casually against the truck, hands stuffed into the pockets of his suit. The final known member of Greg's bruised Cotswolds Crew gang was still tracking their movements with detached interest... or was he? Six glanced in their direction, but his eyes remained fixed on the doors of the barn.

"Is that..." Dante whispered, grabbing Jessie's elbow.

"He's here for Harold. I'm going to—"

Dante looped his arm around hers and dragged her behind the barn. She wanted to protest, but he'd probably done her a favour. Last time she'd followed a Cotswold Crew member, she'd been close to being forced to jump to the bottom of a never-ending well in the middle of nowhere.

"Sorry," Dante said, one hand on the back of the barn as Jessie leaned against the cold corrugated metal. "I should have held back. In the interview, I mean."

"Yeah," she replied, breath quivering as she stared at his lips. "I'm sorry too. I... I don't know. I..." Looking away, she stared off towards the farmhouse. "I think that door is open."

"Huh?"

"The farmhouse door," she said, slipping under his arm and setting off. "Might be worth a poke around?"

"I don't think that's a good idea."

"It's not, but you said it yourself—he's clearly hiding something. You saw how jumpy he got with those questions." Waving over her head for him to follow, she hurried to the door. "Five minutes looking around in *here* while he's distracted in *there*."

Dante looked unconvinced, but he allowed Jessie to tow him towards the converted farmhouse on the property's edge. The heavy oak door was open enough for them to squeeze through without touching anything. They entered a traditional country kitchen with stone floors and a fancy old-fashioned stove like the ones Julia was always looking at in the trade catalogues.

Jessie crept towards a sitting room on the left, keeping her tread soft across the creaking floorboards. She scanned the tartan sofa and landscape paintings decking the walls until a particular display captured her attention. Rows upon rows of licence plates of all shapes and sizes cluttered the walls. Mugs from locations across the globe, too. Seemed like Harold had been travelling, and the guilt twisted again.

It wasn't that she didn't want to go travelling with Dante.

She wasn't sure she wanted to go travelling again. *Full stop.*

"What are we looking for?" he whispered. "I think we should go. Last time we did this at Wellington Heights, we got caught."

"I don't know," she said, dragging open a drawer. "Anything? Something connected to Greg? And we got caught by Richie, not Greg. Richie is on *our* side."

"We found a *gun* in Greg's bedside table, Jessie. A *real* gun."

"And I'm glad you saw it too before Greg got rid of it." Rooting around in the drawer, she was disappointed to find stacks of impersonal 'Best Wishes from All at No.23' Christmas cards sent from neighbours. "That police raid would have gone differently if we'd taken a picture of it. It would have proved we were telling the—"

An angry voice echoed down the staircase in the corner of the room as footsteps padded along a landing above. Exchanging panicked glances, they dashed to cower behind the tartan sofa as Martha Morgan came into view on the stairs. Jessie ducked further while the market organiser fumed into her mobile phone.

"It's *unacceptable!*" Martha snapped. "The market is *already* there. Stallholders are selling as we speak. We've taken pitch fees.... You *cannot* revoke permission now." A pause, and then even louder, "This isn't the *last* minute. This is fifteen minutes *after* the curtain has already risen. I won't allow it."

Jessie struggled to slow her ragged breathing as Martha paced around the room. She heard the drawer she'd opened slam shut, but Martha didn't seem to question who'd opened it.

"*Complaints*? What kind of complaints?" A pause while she listened. "Oh, of course it's *him*. Well, who else could be meddling with town approvals if not *that* man? When Greg is released, he'll put everything right, I'm sure of it. Yes, he *will*. Yes, he *is*! I'm going to visit him tomorrow, so he'll tell me himself. He won't stand for this, and neither will I. You want that market closed down? Over my dead body!"

Jessie edged to peek over the back of the sofa, but Dante clamped a firm hand on her forearm, keeping her pinned behind the tartan until Martha stormed from the room. They emerged at the slamming of a door.

Without a word, they raced out the way they'd entered, boots sliding precariously over the icy flagstones in their haste. Once safely behind the skeletal shelter of a frosted tree, Dante squinted through the barren branches towards the foreboding brick hulk of Fern Moore looming in the distance.

"*When* Greg is released?" he echoed. "Do you think…"

"Wishful thinking," she cut in, hoping she was right. "She's his biggest fan. Let's get back to Peridale."

"Might need to go the long way around."

Six was pacing around the ice cream van. She thought he might be about to tinker with the engine—she'd caught him doing the same to her car on Greg's orders—but like Martha, he seemed to be on the phone. Jessie edged nearer, tugging her arm free of Dante's grip. If Six was creeping around suspects connected to Sebastian's murder case, there was only one person he could be on the phone to.

Ignoring Dante's heated whispers for her to get back, Jessie crept close enough to the stone wall to overhear Six's next words, but she couldn't miss this. She imagined Greg Morgan, worse for wear, clinging to the prison phone while a line of burly men glared at him to hurry up.

But instead of commanding tones, Six's gruff voice emerged with an unusual gentleness Jessie could never have imagined he possessed.

"…I *know*, sweet pea. I promise I'll be home to tuck

you in tonight." He paused, his tone even softer as he said, "Yes, a bedtime story too. I know the flat is cold, but we talked about this, didn't we? Santa likes it that way, so chin up, Mia. Daddy loves you. Now, put Nana back on the phone, will you?"

Stunned by this peek behind the Cotswold Crew enforcer's rough Pitbull exterior, Jessie could only stare. Before she could retreat unseen behind the wall, Six glanced up.

Cursing under her breath, she turned and ran after Dante making his way back up the hill, Six's shouted threats fading behind her.

10

In the calm foyer of Oakwood Nursing Home, Barker nodded at the receptionist as he signed the visitor's log. She glanced up from her book, a well-worn paperback copy of *The Body in the Basement*. Given her disinterested expression, she hadn't noticed he bore a striking resemblance to the man in the brooding headshot on the back page. He pointed towards the 'Visitors This Way' sign, and she waved him through, turning to the next page and pulling the book closer.

He navigated a labyrinth of beige corridors until a lift took him up to the top floor, where things grew even quieter, if that was possible. He wasn't sure why people were so against the idea of moving to these kinds of places in their final years; he could get used to the peace and quiet.

At the end of the corridor, he arrived at a solid oak door proclaiming 'Arnold Jessop' in engraved brass. He tapped a knuckle on the door, wondering how much money he'd need to put away for his retirement years to get a brass nameplate. A firm voice called him in from the other side.

Beyond the threshold, Barker blinked in surprise to find himself transported into a lavish model railway wonderland encased in an even grander apartment. An intricate network of track wove through detailed seasonal landscapes—frost-dusted lawns and lamp-lit cottages dusted with powdery snow. In the centre of this mini kingdom sat a wizened, white-haired gentleman in a red dressing gown, conducting a tiny engine with a whistle emitting tiny puffs of steam.

"Mr Jessop?" Barker began. "I'm..."

"Yes, yes, Veronica's private eye," the old man rasped, milky blue eyes lifting to scrutinise Barker over half-moon spectacles. "One of the nurses informed me you rang ahead. Have a pew, won't you?"

He gestured towards two leather armchairs overlooking the sprawl of his miniature empire. As Barker settled, Jessop rolled his chair over, veiny fingers leaving the wheels to shake Barker's hand in a papery grip. Up close, time had etched deep crags into the old architect's face, sagging the proud bones that must have once exuded confidence and vision. His handshake might have been limp, but his gaze was as sharp as a man's half his age.

"Impressive," was all Barker could muster. "You built all of this?"

"Just a little hobby," he said, with more modesty than required for the impressive structure. "Lest I let my mind go to the dogs. Tea? Coffee? I can have some called in at a moment's notice."

"No, thank you."

"Wise," he whispered, tapping his nose. "For the price I'm paying a month, they should be flying each cup in from the finest Italian barista, but alas, instant." He cleared his throat, casting his eyes over the richly detailed model buildings and streets he'd forged. "So, I expect you're here about that business with Mr Morgan's remains turning up after all this time," he began, jumping straight to the point. "Can't say I knew the lad well myself, but fire away and I'll assist however I can."

Barker collected his thoughts, reminded by Jessop's directness of similar hard-bitten witnesses from his police days—focused and devoid of sentiment. He would take a similar approach, appealing to facts over emotions, and he would need to grapple the reins from Jessop; given the painstaking detail the architect had poured into his tiny empire, he was unlikely to relinquish control.

"As I'm sure you've heard, the working theory is Sebastian was murdered around Christmas of 1979," Barker started, consulting his notepad. "Since you mentioned his sister, Veronica's theory is that Greg Morgan killed his brother to inherit his land. Do you think there could be any truth to that?"

"And *your* theory?" Jessop asked instead.

"Well, that *could* be my theory too, but I need some evidence first." More than just his eye contact remained sharp. "There's a chance Sebastian was killed by someone connected to Vincent Wellington's thwarted development ambitions of the time."

"Which is why you've come to me. The architect." Jessop's bushy brows beetled together as he turned to the window with its views of the snow-dusted tennis courts below. When he replied at last, nostalgia tinged his gravelly voice. "Vincent's vision for that place was *unparalleled*. His passion project—that slice of land held the future in his eyes. I should know." A gnarled finger tapped the temple beneath his thinning white hair. "I'm the fool who spent the best part of a year drawing up the plans for the place. It would have been like nothing the Cotswolds had seen, and I daresay, haven't seen since."

This frank admission sparked Barker's interest. He

glanced at the elaborate model village scaling Jessop's room—this had been a man with grand ideas and even grander ambition.

"So, you'd say you and Vincent were collaborative partners plotting Peridale's future landscape?" Barker pressed. "A landscape that Sebastian wanted to protect."

Jessop let out a raspy chuckle. "Oh, Vincent certainly considered me useful enough, that was, until Sebastian Morgan started throwing his toys out of the pram. I heard he was found when they broke first ground? We were close to that stage ourselves. Vincent had to all but sign on the dotted line, but he lost heart after the disappearance. He became rather paranoid that people would blame him, especially after their altercation."

Barker's mental gears churned. If Jessop carried insider knowledge of shady land deals and Wellington's explosive falling out with Sebastian Morgan, he might shed invaluable light on motives and suspects.

"Altercation?"

"Christmas Eve," Jessop remembered without needing to recall the information. "Wellington Manor. Vincent would throw the most lavish parties, and that one was no exception. Like I said, he was close to signing on the dotted line, so it was a celebration of all of our work. For me, it was a year of my life. For Vincent, perhaps a lifetime. He always dreamed big, and there was something about becoming a father—like he did so late in life—that revved him up to assemble what he called his 'dream team.'"

"You, Harold, and Gwen?"

"The architect, the PR puppet, and the moneybags. What he didn't expect was the thorn in his side—Sebastian." He let out a time-weathered sigh. "Didn't expect him to turn up to the Christmas party, either. Sebastian came in his usual scruffy attire, hair unbrushed, unshaven. It was an outrage, and he walked about the party like he was the king of the manor. Sipping French champagne, scoffing caviar and canapes. It was supposed to be Vincent's celebration, but you'd think Sebastian had just won something."

"Any idea what?" Barker pushed.

"Not specifically, but Sebastian and I had words that evening. Quite the confrontational lad. Passionate, I suppose you could say. He came up to me, bold as brass, asking how *I* slept at night." He chuckled, shaking his head. "Quite well, actually, I told him. He had all these grand notions about preserving country vistas and whatnot, which, mind you, I *fully* support." Leaning in, he whispered, "But you can't protect *every* patch of land, can you? People need homes, and the homes I designed were as perfect for this village as any. Progress marches on whether you like it or not, and he didn't like hearing *that* truth. Threw his champagne in my face and spat his food at my feet." He chuckled again. "Vincent had been keeping a lid on his temper until then, but that act of indecency pushed him over the edge. He grabbed young Sebastian by the hair and escorted him out like he was some common dog."

"And you'd say Vincent had a temper?"

"Ever met anyone that wealthy and ambitious who doesn't?" He arched a brow, wheeling himself from the window to a bureau similar to the antique writing desk Barker had in his office. Using a small key, he unlocked a drawer and flicked through stacks of paperwork. "Sebastian sprung to his feet and swung for Vincent, but Vincent wasn't going to stand for that. He'd put up with almost a year of harassment from that lad by then, so he hit back, and he did not miss."

"Vincent punched Sebastian?"

"Either that, or he had a mouth full of strawberry sauce waiting to spray all over the snow." He continued rummaging, looking up with a glint in his eye. "The people at the party applauded. Everyone was sick and tired of Sebastian's drum beating by then. So few people were on his side. I dragged Vincent off before he could do more damage.

Sebastian drove off into the night nursing his wounded pride and split lip."

"And that was the last time anyone saw him?"

"Seems that way." Jessop sighed, lost in his memories. He resumed his flicking and pulled out some paperwork. "*Ah*! Here they are. My original Wellington Village plans."

Barker joined him as Jessop spread the hand-drawn architectural plans on yellowing paper across his desk, tapping a bony finger on the intricate sketches. "Wellington Village was as close to perfection as anything I ever designed. Truly a shame it never came to fruition. I'll still regret not seeing this realised until my dying breath."

Barker leaned in, examining the clusters of cottages woven among trees and open spaces. He had to admit, it was a far cry from the cramped mini-mansions in Jacobson's blueprints. Jessop's design would have blended in, maybe even become a beloved part of the village by the time Barker's moving van arrived. He might have moved there, never knowing it had once been a contested open space.

"Sebastian was quite worried about developments encroaching on the countryside," Jessop mused. "Concerned about loss of green spaces, increased pollution and the like." He gave a single snort. "A bit ironic considering what we now know about dairy farming's effects on the atmosphere with all that methane. But the lad's heart was in the right place. He was never going to get through to Vincent, though. That man had a one-track mind. Nobody was more shocked than me that Vincent changed his mind. Ironic, really, don't you think?"

"What's ironic?"

"Sebastian tried so hard to stop the development, and yet it was his lack of presence that ground the proceedings to a halt in the end." He gave the plans one last wistful scan before returning them. "Sebastian got what he wanted and didn't live to see it."

"What do you think happened to him in the end?" Barker asked.

The old architect sighed. "You mean, do I think Vincent killed him?"

Barker nodded.

"If he did, I suppose your killer's already dead and buried," Jessop pointed out. "And if Veronica is correct, Greg is already behind bars. Case closed, I'd say."

It would be a convenient ending.

"What can you tell me about Greg Morgan?"

Jessop spread his hands. "Afraid I don't know anything about the other sibling. Greg was never one to make waves over the development plans. He tried cosying up with Vincent. Said he had some land he might be able to sell him, but Vincent was already losing interest by then." Seeming to think the conversation had run its course, the architect wheeled back to the middle of his models and resumed the train service. "Now, if you'll excuse me, I really must get back to wasting my days doing exactly what I want. Don't be offended that I don't show you out."

Leaving Arnold Jessop to his tiny kingdom, Barker left the way he came in, unsure what to think about the architect. He'd seemed open and honest, but he'd appeared eager to wrap everything up in a neat little bow, which never sat right with Barker. Even when he was writing his mysteries, he always like to keep a few ribbons a little loose.

He checked on the receptionist again, the book even closer to her face, and judging by the crease of the spine, she'd just reached the midpoint twist where the detective's daughter was about to be kidnapped. Lost in thoughts of his own stories, Barker bumped into Detective Inspector Laura Moyes on the doorstep.

"Fancy running into you here," Moyes remarked. "Visiting an old relative?"

"Sure," he replied with a wry smile. "And I could say the same for you. Surprised to see you on the Sebastian case. Don't they usually bring in specialist teams for cold cases?"

"Who said *I* was here for the Sebastian case? But I'll take it *you* are too. I know Veronica hired you. She made no secret of it. And don't forget that I was on a specialist cold case team once upon a time, which was good enough for the superintendent. Wanted someone with experience under their belt."

He offered an impressed nod; all his cold cases as the village's DI had been handled by outsiders. "Then it seems we've been tugging at the same ribbons, and I'll assume you're here to speak to Arnold? He has some interesting memories of the Wellington Manor's 1979 Christmas party."

Sitting on the doorstep of the grand nursing home while she vaped away, he relayed the architect's account, including the punch Wellington had thrown and the 'strawberry sauce' in the snow.

"Sebastian seemed like he'd won something?" Moyes picked up on the detail from Barker's account of Arnold's story. "I wonder what? Brave of him to show up."

"Think the punch could mean something?"

She vaped in silence, and Barker gave her a 'I've given you a titbit,' brow raise. "Could line up with the coroner's latest findings. Official cause of death was blunt force trauma to the skull."

"Attended enough messy fights outside pubs and bars during my city days to know one punch can kill."

"Must have been a mean punch because his arms and legs were fractured too. And throw in a couple of ribs. But yes, there's a chance *that* punch could have killed him, which is fantastic." Groaning, she exhaled up to the clouds above. "My prime suspect has been dead for two and a half years and was mute for as many before then, anyway. I have a feeling this cold case isn't turning hot any time soon."

"Experience under your belt, remember?"

"That's what they told me, but we both know that means they didn't want to splash the cash to ship everyone in." She laughed, tucking her vape away. "So, what's Veronica thinking? She must have a theory if she's hired you?"

Veronica hadn't told the police that she thought Greg murdered Sebastian? Barker would have assumed that'd be the first thing she'd do.

"Veronica wants an outside set of eyes," he said, standing up. His offer of an extended hand to help Moyes to her feet was ignored. "I think Jessie told her I haven't had many new cases lately. Probably a pity hire."

"Well, good luck with the pity. And feel free to stop by the station if you ever want to compare notes. Something tells me our paths will cross again on this one, pal."

Back in his car as the heaters warmed up in

seconds, Barker filtered through the pieces of the puzzle Jessop's testimony had provided.

Wellington's explosive temper and violent clash with Sebastian at the Christmas party shone a new light on motives and opportunity. The coroner's report felt like a smoking gun—but only if they assumed Vincent's blow was the sole lethal strike, a theory that might be impossible to prove—maybe it had been more than a single punch like Jessop had said?

Otherwise, someone could have intervened after Wellington's outburst to finish the gruesome job.

Perhaps Greg, hellbent on inheriting that land?

With more questions than answers, Barker set off down the nursing home's winding private driveway. Pinning the murder on a dead man would be opportune for them if true, but only convenient for the killer if not.

First things first, he needed to meet with Julia and Jessie to analyse their interviews and piece together their collective findings.

11

Julia's clammy palms tightened around the steering wheel as she manoeuvred her Ford Anglia into the narrow alley next to the café. Replaying the key details she'd extracted from Gwen during their conversation, she wasn't certain the prickly woman had provided any solid leads.

The glimpse into the decades-old soured business dealings had illuminated a clearer motive. Gwen had been desperate to recoup her investment from Vincent, and Sebastian had stood in her way. But Julia couldn't determine if that made Gwen a legitimate suspect in Sebastian's disappearance or just collateral damage in Vincent's risky property speculation game.

Gwen had mentioned Harold Morgan, Sebastian's uncle, who might have known more about 1979's escalating tensions. Julia hoped Jessie had something concrete from her visit to the ice cream shop over the hill, and that Barker had gained insights from the nursing home. She checked her phone, but neither had been in touch.

Glancing at her watch, she had enough time to help Sue close down the café for the day before the next strategy meeting at their gran's.

Behind the counter, Sue's posture was stiffer than usual as she rearranged a plate of bone-dry scones, avoiding eye contact as Julia approached.

"Everything alright?" she asked. "I know Tuesdays can drag, but did you remember to put butter in the scone mix?"

Sue struggled up a feeble smile. "Not my best batch."

"I'm teasing."

Julia scanned the room for anything amiss but found no overturned furniture or smashed crockery. Evelyn squinted into her teacup by the window. Amy and Shilpa built sugar cube towers at their usual spot. An average, blustery Tuesday.

"Did something happen?" Julia pressed in a hushed tone, leaning over the counter.

Sue shot a nervous glance towards the beaded curtain. "You'd better see for yourself. I don't know what to make of it."

Julia followed her sister through the beads into the gleaming stainless-steel domain she considered her second home. A strong whiff of bleach stung her nose, the cleanliness making the paper spread across the island stand out. A rolling pin and measuring cups weighed down the curling edges of a large architectural plan, accompanied by digital renderings of a crisp modern building and stylish young patrons strolling under a cloudless sky.

The title read 'Peridale – The Howarth Estate: Phase One—Shopping Quarter,' but the modern imagery bore no resemblance to the Peridale Julia knew.

"Where did this come from?"

Sue wrung her hands. "James stopped by about an hour ago. He was asking for you. Seemed surprised you weren't here."

Julia moved closer to the plans. 'Julia's Café' was emblazoned in white and gold above a window as large as a wall on the ground floor of the two-story structure. She scanned down to the patio where a dozen well-dressed customers mingled around wrought-iron tables, lattes and pastries in hand, not a mobile phone in sight. The idyllic scene resembled a lively city side street more than her quaint eighteenth-century café.

"He insisted I show it to you the moment you returned. Refused to take no for an answer. I didn't know what else to do. He wanted me to pass this on. He's offering you the first refusal to own his new café. He's willing to purchase this place from you at a generous price so you can focus all your attention on... *this*."

"Unbelievable." Arms folding tight, Julia turned away from the island. "I can't even look at it."

"I told him you'd never accept. But he said he wants to schedule a proper business meeting to discuss details, and I told him you wouldn't want to do that either. But—"

"He wouldn't take no for an answer?"

Smiling tight, Sue shook her head. Given how shaken she still was, her sister must have endured the brunt of James' obnoxious powers of persuasion.

There was only one thing to do.

Marching to the ghoulish render, she flung aside the rolling pins and the measuring cups. She scrunched the page into a tight ball with such force that her short nails imprinted half-moon divots into her palms. Without hesitation, she tossed the ball into the commercial-strength blender and twisted the dial up to full. A sigh of relief escaped as the glossy paper disappeared in a matter of seconds, sucked down into a muddy slurry. Julia smacked the OFF button, then tipped the grainy contents into the nearby bin.

"Much better." She dusted her hands down the front of her rumpled jumper. "He'll take no for an answer, whether he likes it or not. I'm not budging. Not now, not ever. Pass me that brush, we have a café to clean."

Before following Sue, Julia spared a last glance over her shoulder at the blender. Granules of the destroyed plans still clung to the damp glass like shreds of confetti after a party. His promises of prosperity felt as insubstantial as those soggy bits of paper.

But what had Sue said?

'First refusal.'

If James' imagination came to life, the magical coffee shop with the fancy window and outdoor patio would happen, with or without Julia's name above the door.

It couldn't get that far.

After whizzing around with a brush and mop, they locked up the clean café, ready for the morning rush. Julia, Sue, Evelyn, Amy, and Shilpa wove through the quieting market as vendors packed the last of their wares. One by one they filed into Dot's warm hallway, where Barker and Jessie waited, muted voices drifting from the dining area.

"Interviews?" Julia asked.

"Middling," Barker admitted, helping Julia unravel her scarf. "Arnold gave an eyewitness report of Vincent punching Sebastian the same night he disappeared. Also has a cool train set."

"There's definitely something shifty going on with Harold and the old Morgan family farm. Didn't seem to care about Sebastian either way." Jessie rocked back on her heels, whispering, "And our old shadow friend, Six, is still around. Looks like he's been put on Harold's trail."

"Sounds like Greg doesn't trust his uncle?" Barker suggested, vocalising Julia's first instinct. "Something to look into. How did yours go?"

"Found a woman who had a lot to lose and lost it all. A murderer?" She clung to the ends of her scarf, draping it over the banister. "I'm not sure, but I don't think Gwen told me everything she knows. Seemed in a rush to get rid of me."

"Yeah, mine too," Jessie said.

"And mine," Barker agreed. "Case still open, but I have some information for Veronica, at least."

Julia followed Barker and Jessie into the dining

room, and all heads turned their way. Though glad to see the familiar, concerned faces of her family and close friends gathered alongside a few loyal villagers, Julia's smile faltered.

The group had dwindled from their previous meeting. And that had been their least attended since the early ones following the committee catastrophe.

Dot caught her eye, tilting her head towards the chalkboard, where she had already outlined fresh ideas to bolster their campaign, so Julia joined the others at the table. She took a seat between her father, Brian, and Katie. Julia's four-year-old brother, Vinnie, bounced on Katie's knee, distracted by his colouring book. Across from them, Sue sat beside Neil, while Barker claimed the chair next to Jessie, Detective Inspector Moyes, and her girlfriend, Roxy. At the other end, Evelyn, Amy, Shilpa, Father David, Denise, and Malcolm crowded together on a floral-print sofa pushed under the window.

As Julia accepted a cup of peppermint and liquorice tea from Percy with murmured thanks, Ethel tottered in, pushing a rattling silver trolley laden with biscuits and cream cakes, and Olivia followed her in on two legs. Buttery shortbread and sweet icing wafted over as Ethel parked the trolley within reach and lowered herself into a vacant chair with a groan. Olivia settled on her play mat in the corner with her favourite building blocks to bash together with her cousins, Pearl Jr and Dottie.

Dot rapped her knuckles on the table, commanding the room's attention. "While our toilet paper protest showed James that we're serious, it didn't halt the diggers. If it weren't for finding poor Sebastian, they'd be churning up soil as we speak. We need a new approach, something drastic. Ideas?"

All heads pivoted to Julia. Caught mid-sip of the scalding tea, she gulped too fast and coughed out, "Oh... I..."

Her father's sturdy hand closed over hers, grounding her. "Go on, love. Speak your mind."

"Our flyers and petitions haven't swayed James so far. We need to appeal to him differently, perhaps?" She noticed her dad's approving nod from the corner of her eye. "I'm just not sure how we can get through to him."

"*Nobody* can," Neil said, his pleasant tone uncharacteristically sharp. Brooding eyes remained downcast, fists clenched. "James will *not* listen. I never should've trusted him."

Julia's breath hitched at this rare display of anger from mild-mannered Neil. She exchanged an uneasy glance with Sue.

"What is it, Neil?" Julia asked.

"I'm resigning from the library," he revealed,

eliciting a few gasps. "James is taking over completely. Posters for Howarth Estate are everywhere. My dream job has turned into a nightmare. If I'd known this is how things would have turned out eighteen-months ago, I'd have stepped aside to let the place become the restaurant James wanted it to be."

Sue clasped his rigid hand, and Julia's heart ached. She longed to lift Neil's spirits and reignite his passion for the library, but James' encroachment had already tainted that haven.

A sense of helplessness settled in the room.

"We *are* losing this fight," Julia admitted. Ethel and Dot erupted in outrage, but louder, she said, "James holds *all* the power. Everything we've done seems futile. We're running out of options to stop the Howarth Estate from taking over."

"*Bah*! That's defeatist talk." Dot made them all jump with a smack of the table; Olivia, Vinnie, and the twins laughed. "We'll dig *deeper*, if you'll pardon the pun. Pull out *all* the stops. The toilet roll stunt bought us some time. If we put our heads together, we *can* outsmart James."

"Keep it legal," DI Moyes warned. "We're barely holding onto that field. Once it's released, no protests will stop those diggers."

The detective's warning deflated the burgeoning optimism in the room. Shoulders drooped, faces fell.

Percy, distracted, stuffed an entire shortbread into his mouth, chewing with a sombre expression.

"Alright, we need *fresh* ideas," Julia declared, refusing to admit defeat. What would her mother have done? She mentally reviewed their options. "Jessie had success exposing Greg's misdeeds in the paper. Perhaps we could launch more anti-James campaigns?"

"Veronica's been told to scale back those stories as it is," Jessie admitted. "But I can try to slip some through."

"A fundraiser?" Evelyn offered. "I can read tarot cards. Shilpa's samosas always bring in a tidy sum at church fêtes."

"Happy to contribute," Shilpa agreed. "I can whip huge batches of them up in no time."

"My piano playing usually attracts a good crowd around this time of year," Amy added. "I can play carols. Could even take requests?"

Dot's stick of chalk hovered by the board. "Thanks to our mystery donations, we've got over a thousand pounds in the kitty. We don't need more money... we need *revolution*!"

"Donations?" Shilpa echoed.

"One thousand pounds?" Amy gasped. "From whom?"

"Someone *very* generous," Evelyn said with a knowing nod. "Very generous, indeed."

Murmurs circulated around the group at the revelation of these unexpected cash injections. Julia still hadn't identified the source, and catching Jessie and Sue's eyes, she could tell their nagging suspicions still suggested James might be behind it. None spoke up.

"Whoever it is," Neil broke through the chatter with reasoned volume, "we need to use their money wisely. Dot is right. We need revolution."

"I've had an idea," Ethel said, stirring more sugar into her tea. "Why don't we take some inspiration from Sebastian?"

"And all go *missing*?" Dot replied. "You first, dear. That's the worst idea I've ever heard, Ethel, and that's saying something. You suggested we substitute the beef in a cottage pie for chicken the other day. Who's ever heard of such nonsense?"

"*Camping*, Dorothy," Ethel snapped. "And you have chalk all over your skirt."

Dot looked down to dust off her navy skirt, adding more chalk from her fingers in the process while the rest of them marinated in Ethel's idea.

"He camped out there in protest," Ethel continued. "We could do the same."

"In December? You're already one stiff breeze away from the Grim Reaper, Ethel."

"You're much older than I, Dorothy."

"But much fitter." She rotated her leg on the ball of her foot as though it proved the point. "We'd freeze before James budges."

"Not with the right thermal undergarments, my love," Percy countered with a wagging finger. "I imagine camping equipment has grown more sophisticated these days. Don't you remember that documentary we watched about those pensioners who camped atop Scafell Pike in October? At that altitude, it would be much colder than our ground temperature this time of year."

"And don't you recall what I called them? Lunatics!"

"Lunatics who survived."

"Hmm." Dot huffed before adding 'camping protest' to the board in tiny letters. "We can put it on the back burner, I suppose. Thank you, Ethel."

Unlike her gran, Julia envisioned rows of tents on the disputed field, a human barrier against the construction crews. The land had once hosted a vibrant music festival with tents all over; could it not be a site of protest now?

"If *enough* of us camp there," she said, all eyes turning to her once more, "we'd create a human blockade. The diggers can't dig land that they can't reach. Laura?"

DI Moyes raised an eyebrow. "Not strictly legal. Might end up going the civil route rather than the criminal system. Could create a logistical legal hellscape for James to try to remove you without, in turn, breaking the law."

"It would take a while for that to make its way through the system," Barker agreed. "Still, in the end, only a temporary halt."

"Could force James' hand, though?" Jessie suggested. "Annoy him into giving up? And the donation money could go towards equipment. We could be ready the moment the field is released and on there before he can stop us."

Ethel shot Dot a smug look, which Dot replied to by poking out her tongue.

"So, we're going with more delay tactics?" Sue asked. "How long would we need to camp for?"

"And how many people would we need?" Neil asked.

"Who knows, and a lot," Julia replied to both. "They could keep moving the diggers away from us."

"Not if they can't *reach* to the diggers," Dot said, tapping the chalk in her palm. "If we create a specific formation with the tents... we could gridlock them in.

We don't touch *their* diggers, but they can't touch *our* tents until they have the right paperwork."

"Oh, now you think it's a good idea!" Ethel said.

"Yes, well done, Ethel. Gold star!" Dot conceded with a mock curtsy. "Though the plan has already evolved far beyond your initial suggestion. Okay, so..." She primed the chalk over the board. "We need lots of camping equipment, lots of people, and we need to be ready to go at a moment's notice. Is this impossible?"

"Nothing is impossible, dear," Percy announced, producing a bouquet of plastic flowers from his sleeve; those who didn't know he used to be a magician gasped. "I knew they'd come in handy today."

"Psychic feeling?" Dot asked, glancing at Evelyn. "Girls? You in?"

"Count me in!" Evelyn said, giddy at the idea. "Nothing beats sleeping in the great outdoors under the stars."

Amy pulled her pink cardigan tight. "I'll have to wrap up warm, but I suppose."

"Really warm," Shilpa agreed with a nod. "I'm sure my husband won't mind me not sleeping at home. Says I snore like an old rhino, anyway."

"*Not* sleeping in the tent next to Shilpa," Jessie said, holding up a hand. "I'll try to sneak something into the paper without giving the plan away. Need to keep this low-key. If James gets a whiff, *he* can block *us* before *we* block *him*."

"*Low-key*," Dot repeated, the youthful slang sounding foreign on her tongue as she scribbled the note down. "Okay, great meeting. Might be our best yet. This makes toilet roll look like... well... *toilet roll*! So, yes, very well done indeed, Ethel."

"Thank you, Dorothy," Ethel said, pushing up her lilac curls. "Sometimes my genius astounds even me."

"Don't push it. Anything else before we wrap up?"

"Actually, yes," Jessie said, pushing her chair out and standing. "Don't ask how I know, but I heard the council might be trying to revoke the market's operating permit. Christmas market might not be there for much longer."

The group erupted in outrage, and Julia's mind went straight to the one man with all the money to make such a thing happen. Once they settled and began to disperse, Dot hugged Julia by the chalkboard.

"We're not beaten yet, love," her gran said, rocking side to side in the embrace. "We'll win, whatever it takes."

Julia managed a smile, not as convinced as her gran. She couldn't shake the feeling of impending defeat. They were up against overwhelming odds, once again reliant on a miracle to turn the tide.

Fighting James was starting to feel like scooping water from a sinking ship by hand. But she agreed with her gran about this being the best meeting yet, despite the low turn-out.

Camp Peridale was already a better plan than Operation Toilet Roll, if they could convince the rest of the village to join them.

∽

As the meeting wound to a close, Barker hung back in Dot's hallway. His brother-in-law, Vinnie, nattered to Percy about all the magic tricks he'd been watching on *YouTube* while the former magician indulged him by conjuring never-ending silk handkerchiefs from his sleeves. Katie waited on the bottom step, in no rush to hurry along her son as he squealed in delight as those handkerchiefs erupted from Percy's ears.

"Katie, got a minute?"

She tossed her peroxide curls over her shoulder, meeting his hesitant look with a curious smile. He moved back to let Sue and Neil leave with their twins, waiting until they were alone to continue.

"I wanted to talk to you about Vincent."

"Vinnie?"

"*Vincent*. As in Vincent Wellington Senior."

Katie's friendly expression clouded over. "Father? Why?"

"We're exploring every angle in Sebastian's case." He kept his tone gentle, hoping not to cause offense. "I know it's ancient history, but he was up to something in 1979, and—"

"Ancient history is an *understatement*," she said with a startled little laugh, shaking her head as she helped Vinnie into his puffer jacket. "I was born that year, Barker."

Of course—what had he expected Katie to divulge about an era she'd barely drawn a breath in? Still, he had to ask.

"It's just... there are whispers your father assaulted Sebastian the same day he disappeared." He watched closely for Katie's reaction, her surprise seeming genuine. "Your father never mentioned about wanting to build a new village?"

Katie shrugged, fussing with Vinnie's zip. "Anything my father was up to pre-me is a mystery. He wasn't one to talk about himself like that. Father wasn't the warmest man. He'd talk about our family name, our legacy, but he was always looking ahead. I... I'd rather not go back down that road, if it's all the same."

Barker wished he hadn't had to force her to delve into her past. He'd witnessed her downfall from a life of luxury at the manor, losing her father, bankruptcy, and the struggle to fight for her new life.

"I had to ask, for Veronica's sake. He left no records to you?"

Katie nodded, the ghost of a smile returning as she took her son's outstretched mitten-covered fingers. "Father kept a diary as long as I knew him. I have a box of them in my attic. Haven't read them and don't intend to. Was going to pass them to Vinnie when he was old enough, but..."

Barker couldn't believe the next question on the tip of his tongue.

"I'll think about it," she replied, before he had to ask. "Come on, Vinnie. Time for home. Turkey dinosaurs for dinner?"

Hope buoyed Barker's mood as the mother and son headed out into the swirling snow. If Vincent's own private thoughts betrayed anything sinister from that era, it could break open this decades-old mystery.

Dot popped her head around the sitting room doorframe as Ethel and Percy settled into a game of cards behind her. "Well? Any closer to cracking this puzzle and finding Sebastian's murderer?"

Barker exhaled, hands stuffed in his pockets. "Too early to say. Still gathering strands to weave together. But with Vincent dead these last years, if he *was* involved, the truth died with him. What do you know about Vincent from that time, Dot? Did he have a temper?"

"*Temper?*" Dot rolled her eyes. "That old goat was a walking bomb. I once saw him shake the postman in the street for delivering his mail to the wrong house. That man acted like he owned this place. Jacobscrooge might not be related, but he's a spiritual successor if ever I've seen one."

"Postman is one thing, but murder?"

"Mark my words, Vincent Wellington was capable of *anything*. I'd bet my pension on it."

Dot's bold conviction gave Barker pause. By all accounts, Vincent had been a formidable figure who'd stopped at almost nothing when pursuing his goals. He pictured Katie's stricken face, hoping her father's handwritten diaries didn't reveal a killer's callous admissions; some truths were too heavy.

"Veronica?" he spoke into his phone as he left the cottage. "It's Barker. Are you sitting down? I have some updates for you."

∼

Still in her gran's dining room after everyone else had left, Julia was having a staring contest with the portrait of Duncan Howarth that dominated the space above the fireplace. The painting, a sombre piece by a local artist who had once found solace in Howarth Forest, seemed to hold a secret weight, a silent witness to the village's struggle.

The painting, unearthed from a hidden safe in Wellington Manor, technically belonged to James. Yet, in a twist of fate, his son, Richie, had passed it to them, a hopeful talisman against James' relentless schemes. But the real power hadn't been on the canvas; it was the letter attached, hidden behind the frame's backboard—a deathbed plea from Duncan for forgiveness, an appeal to future generations to avoid his own destructive path.

She'd read that letter aloud in front of most of the residents at the village hall, a plea that had fallen on deaf ears, the vote un-swayed by the words of a man long gone.

"A problem shared is a problem halved." Her father came up behind her. "It's a shame the only surviving portrait of him looks like *that*. We'll never know if he really was that ugly."

Julia managed a half-smile. "Doesn't matter now. It's just a painting. He can't help us."

"At least *we've* got it. A small victory, hiding in plain sight."

"James probably doesn't even remember it's missing. Only cared when it seemed like it might sway the committee."

With a sigh, Julia turned away from Duncan Howarth's lopsided gaze. Nothing more the long-dead industrialist could do for them now. She followed her father, stepping out into the crisp, snowy night, leaving behind the painting and the hope it had held.

Lingering on the snow-covered street, Julia watched as Katie struggled to strap young Vinnie into his booster in the backseat of her baby pink Fiat 500.

"You did great in there," her father said as he blew into his cupped hands. "Fancy a warm-up nip of brandy back at the shop? I have some stock to sort."

Julia managed a thin smile, her thoughts still tangled in the tragic disappearance that had marked her mother's era. The distant laughter from the village hall carried on the breeze, a stark contrast to the village's mood. A brandy sounded nice, but she shook her head. She wanted a warm bath followed by her electric blanket in bed sooner rather than later, but first, she had a question for her father.

"When I asked about Sebastian Morgan, you said you didn't know the name. But Mum knew him, didn't she?"

"If you'd asked me if I'd known that dishevelled hippie, it might have rung a bell. But yes, your mother did get quite close to Sebastian. Can't say I was upset when he left, but I never wanted any harm to come to him."

Julia pulled her coat tighter. "When did you last see him?"

Brian nodded at the lights of the village hall next to the church as more snowflakes fluttered from the abyss above.

"A night much like this," he said, sucking the air through his teeth, "at a gathering not unlike the one we just attended. I was a different man back then, but let me see what I can remember..."

12

1979

Fluffy snow swirled from the inky sky as Brian weaved through the market stalls. The promise of warmth in the village hall beckoned ahead, a welcoming oasis on a bleak winter's night, but Brian would rather have been anywhere else.

He and Pearl had planned to cuddle by the fire with mugs of hot cocoa once Julia was tucked up in her cot. All hopes of a normal night had vanished when Pearl had dropped by his stall that afternoon, insisting they show support for 'the fight.' He wasn't sure when—or how—that hippie's 'fight' had become his wife's too, but she'd been adamant he should attend.

He edged inside, scanning the meagre group Sebastian had managed to rally. His heart sank. The only thing worse than being forced to attend was having no crowd to hide in. And to top it off, the radiators barely took the edge off.

Two farmers, the greengrocer couple from Mulberry Lane, Mr Patil from the post office, and Father Martin from the church were spaced out on the chairs set up for a hundred. So much for their fearless leader firing up the villagers to thwart the land developers. Pearl's face lit up from the buffet table as she waved Brian over.

"You came!" Pearl exclaimed, rocking Julia in her arms. "Your ears must be frozen. Come get warm by the heaters and grab a plate."

"Not much of a turnout, is it?" He kissed his wife's cold cheek before relieving her of Julia's squirming bundle. "And it would be warmer at home by the fire. And not much of a spread, is it? Did you make that cake?"

"I did."

"Small mercies. Did he pay you for it?"

"Brian, it's a protest, not a bake sale."

"You're a fantastic baker, that's all," he replied, picking up a paper plate to grab some of the dry-looking sausage rolls. "You deserve to be paid for it. You're wasting your baking talents working in that hair salon. You could be charging a fortune for your cakes."

"Not everything needs to be a business. Hobbies can stay hobbies, Mr Entrepreneur." She flared her nostrils, bringing out those cute dimples he'd always loved. "Brian... this is important to me. Just tonight, please, try to—"

The doors banged open, and Sebastian Morgan burst through like the snow had carried him in. He had that manic look in his eyes that made Brian feel on edge; like he always knew what was going on, or liked to think he did.

"I'm going to buy him a comb for Christmas," Brian muttered as Sebastian attempted to flatten his wild nest. If Pearl heard his quip, she didn't acknowledge it, drifting towards the seats near the middle. Brian trailed after her, hefting baby Julia higher in his arms.

Sebastian tossed off his coat and rubbed his hands together, scanning the room. "Is this everyone?" When only awkward silence answered, he forced enthusiasm anyway. "Well, good people are often few, I suppose." His restless gaze settled on Pearl and Julia. "You made it, Pearl. Great to see you."

"Brian," he said, holding out a hand. "Pearl's husband."

"Ah, fantastic!" Sebastian shook it, clasping it in both cold hands. "Another soldier for the fight." He let go of Brian's hand and tossed them out to the thin crowd. "And I apologise to you all for being late. I was just at Wellington Manor, and I have some... developments."

"Did Mr Wellington know you were there?" Brian asked. He'd delivered an antique chair to Vincent yesterday, and the man hadn't had a nice word to say about 'that fool in the tent.'

"Well..."

Father Martin cleared his throat. "I hope you've not invited us here to take part in *illegal* activities. As a man of prudent faith, I cannot condone anything that breaks the law." The elderly priest punctuated his sermon by biting into a stale sandwich, glaring over the bread crust. "Your silence speaks volumes, Mr Morgan."

"'Do not judge, and you will not be judged. Do not condemn, and you will not be condemned. Pardon, and you will be pardoned.'" Sebastian's shaky grin grew. "From God's mouth via yours only last Sunday, Father. Drastic times call for drastic measures."

Brian experienced an unexpected surge of camaraderie with the old cleric, whose sermons often sent him to sleep when he found himself with nothing better to do on a Sunday morning. Trust the man living in a tent to drag them into his crimes when they were there to 'support' him. Pearl shot Father Martin a quelling frown.

"I just had a *little* look around," Sebastian admitted, a little less frantic; he seemed to notice he was losing the small crowd. "Nobody got hurt, and it was worth it. Oh, it was worth it!"

"You'll be robbing graves next," Brian muttered, eliciting another stern look from Pearl. She lifted Julia from his arms and edged closer to Sebastian in her seat. The baby grabbed at Pearl's dark curls, enthralled by the madman's pacing.

"I scoured Vincent's study from top to bottom," Sebastian proclaimed, milking the suspense. "I just wanted to find something. I keep hearing about secret 'contingencies' that would stop any developments being built on that land."

"Did you find them?" Pearl asked. "This could change everything."

"No!" His grin widened. "But... hidden away in a safe behind an oil painting—an unlocked safe, might I add—I found something." With a dramatic flourish, he revealed a yellowed scroll bound in red ribbon. "*Borrowed*, I assure you. I do plan to give it—"

"I did not agree to be an accessory to a theft," Father Martin announced, slapping his knees before pushing himself up. "And I encourage those of you who are people of faith, who want a clear conscience tonight, to follow my example."

The farmers and greengrocers followed Father

Martin out, leaving Mr Patil, Pearl, Brian, and Julia, with Brian only staying for his wife. Sighing, he tossed a prawn vol-au-vent from the buffet into his mouth.

"So," Brian muttered through his mouthful as the doors finished swinging, "what did you steal, Morgan?"

"*Borrowed*," he repeated, unwrapping the ribbon of the scroll. "I *will* give it back. *Tomorrow*. It was in amongst a stack of Wellington family records from the 1800s. Lineage maps, property divisions, bank statements. But this stood out."

Sebastian unfurled the scroll to reveal spidery writing and a family tree brimming with circles, crosses, and scribbled annotations. Beside the faded names of Wellington ancestors, someone had drawn cryptic symbols in red ink. Brian craned his neck, but couldn't decipher the ancient scribbles.

"Vincent is *obsessed* with legacy," Sebastian explained. "Look at this from 1849, from the year Clarissa Wellington died."

"Who?" Brian asked.

"Don't you know anything about our local history?" Mr Patil spoke up, tossing a lazy finger in the direction of the back of the stage. "Duncan Howarth built that grand house in the forest for his love. Influenza got her before they married, and it sent him mad."

"So... a woman died in 1849... and...?"

"Look here," Sebastian said, running up to Brian with the scroll outstretched like some valued prize. "Under Clarissa's name. Do you see it?"

"I only see scratches."

"*Precisely*! A redaction."

"Are you saying Clarissa had a child?" Pearl asked.

"Why else would there be scratches under her name?"

"An incorrect entry?" Brian laughed off the suggestion. "And if not, some woman had a baby in the 1800s. So what? Long-lost history."

"You know, Brian, for a man so interested in antiques, I thought you might have more of an appreciation of the historical significance of this discovery."

Brian's neck hairs bristled.

So, that's how it was going to be.

"Yeah?" Brian said after clearing his throat. "I still don't see why it's so important."

"Duncan Howarth never had an heir," Mr Patil sighed.

"So?"

"Well, he used to own that field Vincent Wellington wants to build on," Sebastian continued, staring at the family tree with all the wonder of how Brian imagined Julia would look on Christmas day.

"The records of how the land went from his hands to those who built the market in 1869 are as lost as the 'contingencies'... contingencies that *I* believe Duncan Howarth put in place when he left that land to his heir. An heir hidden from history... hidden in Vincent's safe. The question we should all be asking is 'why?'"

"I *am* asking 'why?'" Brian replied, scooping up Julia from Pearl's arms. "Why I bothered coming to this meeting? C'mon Pearl, it's time to go."

Brian looped an arm around his wife's shoulders, but she shrugged his arm away, focused on Sebastian and the stolen scrap of paper. Jealousy flamed deep in Brian's gut.

"He belongs in the looney bin," he whispered to her. "Let's get home in front of the fire. Or, even better, it's not too late for a drink at The Plough?"

Pearl angled a reproachful look his way. "I already told you I needed to be here tonight. This is important to me."

"But I'm your husband," he blurted out. "I think you should—"

"This is *important* to me," she repeated, firing him the stern look he knew not to question. "I thought if you came to a meeting, you might want to help protect our village too, but you've acted exactly as I thought you would, Brian. I think you should go."

Face burning, Brian gathered up his coat and Julia's pram. While Sebastian continued to blather about land rights and inheritance, Brian backed out through the doors. Hunched against the cold and his humiliation, he walked the short distance to his mother's cottage.

"What an idiot your dad is, eh, Julia?" he murmured into the pram as they left the hall behind. He crooned a few lines of 'You Are My Sunshine', but she didn't make a sound. "You're right... I should have kept my mouth shut."

In his mother's cottage, he found her exactly as expected—in the dark on the sofa, watching an old film on the black-and-white television she refused to update. Brian crept upstairs and settled Julia in her cot next to the bed he shared with Pearl in his childhood bedroom. He'd be sneaking down to sleep on the sofa once his mother drifted off and could be prodded to retreat to her bedroom.

"That you, Brian?" she called.

"Me, Mum."

"Why don't you come down?" She sounded tired. "You used to love this film."

After changing from his busy day at the market and checking on Julia again, he joined his mother in the sitting room, flicking on a lamp on his way in. Two steaming teas waited on the coffee table next to a plate of fig rolls. She patted the empty space next to her, sitting in the middle as she always had. On her other side, he could still make out the dent from where his father would sit—and nobody ever dared disturb. *Help!* by The Beatles flickered on the television; he'd gone to see it half a dozen times when he was a teenager.

"Took Pearl on one of our first dates to see this," he said, hugging a pillow close. "I think I'm making a right mess of things, Mum. You're right. She seems more taken with that scruffy bloke these days."

She offered him a fig roll. "Jealousy isn't a good colour on you, son. And maybe I was mistaken. Whatever would make you think he could replace you? Pearl started a family with you."

"He just... Pearl was totally spellbound, hanging off his every word while he prattled on about Duncan Howarth having some secret child with some old Wellington?"

"That bloke who built that house in the woods?" Dot asked, though she sounded as curious as Brian had felt at the meeting. "Pearl loves you. I know that for a fact. It was only the other day she gushed about what an amazing father you are to little Julia."

"Really?"

"Oh yes. She knows you're a good man. Just a bit of an idiot now and then." Her eyes crinkled with gentle humour. "You get that from your father, God rest his soul." She rested a hand on the empty space. "She loves you, make no mistake about it, but she loves this village too. She just wants what's best for your future here with Julia, and any other little ones you'll have running around one day."

"You think?"

"Mark my words, dear," she said, patting his knee on her way up. "You two are in it for the long haul. I can feel it in my waters. I'm off to bed, love. Try not to sleep on the sofa again, will you? An apology goes a long way, you know. Your father was always good at those."

Brian clung to her optimism as she shuffled upstairs, intent on staying awake until Pearl returned from the meeting, but as the title song started playing after Ringo escaped being sacrificed on a beach in the Bahamas, his drooping eyelids finally closed.

How could some secret child from the 1800s be so important?

It was the here and now that mattered to Brian, and the truth was, unlike his wife, he didn't care if they lived in Peridale.

As long as they were together, he'd live anywhere...

13

Wrapping her fingers around a mug of hot chocolate, Julia felt the warmth seep into her skin, unsure of what to say to her father. Across from her in the darkened café, with only the lights on the Christmas tree illuminating his lined face, he blew on his drink, his gaze distant. In all the years since her mother's death, Julia had heard nothing but happy stories about their marriage from her father.

"So, that was the last time you saw Sebastian?" she asked when the silence became unbearable.

Her father nodded, his eyes still far away. "I waited up for your mother that night. When she got home, we talked for a long time about the village, the future. I think that was the moment I realised how much

Peridale truly meant to her. How much she was willing to fight for it. I promised I'd support her properly, but I don't think she believed me."

"Did you sleep on the sofa?"

"I..." He took a sharp slurp, avoiding her eyes. "Can't remember."

Julia swallowed against the lump in her throat. She hadn't asked her father about 1979 to pry into their early marital problems in the months after her birth. She'd be lying if she said those months with Barker were the easiest of her marriage, given the sleepless nights and sudden shake-up of their routines. But she still cherished the memories of that little bubble of time when they'd been cocooned in their cottage; flaws and all.

"Do you think Sebastian really found proof that Duncan Howarth had an heir?" she whispered into the shadows.

"A secret heir, after all this time?" He offered a heavy shrug. "It still seems far-fetched to me. And I don't know why it was important then, nor do I now."

Far-fetched, Julia agreed. And yet she sensed there were more secrets in Peridale's past connected to Duncan Howarth than she'd ever imagined when staring at his portrait earlier.

If Sebastian thought the discovery could help

them win against Vincent in 1979, maybe it could help them against James in the here and now.

∽

Julia dumped another shot of espresso into her gingerbread latte. In the stillness before opening, she yawned, glancing at the donation tin where she'd dropped that morning's mysterious donation.

"Seven hundred pounds this time."

She couldn't silence the nagging voice insisting it was James' doing—an elaborate scheme to toy with her.

"I've found a cheap supplier for the tents," Jessie announced from the other side of the counter on her laptop. "If we buy fifty, they're basically half price."

"Fifty? More like fifteen," Julia thought aloud, recalling the low attendance numbers at last night's meeting. "Even that might be pushing it. Let's wait until we know for certain when we'll need them. You never know what might happen next."

"Earthquakes?" Jessie suggested. "Floods? That would be handy. Might ask Evelyn to cast a weather spell."

Julia chuckled, blowing her latte. "I don't think Evelyn is in the business of casting spells."

"I could always ask." She continued typing.

"Thought anymore about talking to the suspects again? Gwen, Harold, Arnold? Was thinking we could force them all into a little reunion and see what happens. Might be entertaining *and* enlightening."

"I'm not sure any of them would agree to..."

Julia's sentence trailed off as she placed the extra-strength latte on the counter and hurried to the front window. An army of police officers descended on the subdued Christmas market. They fanned out between the stalls as the merchants prepared for the day, and a line of suited individuals with ID badges stood along the edge of the green, faces surly; Julia recognised some of them.

"That's Martin and Richard from the corrupt committee meeting!" Jessie said, joining her. "They're in James' pocket, and I bet the rest are. They *all* voted to approve the Howarth Estate. What's going on?"

"What was it you overheard about the market permission being revoked?"

Martha Morgan emerged from the market with her clipboard as the officers continued to fan out. Outnumbered, Martha held her chin high, like a general ready for battle. Her strident voice carried to the café over the market's churning chaos.

"...*no* legal grounds for shutdown! On whose authority?" Martha bellowed, a note of desperation in her voice as she brandished a clipboard under the lead officer's nose. "These are *binding* approvals. Look here. We have permission until at least the second of January. *At least!*" She raised the clipboard like a battle-axe. "This market harms no one. It's here *every* year."

"How can they do this?" Jessie asked. "I'm not Martha's biggest fan, but she's got a point. People have been talking about the Christmas market coming to the village since before Halloween."

"Maybe there's been a mistake?"

"I admire the optimism, Mum, but this many police officers for a mistake?"

Julia murmured her agreement. Behind Martha's sparring form, resignation replaced the fight across the market. Stall owners wore identical expressions of weary defeat, beginning to pack up under the smirking officials' duress. Julia felt a deep pang of empathy for the saddened faces peeking out of scarves and hats. The handmade crafts, delicate wreaths, and homemade food... all left unsold.

A beefy officer gripped the arm of a defiant pickle seller, refusing to pack up. Horrified, Julia watched Martha leap to intervene. She grabbed the officer's arm, pulling him away, causing him to teeter into a crate of potatoes at Denise Coleman's farm produce stall. The officer regained his balance before the potatoes, but that didn't stop nearby officers from swarming around the spilled spuds.

"You just *assaulted* a police officer!" one yelled. "Hands above your head. *Now!*"

"I did no such thing!" Martha cried, stepping back, hands on hips. "That brute had hold of Angie's arm for no reason. I was just—"

Two officers jerked Martha's arms behind her back. In a blink, they marched her in handcuffs towards the police station up the lane.

"Everyone stay behind their stalls!" Martha's cry echoed across the silent green. "This isn't *fair*. This isn't *right!*"

Julia hugged herself against the chill, wishing to erase the ugly scene. She met Jessie's equally appalled stare as officers continued dispersing confused stallholders.

"Bit rich from her, given her support for her cousin," Jessie said, shaking her head, "but she's not wrong. This *isn't* right. What's happening around here?"

Outside Richie's, James leaned nonchalantly against a lamppost, watching like he was catching up on a juicy drama on the TV.

"Ethel was right," Julia said, her lip curling. "He does have a slappable face. I'm going to see what—"

"And get yourself in the cell next to Martha?"

Jessie raised an eyebrow, pulling her from the window. "C'mon, we've enough to handle without worrying about the market. Those Christmas brownies smell like they're ready."

Ignoring her instincts, Julia sliced the cinnamon and nutmeg flavoured brownies in the kitchen, her gaze fixed on the shiny steel surface where James' plans had rested. Perhaps accepting his offer, moving away, opening a new café elsewhere was wise.

A sickness had taken hold, one that had watched events unfold while leaning against a lamppost. Julia slammed the tray, now crumbed with brownie pieces, into the sink. The sound echoed like a deafening bullet. She clung to the hope of fate. If it was real, something was coming for James Jacobson—something he truly deserved.

14

Later that afternoon, Jessie couldn't believe her stroke of luck as she crouched behind a graffitied column in Fern Moore's concrete courtyard.

After catching a glimpse of Six lurking around Harold Morgan's ice cream barn, she'd put two and two together from the conversation she'd overheard. Couldn't afford to turn the heating up in his flat? Had to be Fern Moore. Maths had never been her strongest subject, but her hunch had given her the correct answer.

Pushing little Mia up and down on the swing, Six looked unrecognisable. A woollen hat capped his shaved head, while a scarlet scarf swaddled the lower half of his face. His eyes—normally so cold and detached—sparkled as he pushed his giggling daughter. She appeared to be around six or seven, and judging by her carefree smile, had no idea what Daddy did for a living.

Jessie would have walked past him in the street without recognising him. The last standing Cotswold Crew gang member had succeeded in hiding in plain sight.

She hadn't recognised him in CostSavers ten minutes earlier, either. She'd gone into the mini-supermarket on the corner to ask if anyone knew of a mysterious bald bloke named 'Six.' But before Jessie could open her mouth, a familiar voice rumbled from the chocolate aisle.

"You'll have to choose the white chocolate or the milk, Mia. You can't have both. You have to save some for the other kids."

Jessie had peeked around the corner to glimpse Six selecting chocolates with a beaming young girl before trailing the unlikely pair to the play park.

Safe and unseen, Six didn't notice Jessie peering around the concrete pillar to capture a few photos. She imagined this must be how Six himself lurked, invisible while tracking his own marks over the years. How ironic that she now watched his most unguarded moment—a tender scene Jessie never could have pictured the notorious thug participating in.

Yet there he was, grinning and pushing little Mia's swing while she squealed for him to go higher. Jessie snapped some shots of Six's smile, softening his brutish features. Some things needed to be seen to be believed. She sent the picture to Veronica straight away.

JESSIE

> I spy with my little eye, something beginning with SIX... and he's not the man I thought he was when he's off the clock.

The man laughing and playing with his daughter was the same man who'd stalked Jessie on Greg's orders, cut her brakes, and even marched her to a well wielding a giant knife, an ordeal she'd barely escaped from alive.

All that.

And a family man.

She had to laugh.

A sharp jab in her ribs launched Jessie out of her skin. Whirling around with clenched fists, she almost swung before seeing the silly grin of her ex-boyfriend, Billy.

"Hold your horses, Rocky Balboa!" he cried, peering around the column. "Who are we spying on?"

"Who said I was spying?" Jessie deflected with an eye roll, pocketing her phone. "I was... looking for you, actually. Thought I'd drop by the food bank and see how you were getting on. I was in the area. Cash-and-carry run for the café."

Over-explanation or not, Billy's eyes lit up. Guilt squirmed in her stomach; he'd always been more gullible than her.

"I'm just on my lunch break," he said, jerking a thumb over his shoulder. "Paige is waiting at Daphne's for me with the girls."

Jessie followed his gesture to the flaming cherry-red headed woman ushering two kids in colourful hats into the café.

"Look at you, all grown up and playing happy families," she said, giving him a playful jab in the arm. "Who'd have thought bad boy Billy would turn so respectable on me?"

His cheeks tinged pink despite his returning grin. He scuffed one toe along a crack in the pavement, almost shyly.

"Just took finding the right girl, I guess. Paige is a firecracker, but she's got heart. The girls too—they're little monsters, but I love them to bits like they're my own." He checked his watch, then flashed Jessie a sheepish look from under his lashes. "If I leave them too long, they'll tear the place up. You're welcome to grab a bite with us? Might be nice."

She considered lunch with her ex's new girlfriend

and her kids. Too weird, even for her. "Already eaten, but I won't keep you. Catch up another time?"

Billy nodded, though he hovered for a moment, shifting his weight between his feet, hands tucked in his pockets.

"A couple more minutes won't hurt," he said with a wink. "So, how's things going with that new fella of yours? Danny, was it?"

"Dante," Jessie corrected. It was her turn to shift her weight. After Dante's abrupt travelling suggestion and her clumsy reaction at the ice cream shop, neither had contacted the other since, and Jessie wasn't keen to confess as much to her very first ex-boyfriend. "We're still just, you know, figuring things out. Nothing serious yet."

An unexpected ache poked her chest at the downplay. She thought about how happy they'd been at the mulled wine stand only a few days ago. Why'd Dante have to complicate things?

"Quick question before you go," she asked, nodding at the swings. "You know that guy over there? With his kid?"

Billy followed her gesture to the anonymous bundled figure. "Chris? Moved here before I left for the army. A couple of years?"

"Chris...?"

"Dunno. Just 'Chris.' Keeps to himself but seems

like a decent bloke. His kid is sweet. Goes to school with my—our—*Paige*'s girls." His cheeks and nose flushed red. "What's her name? I always want to say Abba? But I know it isn't...?"

"Abba?" Jessie laughed. "It's Mia. As in..."

"*Mamma Mia!*" He clicked his fingers. "Paige's favourite film. Always get there in the end." Scratching the back of his head, his blush deepened. "Had Mia 'round for dinner a few times when Chris is working."

"Working?" Jessie nodded, stealing a glance at the swings. "Know what he does?"

"Delivery driver, I think? Works funny hours. Why are you asking? Has he done something?"

"Oh, just..." she deliberated, reluctant to fully expose Six's—or Chris'—identity and risk Billy playing the misguided hero. "I think he might be loosely connected to my dad's Greg Morgan case." At Billy's clueless look, Jessie waved a hand. "Doesn't matter. But say... I mean, just theoretically... if you had a kid of your own, would you commit crimes or do dodgy stuff to support the thing?"

Billy stared into the corner of his eyes as he considered the unexpected question. "Dunno. Has Chris done something bad? Seems decent enough to me, but you never know with types round here. I could have a word, subtle like. If he's giving you trouble..."

"The question, Billy."

"Yeah, I think I'd do anything for my kid if I had no other choice." He bit back a grin and winced like he was sitting on a pincushion. "I—No, doesn't matter."

"Go on," she said, nudging him. "I know that face. Spill..."

Billy shrugged, stuffing his hands deeper in his pockets.

"That question might not be so imaginary. It's early days. We're keeping things quiet, so you can't tell anyone, but..." He glanced around the column towards the café. "But there's gonna be one more little monster running around before long. Paige is pregnant... I'm gonna be a *dad*, Jessie!"

Jessie's heart wobbled like it never had as she fought to mirror his brilliant smile. *Pregnant*? Billy was still a teenager in her mind, but he wasn't, was he? He was twenty-three, and Jessie would be twenty-two in a few months. The age that people did this stuff. The baby talk had been part of the reason she'd ended things before her travelling days. She dragged him into a hug, not sure which of them was more stunned.

"Congratulations!" she said. "I'm really happy for you both."

Over his shoulder, Jessie glimpsed Paige waiting at the café door, scanning the courtyard—an all-too-vivid vision of the future Billy had wanted for them: prams, packed lunches, domestic bliss. She swallowed hard.

"It's everything I've ever wanted. Feels like it's all coming together."

"I'm so pleased for you, but I just remembered... I said I'd get back to the café before my break was over, and I..." Glancing at her watch, she backed away. "I won't keep you. But congratulations again. We'll have a proper catch-up soon. And pass on my congratulations to Paige, and... *congratulations*."

With a departing wave masking her chaotic state of mind, Jessie ducked out of sight. Catching her breath against the cold brick, she wasn't sure what her reaction had been, but she'd caught the confused pinch of his brows before she'd sprinted away. She pulled out her phone, not sure whom to text, but a message was waiting for her.

> VERONICA
> Know where he lives? Police might want to know...

Jessie peered around the corner. Six had stopped

pushing Mia on the swings. They were walking towards one of the stairwells, and for the moment, forcing thoughts of Billy Matthews and his pending offspring from her mind, Jessie returned to her column as Six and his daughter vanished from view. She stole a glance at Billy through the foggy café windows as he spun one of the girls around.

She *was* happy for him, and she already regretted acting like a total doughnut; she'd apologise later when she'd figured out why.

On the second-floor stairwell, she watched as Six unlocked the door of the fourth flat from the left. He scanned around, as if expecting to be followed, but he didn't look in Jessie's direction. When he was off duty, he was off-guard, and she didn't blame him. She'd never have recognised him, so why should anyone else?

But Jessie knew what nobody else did.

The location of the last member of the Cotswold Crew gang wouldn't be shared with the police. Not yet, anyway. She now had leverage, and maybe the secret ingredient to keeping Greg Morgan behind bars if the trial and murder rumours didn't stick.

> **JESSIE**
> Not sure where he lives, but his real name is Chris. No surname yet. Side note… is it normal to act like a total numpty when finding out your first boyfriend is about to have a baby with someone else?

> **VERONICA**
> You're asking me about normal? O, beware, my lord, of jealousy. It is the green-eyed monster which doth mock the meat it feeds on. (Othello, Act Three, Scene Three). I'm in the office if you want to talk more…

> **JESSIE**
> Need to get back to the café. Later. And I'm not jealous. Idk what I am… :s

> **VERONICA**
> *I don't know. (And it's probably normal to feel jealous?)

Was Jessie jealous?

Did the green-eyed monster explain the squirming?

No, she didn't want a baby, but she was feeling *something*. She flicked between her text conversations and decided to send another, this time to Dante.

> **JESSIE**
> Hey, just me. Drink at Richie's tonight? Think we need to talk.

Dante read the message, and three text bubbles popped up, signalling he was typing a response, then disappeared, and reappeared. She waited behind the column for almost five minutes, awaiting a reply that never came. A sigh escaped her as she pondered if she'd botched everything. Resigned, she headed back to her car, discreetly parked around the corner outside McSizzles chicken shop, the venue for many of her dates with Billy.

She shoved boy troubles aside as she drove back to Peridale, her mind fixed on Chris 'Six'—Father of the Year. She recalled his undefended smiles shared with his daughter, as vivid as the blue sky above. Maybe this ruthless enforcer did have a moral boundary he wouldn't cross for Greg Morgan. Her mission was to find that line.

She needed to press Six's pressure point to force his hand.

If anyone knew where Greg Morgan's bodies were buried, it was Six, and if the flung mud of the corruption trial and Veronica's murder claims didn't stick, Jessie might have just discovered the strongest cement to keep Greg locked behind bars for good.

~

Barker winced as Katie ripped away another wax strip in her pink palace salon on Mulberry Lane. She tutted under her breath, reusing the same strip several times on the same spot.

"Honestly, for an ex-detective, your pain threshold is terribly low," she remarked, scrutinising his brows. "Almost done taming those bushy beasts."

He shifted in the plush salon chair, wheels rolling along the floorboards of the office above. He needed to redirect the conversation before Katie suggested—or forced—further cosmetic procedures.

"I was rather hoping we could discuss your father's old diaries, if you've found them?"

"Almost finished. It's about time someone sorted out that... *problem*." Her finger wafted in the space between her defined brows, sporting an unnatural arch as she tilted her head to admire her handiwork. After another smear of wax, she ripped off more hairs, then spun him to face the gilded mirror. "Wait until Julia sees you, you handsome devil."

Barker had to admit, his subtly shaped brows and smoother skin, thanks to the sharp blade dragged across his entire face, had rejuvenated him somewhat. He ran an experimental hand over his jaw, smoother than ever.

"The redness will go down, won't it?"

"In an hour, you'll look like a twenty-five-year-old," she whispered, patting his shoulders. "I'll book you in for a rolling monthly. Our little secret. I can take care of those greys too? I do my Brian's roots every Thursday." She held a finger to her lips and giggled. "I never said that."

"I think I'm happy embracing the salt and pepper."

"Suits you, anyway," she said, patting his shoulders. "Brian looks like Rod Stewart without his touch-ups. Now, those diaries. *Yes*, I found them. *No*, I haven't read them."

Teetering on her pointed shoes, Katie dragged a thick archival box from under the acrylic reception desk. She heaved it over to the chair and dumped it in Barker's lap. He groaned under the weight, the faint smell of mildew clinging to the cardboard.

"Father would scribble his thoughts down every night in his study before bed," Katie said, gazing out the window as the sun set. "Could be pointless ramblings, medical gripes, or financial records for all I know. But take them, read them, and... don't tell me what they say." Eyes closed, she turned to the mirror. "Unless there's something nice about me, or my brother, or... probably not. You know what dads are like."

"I don't, actually," he replied with a tight smile. "Except for being one."

"*Right.* Sorry." Her neon pink cheeks flushed maroon as her eyes clenched tighter. "You don't know who your dad is, do you?"

Barker shook his head, lifting the lid of the box to peer inside. He wanted to talk about his father as much as Katie wanted to read the diaries. The box overflowed with tiny journals of all colours, stacked in rows, each year embossed in gold on the spine. He reached in to pluck out a volume, but Katie slammed the lid back with clawed nails, painted to resemble jolly snowmen.

"Not in here," she pleaded. "I still don't feel right about this. I'd die if someone read my diaries, but I suppose Father is already dead, so... I'm only really doing this for Veronica." Glancing up at the ceiling, she whispered, "I've been hearing her cry up there, and she never wants to talk to me about it. Well, she doesn't want to talk to me about much, to be honest, but I like her even if she doesn't like me. And I still feel guilty about selling Wellington Manor to Jacobson. If not for me, he might never have settled here. Jessie said nailing Greg might help bring down James too, so... if these can help the case, do what you need to."

Barker lifted the box, his hunch pointing less at Greg and more at Katie's deceased father. "I'm sure they will be helpful, Katie. Thank you. And don't blame yourself for James. He grew up over on the Fern Moore estate. He might have come back at any time, even without the manor sale. I'll return these once I've found what I need."

"You'll want to leave before Mrs Coggles arrives for her weekly moustache wax," she ordered, hooking a thumb for him to get out of the chair. "Last time my Brian was here for his bi-weekly pedicure, she expressed some rather *strong* opinions about men having treatments."

Considering the pain he'd endured, Barker might have agreed with Mrs Coggles, but obtaining the box made it worthwhile. Opting against taking the diaries to his car, he had a better plan.

Three sets of eyes were better than one.

After ascending the narrow staircase to *The Peridale Post* office above, he knocked and then pushed open the door. Inside, Veronica and Jessie were curved over their desks. A vibrant mural of Peridale adorned the walls, failing to brighten the serious atmosphere. Both glanced up with glum expressions as he placed the box next to the worn-out sofa.

"What happened to your face?" Jessie asked, peering at him. "You look like you've been hit with a snowball."

"Katie's wax pot happened. She said I'd look twenty-five."

"Sure, Grandad." Laughing, Jessie rolled her eyes. "What's in the box? A lifetime supply of Werther's Originals?"

"Vincent Wellington's diaries. They might contain insights into what happened to Sebastian," he said, distributing some 1970s volumes. "Perhaps even a confession."

"You won't find one because *Greg* killed Sebastian," Veronica stated as she received her share.

Barker cracked open a 1979 volume at a random page and began reading.

"Aren't you going to tell him?" Jessie called, propping her feet on her desk.

"Tell me what?" Barker muttered, absorbed in the diary.

Veronica remained silent, but Barker was fixed on the page. As he squinted and pulled his reading glasses from his pocket, a sense of disbelief washed over him. What he read wasn't a confession, nor did it pertain to Sebastian or the case. Instead, it was an unexpected revelation about Katie Wellington, something he wasn't sure she was aware of.

"Greg has sent me a visiting order," Veronica announced, prompting Barker to close the diary with a snap. "I won't be going, but perhaps you'd like to? It's unnamed, so presumably, anyone can use it. Just have to call the prison to confirm."

"Like a golden ticket," Jessie said. "Don't fall in the chocolate river and leave the fizzy lifting drinks alone. And if tiny orange men with green hair start singing, you're probably about to die, so run."

Slipping the shocking diary volume into his back pocket to ensure its contents remained private, Barker turned his attention to the visiting order on the desk. Why would Greg seek a meeting with Veronica now?

"Would be helpful to understand Greg's perspective," Barker said, flapping the card against his palm. "Even if it's a web of lies. Now, let's delve into these diaries. There's no telling what secrets they might hold."

～

Jessie rubbed her tired eyes, skimming through Vincent Wellington's pretentious ramblings from 1980. The man loved to talk about himself at great length, sometimes even in the third person. She endured a third page of 'Vincent adores his new Rolls Royce' before slapping the book shut to skip to the next one. And when he wasn't talking about his new cars, clothes, antiques, and foreign holidays, he was obsessed with writing at length about his legacy and lineage.

Stock.

Pedigree.

Status.

Gross.

Across the office, Veronica yawned, sinking further over an open diary. Neither had moved in hours, and Barker had long since left with the bulk of the 1979 entries. Pushing the diary away, Jessie swivelled her chair towards her editor.

"Feel like a break? It's just past midnight."

Veronica didn't look up, giving a slight shake of her head, still reading. She'd barely spoken since Barker dropped off the diaries, and Jessie was tired of trying to pull things out of her like a dentist yanking out a tooth of someone with clenched lips. She recalled some advice from her brother, Alfie, given while they were travelling.

"Don't expect to make friends without an offering," he'd said in Paris, noticing her struggling with the many people they'd met daily. "Strangers are more likely to open up if you reveal something. Stories are currency on the road, so invest wisely."

Clearing her throat, she said, "I wanted to talk about something that happened earlier…" Veronica still didn't glance up, but her subtle nod encouraged Jessie to continue. "You know how I've been seeing Dante recently?"

"Sort of?" Veronica offered a dry smile. "I thought

you two were official. Boyfriend and girlfriend, or does your generation not like labels in the same way you don't like drinking milk from a cow?"

"*Whatever* we were, I think I've jeopardised it with my mouth."

"What did you say this time?"

"It's more what I *didn't* say." She stared at the spray-painted mural, drifting to the lurid green fields. "When we were walking to your Uncle Harold's ice cream place, Dante mentioned travelling together, and I didn't know what to say... Then I ran into my ex, Billy, found out he's having a baby, and now Dante is completely ghosting me, and—"

"Isn't this what diaries are for?" She flapped the book. "What do I know about romance, Jessie? My first and only husband left me for being a 'heartless witch'... maybe Martha was right."

Jessie threw a scrunched-up post-it note across the office. Missed by a few inches. "You're not heartless. And it might be stupid and trivial, but it's *my* stupid and trivial." She threw another crumpled post-it and it bounced off Veronica's spiked hair. "I would have killed for trivial problems once upon a time."

"Then be careful what you wish for." She removed her glasses, placing the diary down and looking at Jessie. "So, you're torn between your ex and your new love?"

"I never said it was love," Jessie replied swiftly. "And Billy's moved on. *I've* moved on. And I—"

"Do you still love him?"

"No," Jessie answered quickly. "Only in the way you love a first love, you know? I want him to be happy, and that's not with me. We didn't want the same things. I thought Dante did. We share a job, have a laugh, but..."

"He wants to go on holiday?"

"Travelling."

"A *long* holiday, then."

"Long holiday or not, I've already done that," Jessie admitted. "Said he wants to go and find himself. He thinks that's what I did. I don't think I found myself." She considered it. "It was kind of just a long holiday."

"Travel broadens the mind and changes you, but you always have to come home." She peered over her glasses with a knowing smile. "Be grateful you have somewhere to call home. You could always do another lap? Don't you still have the travel bug?"

Jessie shook her head. "I wanted to come home. The thought of leaving again, or Dante leaving, leaves me feeling..." She searched for the right word. "Lost? I dunno."

"Don't know," Veronica corrected.

"Regardless, I *don't know* where I'm going right

now. My ex is having a child. A *child*, Veronica. A *real* one, with all the crying and screaming."

"Babies are known for that." Pursing her lips, Jessie could tell she was irritating her; maybe it was trivial. "Look, I'm hardly the go-to for relationship advice, but I've been around the sun a few times. Here's a piece of advice that works for most things. When unsure of your next move, carry on as you are and wait for clarity." She stretched, yawning. "Avoid rash decisions or sudden shifts. Just be. If you're lost, be lost. Who says you need to be found, anyway?" She caught the echo of her words, no doubt thinking about Sebastian in an instant. "I'm definitely buying you a diary for Christmas."

"Flow like water."

"*Precisely*! See, you know the answers deep down. That's why you're here. Love can cloud even the sharpest minds. Trust your heart, but don't let it walk you off a cliff."

Jessie appreciated the advice, especially as it wasn't wrapped in a Shakespearean quote like a pig in a blanket at Christmas. She'd opened up hoping for reciprocal openness, but she'd needed to hear those words. Maybe she did have the answers, but she still didn't know why she'd acted like she did with Billy.

"So, is that what you did? When Sebastian vanished?" Jessie prodded. "Just carried on?"

Veronica's gaze drifted. "Never stopped thinking about him. Even if only a passing thought, it's every day. I see a man with long hair on the street, and I stop in my tracks. I hear a Beatles song, and I hear them echoing around the farmhouse." A fond smile softened her tired face. "Oh, Mum and Dad couldn't *stand* them, but once they died, Sebastian played his records so loud the next farm over could hear them." She laughed, but it soured into a sad smile just as quick. "I *had* to carry on. Have a normal life, for Sebastian."

"When I asked about him, you—"

"Claimed he was dead?" She nodded. "I knew he wouldn't run away without leaving me some kind of hint. I've known he was dead from the moment I found out he was missing. He was ruffling too many feathers, and..." Blinking, she looked around the room like she didn't know where she was for a moment. "Forty years later, and here I am. I'm not even sure how I got here."

"Because Johnny Watson thought you were the best person for the job. He wanted to put the paper's reins in steady hands. Told me you were the best teacher he ever had."

"Really?" She huffed a disbelieving laugh. "That, and he knew Greg was my brother. Johnny could smell what was coming *long* before anyone else. I didn't mean to tell him, but after Greg won that by-election in January, I found myself in the pub drinking my sorrows away. I think Johnny had already left the village by then, but he'd come back to try to steady *The Post* ship after the first few new editors quit. I told my old student everything. He was one of my best, but he was a fool for thinking *I* could be the one to bring Greg down."

"But Greg *is* in prison now."

"For the time being," she said, fidgeting as she dragged herself closer to her desk. "And here I am, scouring through old diaries in the dead of night, still trying to uncover evidence linking Greg to Sebastian's death after all these years."

Jessie left her chair and perched on the edge of Veronica's desk, nudging a satsuma towards her; she'd barely touched her soggy chips from hours ago. "There's still a mountain of diaries to sift through. Perhaps Vincent Wellington paused his ego-stroking long enough to admit to his crimes in a later entry... say, 1984... 1991... 1999... 2003..."

Veronica, sceptical, turned a page and scoffed. "Just more self-aggrandising drivel. Vincent was always an insufferable—" She stopped, eyes narrowing at the page, lips following the curly script. After a moment, she cleared her throat, and read, "'At last! The evidence I've sought! Earl Philip's letters revealed the truth about Edward Wellington's birth. His true lineage. As I suspected, after discovering the falsified family tree, Edward wasn't Jonathan Wellington's son. Like myself, Jonathan was a bachelor without descendants. The boy he raised, my great-great-great-grandfather Edward was Clarissa Wellington's son. That land rightfully belongs to me.'"

"Clarissa?" echoed Jessie.

"Duncan Howarth's beloved, the woman who died before he finished her forest home." She re-read the passage. "This is the first time Vincent showed excitement for something beyond his own greatness or possessions."

"I remember a museum exhibit on them from that small place around the corner," Jessie said, wishing she'd taken some pictures before the place shut down. "I'm distantly related to Clarissa through Katie—via marriage—via adoption. But the woman at the museum was adamant Clarissa had no children."

"But why would Vincent think he had rights to land sold off in the 1800s because of that?"

"What if it doesn't need to make sense to *us*?" Jessie suggested, closing her laptop. "It mattered enough to Vincent for him to keep it secret, hidden away in his diaries. He wouldn't tell *The Peridale Post* why he had a claim to the land, but he was trying to sort it out privately with the council. The man was *obsessed* with lineage and legacy, and Duncan and Clarissa weren't married. What were the attitudes to having babies out of wedlock in 1979?"

"Still a few too decades too early for it not to be frowned upon. Only marginally moved on from the Victorian morality panic of the 1800s when this was first hidden. Are you suggesting—"

"What if Sebastian found *this* out?" Jessie said. "A secret shame big enough to die for? It wasn't like Vincent and Sebastian were the best pals before that. He did punch him at that party."

Veronica stared down at the floor as though she could see Katie drilling away at someone's nails from earlier in the day.

"Could I have had it wrong *all* these years?" Veronica said in a strained voice. "I've always been *so* sure that Greg killed Sebastian to inherit the farm for the money, but if Greg wasn't the one to murder Sebastian... *could* it have been Vincent Wellington?"

15

Jessie wanted nothing more than to stay in bed the next morning, wrapped up in her duvet, but her fourth alarm annoyed her out. After a quick shower to blast away the sleepiness from flicking through a dead man's diaries until the small hours, she ran out of her flat with only minutes to spare before the café opened.

The silent village green greeted her. Stalls remained, but no merchants had turned up for the few confused shoppers wandering around. Given how much of a rush the council had been in to shut down the market, she'd have expected the offending stalls to have been dragged away as fast as Martha.

At Richie's, James enjoyed his morning coffee at the window, looking out at the deserted market. She had to resist the urge to bang on the glass to ask why he'd done it, not that it would make a difference. There were only two reasons in her mind: he was getting ready to start work on paving over the green with a roundabout for when he finally found his road access, or it was petty revenge. Why should the people of Peridale have a Christmas market when they weren't stepping aside and allowing *him* to have what *he* wanted? She scooped up a ball of the melting snow and tossed it at the window. James jumped in his seat, spilling coffee down his white shirt.

Better than a conversation.

Jessie spun to run to the café, but silver hair further up the road caught her eye. She spotted Veronica outside the police station, coat collar turned up, arms clasping a tatty old box to her chest. In the café, Julia was already hard at work in the kitchen, whipping up something for the oven. Knowing the super baker could spare her a few minutes, Jessie hurried up the street to intercept Veronica.

"Sebastian update?"

Veronica shook her head, features grim. "I wish. No, I was inspired by Barker getting those diaries. Requested a copy of all the original case files from when Sebastian first vanished. My statements, witness statements... DI Moyes was surprisingly happy to provide them, as long as I didn't print them in the paper."

"Oh." Jessie nodded, peering into the full box. "Did you tell them about the diary?"

"I did. They didn't seem as keen about that, but can you blame them? Proving someone living committed a murder forty years ago is hard enough without the accused already being six feet under." She hoisted the box up and said, "Breakfast at The Plough? My treat? I owe you."

"How about the café? My treat, and you don't owe me anything. But I'm about thirty seconds from being late for work for the second time this week."

"Then I won't keep you. I'm not in the mood for the Old Age Pensioner Inquisition today, so I'll keep this brief." She lowered her voice and said, "They released Martha this morning after her antics at the market yesterday. Gave her a slap on the wrist, once she calmed down from ranting about getting everyone fired thanks to her 'important politician' cousin."

Jessie rolled her eyes. "Typical. What does she think Greg can do from behind bars?"

"According to Moyes, she had changed her tune by this morning. She visited Greg before the scene at the market. And after a nap and a cup of tea, Martha said that 'maybe Veronica was right about him...'"

Before Veronica could speculate further, Detective

Inspector Laura Moyes emerged from the station clutching a takeaway cup of coffee from Vicky's Van on Mulberry Lane.

"Condolences," Jessie said, nodding at the cup. "What's this I hear about Martha's change of tune?"

"You're right, it's foul," Moyes said after a sip. "And she was acting different every hour. Think she was in shock. Sometimes happens with first time arrestees." Sipping the coffee, her top lip snarled. "Thought you'd be back at your office digging through those by now? Like I said, if your fresh eyes see something we've missed, don't hesitate to call. Any leads right now would be helpful. And shouldn't you be at the café, Jessie?"

"On my way. What did Martha have to say about visiting Greg?

"That he wasn't the man she thought he was." Moyes rolled her eyes, popping the lid off to pour the pale coffee into the road. "I think she genuinely thought Greg was going to save her somehow. But by the end, it's like she'd lost all faith in him."

"Maybe the time alone let her stew," Veronica suggested.

"Seems like it, and you might want to warn your mum, Jessie," Moyes said, throwing the coffee cup into a nearby bin in one shot. "Martha asked when the 'café down the road' opened, and it seemed important. If trouble kicks off, you know who to call."

Jessie and Veronica exchanged a surprised look as Moyes ventured back into the station.

"Martha might be there already. Need a hand carrying that box to the office?"

When Veronica confirmed she was fine, Jessie jogged to the café, mind spinning over Martha's unexpected shift regarding Greg after how adamant she'd been that first day at the market. She went in through the back door to the kitchen, as Julia slid a tray of gingerbread people into the oven.

"Is Martha here?"

"Market Martha? No, why?"

"Then you might want to buckle up," Jessie said, tying her apron behind her back. "She visited Greg yesterday, and according to DI Moyes, she's keen to talk to you about something, and…" Parting the beads, Jessie stared at the doormat. "Bit early for mail, isn't it?"

At the door, Jessie scooped up another envelope. Plain white paper like the others, the same 'For the cause' scribble on the front, but this time, something different. Not only was the envelope thicker, but it also carried a scent.

A familiar scent.

Sunlight glinted off the donation tin as Julia thumbed through the stack of crisp banknotes, her pulse racing—one thousand pounds this time.

"It *has* to be him," Sue whispered, arriving late for her shift after waiting at home for the plumber. "He's messing with you, Julia. You don't want to let yourself be bought by James. Trust me."

Julia sniffed the envelope, as Jessie had before she ran out of the café. The faintest hint of a scent lingered on the paper, not that Julia had smelled the others. She wasn't sure what—or whom—it reminded her of.

"Perfume?" Julia asked, wafting the paper under Sue's nose across the counter. "You know this stuff better than me. Recognise it?"

Sue wrinkled her nose. "Sickly sweet. Like something Katie would wear?"

"We know it's not Katie."

"Do we?" Sue arched a brow. "Her salon is always busy. She bought the place outright with the manor money and she's renting out the top floor to the newspaper... she's probably got more money than any of us right now."

"But over two thousand in one week?"

"This is the woman who used to spend that in a

day on one pair of shoes."

Julia considered Katie might be sending them the money, but it didn't stick. "No. Katie learned her lesson. She wouldn't throw her money away like this. She'll be saving it. For Vinnie's future."

"All I'm saying is," Sue whispered, sniffing the envelope again, "you know Katie has been blaming herself for handing James the keys to the manor. Maybe this is her way of trying to put things right?"

While waiting for the first customers on the quiet morning—thanks to no market and Sebastian's unsolved murder becoming old news—Julia continued to wonder if their secret benefactor could be Katie. She would be grateful for the generous donations, but she couldn't accept them knowing the sacrifice Katie had made to turn her life around after nearly losing everything.

"Julia, I thought you said they cancelled the market?"

"They did?"

Julia tossed the money on the counter and hurried over to Sue as she filled sugar pots by the window. Outside, the vacant stalls had erupted with activity as market sellers scurried about, their wares cluttering the village green once again.

And Martha Morgan wasn't the one leading the charge. Instead, Dot's shrill voice cut through the din with the aid of her megaphone as she ordered sellers this way and that, while Ethel and Percy hustled to unload boxes. Julia grabbed her coat and gloves and pushed out into the cold, flagging down Dot for an explanation amidst the controlled chaos.

"We were up *all* night!" Dot announced in her no-nonsense tone, rushing between stallholders to guide them into position. "No permits or not, we're not going to let the festive season pass without a full market. We're staging a *protest* market. These hardworking people deserve to sell their goods, and we need foot traffic here to spread awareness about the awful, corrupt individuals pulling the strings in this village." Her eyes flashed with defiance. "It was all Ethel's idea. She has at least two good ones a year, if she's lucky."

Ethel shot Dot a side glance, but her smile was pleased before she barked at the woman selling jarred pickles to straighten her sign.

"But this is illegal," Sue called, joining Julia on the edge of the green. "You're going to get in trouble."

"My old neighbour made bootleg DVDs on his computer and had control of an entire black market in Peridale, and the police never sniffed him out," Ethel exclaimed, waving for Denise Coleman to take a prime stall near the café. "People have got away with worse around here."

A makeshift market without permission from the council was a little different in scale, Julia thought. And despite their gusto now, the police had shut down the official market just yesterday with force.

"This won't last long," Sue said to Julia, and she felt just as pessimistic.

"It'll last as long as we remain bold!" Percy proclaimed as he rushed past with boxes of leeks for the veg stall. "We shall not, no, we shall not be moved! We shall..."

Dot hurried to cram the megaphone to his lips, and his reedy voice rang out across the green. A chant erupted amongst the stallholders as more villagers arrived to support the effort.

Despite her doubts about the longevity, Julia's heart warmed to see everyone banding together, fighting for this space that meant so much. For what they knew was right.

She couldn't argue with that.

"Get those ovens firing," Dot barked at her through the megaphone as the chant carried on. "You can have a stall for the café, free of charge. Nobody pays a penny until the council reverses their decision. *And to everyone else*," Dot called, turning the megaphone towards the street running through the village, "*spread the word*! The Christmas market is back on, and we shall not, we shall not be moved!"

James barged out of Richie's, his face mottled crimson as he shouted into his mobile, drowned out by the chanting. Behind him, his son, Richie, lingered in the doorway, looking amused by his father's reaction.

Cupping his hands around his mouth, Richie called, "Free drinks for *all* stallholders! As many winter warmups as you want."

A cheer rang through the market, and a couple of people abandoned their unpacking to take him up on the offer. James turned to snap something at Richie, whose response was an eye roll, jerking his head at his father to move out of the way of the door. James stepped closer to the road, but his furious gaze tracked everyone walking into the bar for a free drink on his coin.

Jessie exited the bar next, and Julia waved, surprised to see her daughter there; she hadn't said where she was going after handing over the envelope.

"We should get started," Sue said, tugging on Julia's sleeve. "Could be a good business opportunity, and if not, at least it's ruining James' morning."

"Simple pleasures."

The sisters shared a laugh as they turned towards the café. The illicit market wasn't the organised resistance they'd planned, but seeing the hopeless fury on James' face was enough for Julia this morning.

A war yet to be won, but they'd won this small battle, for now.

"Mince pies, gingerbread, and—"

A blood-curdling scream pierced the crisp morning air, followed by another further up the street. Julia's head snapped up to see an out-of-control green estate car swerve around the corner from the direction of the library, picking up speed as it tore through the village. It crashed through a wheelie bin in front of Evelyn's B&B, erupting rubbish all around. Evelyn popped up from behind her garden wall, her turban askew, as she watched in horror as the car pummelled on.

The car veered violently past The Plough, narrowly missing a woman walking her dogs as she jumped back onto the pavement. More screams rang out as pedestrians darted out of the way, muffled by the stallholders who hadn't noticed what was happening and continued their jovial chanting.

"*Stop!*" DI Moyes yelled, rushing from the station.

But the car maintained its frenzied pace, weaving towards the market. Ice flooded Julia's veins when she noticed Jessie was halfway across the road, eyes glued to her phone as she tapped out a message with quick thumbs. She was right in the car's chaotic path.

"*Jessie!*" Dot's shrill cry echoed through the megaphone. "Get out of the way!"

Jessie's head jerked up, her phone tumbling from her grasp. Julia saw her mouth open in a silent scream, deer-in-headlights terror paralysing her limbs. The car bore down on her, mere feet away. James grabbed Jessie's coat in two fists, yanking her back onto the curb with seconds to spare.

In a blur, the car streaked past where Jessie had stood only seconds before. But there was no time to let out the sigh of relief choked in Julia's throat. The car was still headed straight for the market full of unsuspecting people. Stallholders screamed, scrambling to get clear. With an awful crunch of metal and splintering wood, the car smashed through Denise's vegetable stand, obliterating it in a spray of produce and wood. It ploughed through two more stalls, leaving chaos in its wake before crunching to a forced stop near the church, smoke spewing from the mangled hood.

"What the...?" Barker came rushing from his office. "Did something explode?"

Julia grabbed Barker's hand, unable to tear her eyes away as the car's wheels spun ceaselessly, churning up mud and grass as it dug deeper into the wreckage. The vehicle edged closer towards the ancient church with each violent rotation. Then a man burst forward, wrenching the driver's door open.

He yanked the keys from the ignition, and the engine cut off, the wheels shuddering to a standstill.

Behind the cracked windshield, Martha Morgan lay motionless over the steering wheel. Blood trickled from a gash on her forehead, dripping into the deflating airbag.

Julia released Barker's hand and rushed across the road to Jessie. Her daughter stood stunned on the curb, trembling as all the colour drained from her cheeks. Julia grabbed her in a fierce embrace.

James Jacobson lingered a few steps away, glancing between Jessie and the smoking wreckage he'd saved her from. Julia met his eye, the words stuck in her throat. But she managed a silent mouthed 'thank you,' hoping her conflicted gratitude shone through. James gave a terse nod, his face unreadable, before retreating into the bar without a word.

Over Jessie's shoulder, Julia took in the devastation cluttering the green. The defiant little market they'd rallied was now matchsticks and rubble strewn across the grass.

Peridale's idyllic postcard image had warped into a disaster zone in mere seconds. But Jessie was safe, thanks to the last man Julia had thought would try to help her. She squeezed her eyes shut against the complicated swirl of emotions, holding Jessie close amidst the chaos.

16

Julia couldn't take her eyes away from Jessie as she put on a brave face for the customers behind the counter. Her daughter insisted she was fine despite her near brush with death the previous afternoon. The café offered front-row seats to the crew clearing the destruction on the village green, keeping Julia occupied enough; she'd been catching snatches of the speculation around the vehicle's destructive tear through the village.

Why had Martha Morgan's car lost control?

Had her brakes failed or been tampered with?

And who might be to blame?

Julia suppressed a shudder, picturing the smoking vehicle wreckage and her panic-stricken daughter on the curb. She slid the last teapot onto Evelyn's table and made her way back to the till.

"You should take the day for yourself. After a trauma like that..."

"For the *tenth* time, I *wasn't* hit, Mum. Honestly, I'm okay." Jessie flashed her a smile that seemed more strained than reassuring. "The café needs all hands on deck today. Busy, busy, busy. I'll rest later."

Sue zoomed past. with trays laden with empty mugs and plates. "At least sit down for a few minutes. You look peaky. Could be delayed shock. I'd see it all the time at the hospital after car accidents."

She rolled her eyes. "*I* wasn't in a car accident. You know what's shocking? *This* harassment in the workplace. Don't make me fill out a form. What does everyone expect me to do? Stare out the window for hours? Rock in the corner? But since you're trying to get rid of me, I'll finish at three. Something I need to do."

Before Julia could question her daughter's plans, DI Moyes pushed into the café. A dozen questions erupted about Martha's crash. Julia noted the babble carried more curiosity than compassion.

DI Moyes raised her hands, waiting for the chatter to subside. "We're still waiting for the vehicle report, but eyewitnesses suggest the brakes did fail, causing Miss Morgan to lose control."

"Fail... or were cut?" Jessie asked.

Moyes hesitated. "No evidence either way yet."

"*Really?*" Dot elbowed her way forward to stand eye-to-eye with the detective. "Because *I* heard a rumour that the politician that Greg Morgan replaced had *his* brakes cut too."

"You mean Hugo Scott?" Sue said. "I worked that shift. He died almost as soon as he arrived. Nasty crash."

"Greg offed him to win that by-election," Jessie chimed in. "And he had his Cotswold Crew pet tamper with my brakes when I was getting too close to the truth before that committee meeting. Why would the puppet master let something like being behind bars stop him from pulling the strings?"

Murmurs of agreement rippled around the room. Julia noticed Moyes shift her weight at this line of accusation.

"There was *no* evidence that Mr Scott's brakes were deliberately tampered with. Let's try to stick to what happened yesterday."

"But was it deliberate yesterday?" Shilpa suggested. "It looked more like an awful accident."

"I'm not so sure..." Evelyn mused, swirling her teacup. "I overheard Martha tearing strips off James in defence of Greg Morgan at my tarot stall this week."

"Could be she decided to get even and things went

too far?" Amy suggested. "Everyone is saying Jacobscrooge was behind the market shut down. What does Martha have to say for herself?"

Moyes cleared her throat. "We'll be exploring every angle, I assure you. For now, Miss Morgan is still unconscious, so questioning will have to wait."

As Moyes stepped up to the counter to order coffee and mince pies to share with her team at the station, Julia continued assembling the plate she'd been putting together to take down to Barker's office.

"I'm not trying to scare you," Moyes said, nostrils flared, "but just to be on the safe side... steer clear of driving anywhere if you don't need to."

Unease pricked Julia's skin at the warning. She hadn't considered herself potentially in harm's way as well.

"Dot's right though," Jessie whispered after they sent the DI on her way. "*Has* to be Greg, even from behind bars. He's done it before, and now he has the perfect alibi."

"It is looking that way, but how do we prove it?"

"There might be a way," Jessie said, glancing at the clock. "You'll want to take that tray down, or you're going to miss everything. They've been down there for ten minutes."

Picking up the finished tray, Julia gave the demolished market one final glance as the noise in the café switched from Martha to James' upcoming Winter Gala. As villagers debated if they were going to attend, Julia left through the back door.

She descended the creaky wooden steps to the murky office armed with tea and coffee, along with plates piled high with cakes and pastries.

Barker had gathered their key suspects—Gwen Dean, Arnold Jessop, and Harold Morgan—though none looked pleased with the forced reunion. Gwen sat rigid in her chair by the vinyl player, draped in fur and jewels, her back-combed beehive sagging. She refused to look at anything but her nails. Across from Gwen, Harold slouched with arms crossed over his barrel chest on the Chesterfield sofa, shooting hostile glares towards Arnold. The elderly architect seemed oblivious, glancing over his half-moon spectacles as he sketched on a notepad across from Barker.

After distributing the drinks and cakes, Julia lingered by Barker's side as he let out an irritated sigh.

"I'm grateful you all came, but we can't sit in silence *all* afternoon," he announced. "Who tampered with Martha's brakes?"

Gwen flapped a dismissive hand "How could Martha's reckless driving be connected to Sebastian's death forty years ago? *Ridiculous* question."

"I'll remind you that Martha was Sebastian's cousin," Barker said evenly. "And up until her accident, she was still aligned with Greg Morgan. I find the timing rather suspect."

Arnold smoothed his white hair, regarding Barker over his specs as he set the pad down. "Perhaps Martha herself orchestrated the crash? I heard that she was quite outraged over the Christmas market permit being revoked."

"How *dare* you!" Harold erupted, half-rising from his chair. "My daughter is *no* radical! If her brakes failed, you can bet someone cut them. The question is who..." His accusing glare swung between Gwen and Arnold.

"Yes, Harold, dear, *you* were always handy with spanners." Gwen palmed up her deflating beehive. "And desperate people make foolish choices when they have much to gain."

Before tensions could escalate further, Julia decided she needed to intervene. "Harold, how is Martha faring? We're all worried about her recovery."

He scrubbed a weary hand down his face. "Still unconscious. Lots of broken bones, a collapsed lung, a slight skull fracture, and who knows what else. She survived a four-hour surgery, but it's too soon to know if she'll..." His voice cracked. "I shouldn't be wasting time with pointless questions when my daughter is fighting for her life."

"Then I won't take much more of your time,"

Barker said, consulting his notes. "I'd like to establish where each of you were on Christmas Eve, 1979—the night Sebastian disappeared."

"At that dreadful Wellington Manor party, of course," Gwen said. "Though I left rather early after Vincent's outburst."

"Most people did," Arnold interjected, finally dragging his gaze from Harold. "After witnessing Vincent punch poor Sebastian, the party atmosphere died."

"No need to rehash the party itself," Barker redirected. "I want to know your whereabouts *after* things ended sourly there with Sebastian driving off into the night."

Gwen snatched a flaky croissant, spilling crumbs down her fur collar. "Went straight home to my boyfriend's cottage. Had it all to myself while he was away on business. Now long dead, God rest him."

Arnold helped himself to tea with trembling hands. "And I stayed on at the manor. Vincent offered his guest quarters following the unpleasantness." He slurped loudly, continuing, "He and I were the sole guests remaining as the staff cleaned up."

All eyes swivelled to Harold, whose thick moustache twitched over pursed lips. After an extended pause, he pushed to his feet. "Don't have to sit here listening to this nonsense. I'm going back to check on my Martha."

"Mr Morgan, please. Just tell us where you went after leaving Vincent's party. It's a simple question."

Harold's jaw tightened. "Simple answer is, I went to the farmhouse. Now can I go?" Without waiting for confirmation, Peridale's gruff ice cream baron stormed towards the exit.

Gwen made a scolding tsk sound. "Ever the hothead, that one. Small wonder he and Vincent were thick as thieves with tempers like that." She shot a pointed look at Arnold. "Don't you agree?"

The architect made an evasive noise in his throat, slurping more tea. Julia gave Barker's shoulder a sympathetic squeeze. His brooding stare remained fixed on the doorway, churning over unanswered questions.

"I noticed your crime board," Julia said, crossing the office to where Barker had pinned up various documents, photos, and scribbled notes connected by a chaotic web of multi-coloured strings. "Found a lot in Vincent's diaries?"

Barker blinked, drawing his attention back to her with a hint of an appreciative smile. "Just trying to connect threads. Making progress unravelling the past, at least."

He first landed on the letter penned by Duncan

Howarth. The letter found concealed behind the portrait now hidden in her gran's dining room. The impassioned plea for forgiveness and wisdom she'd read aloud to sway the planning committee. Next to it hung an aged map of Peridale depicting a familiar crop of buildings, with a name she wasn't expecting to see attached to the ownership of the field behind the café.

"Duncan owned that field?" Julia exclaimed.

Arnold dabbed cake crumbs from his whiskery lips. "Ah, therein lies a tangled drama. When Howarth lay dying in that ramshackle forest house, he received a most unexpected visitor—"

"Earl Philip Wellington, father of his lost lady love, Clarissa," Gwen interrupted. "You know he wasn't a real Earl, right? Faked the title and nobody bothered to check back then."

"Philip revealed a startling secret kept from Howarth following Clarissa's death," Arnold continued. "It seems Clarissa had a child she bore in secrecy before her untimely death—a son fathered by Duncan Howarth himself."

"Howarth had an heir?" Julia murmured. "Maybe that's what my father overheard at the village hall on that night all those years ago. I think Sebastian knew about this. Vincent kept the records in his safe. Wanted to keep it secret."

Gwen huffed. "What else might one expect from such imperious men? Ordering helpless women about to conceal their misbegotten offspring. The honourable Wellingtons have always considered themselves above reproach."

Arnold gave a tilt of his head. "Social standards were rather rigid in those days regarding matters of decorum and class." He adjusted his spectacles. "In any event, Philip ensured his grandson, Edward, was safely raised by Jonathan, Clarissa's brother... not that Howarth lived more than a few days beyond that melancholy discovery."

Barker cleared his throat, re-joining the conversation. "Vincent Wellington's diaries reveal the sticking point—Duncan left that land to Edward in his final days, but Jonathan sold off the land Edward should have inherited before the boy reached maturity."

"On the verge of losing the manor," Arnold said with a waft of his hand. "Or so Vincent said."

"Wellingtons are good at that," Julia muttered.

"After Katie arrived on the scene," Arnold continued, not hearing her, "Vincent convinced himself the land's chain of ownership after Jonathan's initial sale was invalid. Once he had the proof of Edward's true parentage, Vincent spent every waking hour obsessed with reclaiming that land. After all, the land wasn't Jonathan Wellington's to sell. And that's where *we* came in. To help design his vision."

"And *pay* for it," Gwen grumbled.

Julia's thoughts tumbled over this new information. She pictured young Sebastian grasping at similar dusty threads back in 1979—clues too abstract to halt Wellington's imposing plans.

Unease pricked her skin. She turned back to her husband, whose own restless gaze remained fixed on the letter penned decades ago by Duncan. He'd made no mention of an heir, claiming those to be his final days, but it seemed Earl Philip saved the biggest surprise for Duncan's last gasps.

"Fascinating as this history lesson is," Julia began, "I'm unsure how it gets us any closer to why Sebastian died or who killed him, or what happened to Martha."

Barker raked a hand through his hair. "There must be a connection. I just haven't found it yet. Still half a box of diaries to go through. He's rather verbose."

Gwen lumbered to her feet, coat shedding crumbs. "I wish I could assist you further, but I'm afraid I must be off." She wrapped the leftovers from the tray in napkins and stuffed them in her pockets. "Sorry that I couldn't be of more use."

As Gwen waddled towards the exit with her bounty, Julia felt a tug of disappointment. Like after their first meeting, she doubted the prickly woman had revealed all she knew.

"If you know anything else," she called after Gwen. "You know where we are."

Gwen paused, manicured fingers tightening on the doorknob at the top of the stairs. For an instant, Julia thought she detected deep sorrow in the woman's eyes as she glanced back, but then her expression shuttered.

"If I don't set off now, I'll miss my bus," she said, opening the door to the bright light. "Can't be missing *Bargain Hunt*, can I?"

The heavy door closed behind her swish of furs, leaving a faint silence. Julia stared at the empty tray, wondering if a pivotal clue had just walked out. With a sigh, she moved to help Arnold upstairs while Barker tidied his disappointing notes. After helping him into his chair, she wheeled him to an Oakwood-branded car and waved him back to the nursing home. On the green, all but a couple of stalls remained.

Rather than rush back to the café, Julia joined Barker in the office.

"What do you make of all this?" She perched on the edge of his cluttered desk, rearranging the haphazard piles of paper. "Scandals from a bygone era, family secrets, ownership claims... where might it all be leading?"

"If I knew, I'd sleep easier tonight. I... I'm visiting Greg Morgan in prison in two hours."

"What? How?"

"Courtesy of a visiting order from his sister. Veronica didn't want it, so I arranged a meeting, and he accepted."

"What do you think he wants to say to you?"

"That's what I hope to find out. Might help to hear his side of the story, even if it's not entirely true, but before then... I wanted to ask you something about Katie."

"Katie?" Julia's stomach lurched. She hadn't given much thought to her father's wife since the disaster at the market. "Is this about the money?"

"Money?" He shook his head. "No, it's about her mother."

"Katie's mother? Oh, I..."

"Don't know who she is?"

"Katie must have mentioned her, but..." Julia searched her memories for something—anything. "In all the years I've known Katie, I don't think she's ever once mentioned her mother, and I... I've never asked. Oh, that's not good. Why, Barker? What have you found?"

"Another time," he replied, checking his watch. "I

need to set off to the prison, but there's one more thing. If Vincent's theories about having ancestral rights to that land have any merit to it, you know what that means?"

The penny dropped.

"Katie is Duncan Howarth's descendant," Julia spoke the theory aloud. "She and Vinnie are next in line."

Arching both brows, he nodded, holding his palms out. "It's a long shot, but it's something. Finally, something. But I need to set off. If you see Katie before I do, ask her about Howarth, and don't mention her mother…" Sighing, he rubbed at his stubbly jaw. "I need to talk to her."

Leaving Barker to get ready for his visit to Greg, Julia climbed the staircase, wondering if they'd just found their chink in James Jacobson's armour. The thought of Katie having any right to the field felt as far-fetched as Katie being the one behind the donations, but like Barker had said, it was something, and when they'd had so little to cling onto, Julia would take any 'something.'

17

Jessie lingered in the shadow of an oak tree outside the gates of St. Peter's Primary School. Kids tugged on sleeves as gossiping mothers refused to give up their speculation.

"Absolutely *crazy*, if you ask me, Sharon," one of them said in an exaggerated whisper. "*I* heard that woman who crashed into the market killed the guy they dug up, and that was her trying to take her own life."

"Didn't work, though, did it, Trish? Because *I* heard she survived, but she lost *all* her limbs."

"Oh, the poor lamb!" Trish gasped. "But *I* heard it was only an arm?"

"*All* her limbs, that's what Jaden's mother said, but

we all know she likes to..." Sharon said, pausing to mime a chugging bottle at the side of her mouth, "...and not just because it's Christmas."

"Oh, *don't*! I woke up with the worst Baileys headache this morning. Felt as legless as that poor market woman."

"Trish, you're *wicked*!"

"*What*?" Trish held up her palms. "I'm not the one who steamed headfirst into a crowded market. Did you hear that she hit *three* people?"

"Really? *I* heard it was seven."

The women passed by Jessie's tree, and she resisted the urge to put a foot out to trip them up as they teetered on heels on the uneven gravel path. Jessie had assumed the café always attracted the worst gossip, but it turned out that honour belonged to the school playground.

Across the hopscotch, Roxy Carter, Jessie's mum's old friend and Moyes' other half—and Miss Carter to the pupils—was with a young girl on the bottom step. The young girl, whom Jessie had recognised as Mia from the first rush through the doors after the final bell rang, twiddled her tinsel-tied pigtails.

Jessie checked her watch at the sight of a tall figure in a bulky puffer jacket jogging past her hiding place, a hood concealing his face. Mia's sullen expression evaporated, replaced by wide-eyed delight as the latecomer scooped her up and spun her around. Roxy said something to the man that made him wave a hand and set off across the playground, Mia's hand in his. Shaking her head, Roxy walked towards the school doors now that the last child had been picked up.

The man and Mia walked past Jessie's tree, and she glimpsed his Pitbull-like features hidden by the hood.

It was him.

Six.

Jessie gave her accomplice waiting in the bushes the thumbs up, pushed away from the oak, and trailed after father and daughter as they set off in the direction of St. Peter's church.

"...*then* we learned about Ancient Egypt until lunchtime," Mia said, skipping between steps, her hand swinging in her father's. "Did you know they used to pull your brain out through your nose after you died?"

"I'm sure *you* did," Jessie called as she matched their pace. "That's one of your specials, isn't it, Six?"

Six's sharp swivel betrayed his astonishment at Jessie's sheer nerve. Before he could spit venom, Jessie tilted her head at Mia as she skipped alongside.

"Mia, run up ahead, will you?" Six said, his voice

wavering. "Daddy needs to talk to his friend about something."

"Can we get ice cream on the way home?"

"As much as you want."

Six bit back whatever colourful tirade perched on his tongue as Mia skipped ahead a few steps. Jessie held his glare with her jolliest smile, determined not to show a sprinkle of intimidation even as her pulse raced out of control.

"I suggest you turn around and leave right now," he ordered in a low growl. "I don't know who you think you are, but I won't—"

"Would that be Harold Morgan's ice cream place, by any chance?" Jessie charged on, doing her own skip to keep up with his quickening pace. "I saw you there the other day, didn't I? Sneaking around the place? I thought you were there to track Harold Morgan, but you weren't, were you? You were there for his daughter, Martha." She paused, ducking to catch his eyes averting hers in the shadow of the hood. "*You* cut them."

"You don't know what—"

"I think I *do* know what I'm talking about," she continued. "Of course, you didn't cut them because *you* wanted to. You cut them so you can buy little Mia over there some ice cream without telling her she can only have one scoop. Or something as simple as putting the heating on so she doesn't have to sleep in a cold flat." She paused, but he didn't say anything. "The timing is too perfect for you to deny it. Martha visited Greg before she crashed in the same circumstances as Greg's former rival. She changed her tune on her cousin, like she'd learned something she wasn't meant to know. Did she figure out what really happened to their cousin forty years ago? Or did Greg not like the colour of her shoes? Doesn't take much for him to set his last soldier on his enemies, does it?"

Six's lips peeled back from his teeth, but his rebuttal never took shape.

"The way I see it, pal, you have three choices," Jessie pressed on. "Keep your head down and hope you never get caught. Go on the run and force Mia to live in hiding for the rest of her life or... you can come forward with everything you know about Greg's dodgy dealings, and maybe they'll go easy on you." She paused before adding more gently, "Might not miss too many of Mia's birthday parties. The police couldn't get any other crew members to talk and look how it ended up for all of them."

Six shoved his hands deeper into his coat pockets but didn't break stride. Mia waited for her father at the top of the lane, her attention fixed on the workers tossing fragments of wood into a skip at the end of the green.

"You're playing a dangerous game, lass."

"So are you."

Six didn't argue.

"And you've got a chance to make things right." Jessie slowed her brisk walk as they neared the end of the lane. "I know you care about her not knowing who her daddy really is, but she's lucky to have a parent who loves her. I wasn't so lucky at her age. You have until the end of the week."

"Oh yeah? Or else what?"

"I'll tell the police you live in the fourth flat from the left on the second row at Fern Moore, *Chris*."

Six's knuckles thickened into a fist, but Jessie tapped on his shoulder and nodded behind them. They both turned to see a figure in a balaclava filming their every move.

"Doesn't feel so nice to know you're being followed, does it?" she said, taking a step back. "End of the week, for Mia."

With that parting shot, Jessie dropped back. She loitered at a distance, watching Six steer Mia across the road and out of sight without a backward glance. Only once they vanished around the bend did Jessie release an enormous exhale. Legs quivering, she leaned against the low stone wall as her balaclava-clad accomplice did the same a few feet away.

"You can take that thing off," Jessie called to him. "He's gone."

Dante pulled off the balaclava with a pant.

"Thank you," she said.

"Wasn't going to let you go in on your own, was I?" he offered with a shrug. "He could've ripped your head off. He still might."

"Had to rattle his cage. Greg's secrets can't stay buried forever, and time is running out." She summoned a faint smile for her uneasy ally. "I do appreciate you coming."

Dante scuffed a boot. "Wasn't sure I would. Listen... I... I want to talk. Fancy a quick drink at Richie's?"

Jessie almost told him she'd have to get back to the café, if only to avoid the awkward conversation they'd have, but she couldn't put it off forever. Besides, her mum and Sue had been trying to get rid of her all morning.

"Has to be quick," she said, kicking away from the wall. "On me. I owe you."

Dante nodded, and they headed for the warm glow spilling from Richie's onto the snow-dusted pavement. For once, there was no sign of James lingering in the quiet bar.

They sat at the bar under the safety of the glowing

pendant bulbs, taking their time to scan the menu while Richie finished unloading a crate of gingerbread liqueur. The stuffy silence between them was unfamiliar, more like two wedding guests from different sides of the family forced to mingle. She sucked in a bracing breath, unable to endure the tension a moment longer.

"I'm sorry for being rubbish after you asked me to go travelling," she confessed in a rush. "It's not a bad thing that you want to go travelling. It's a great thing, actually. Highly recommend it, but... you obviously want adventures, and you should go and find them, but I... I *won't* be coming with you." She paused, and like with Six earlier, no response came. "I want to stay here, in Peridale. I spent so long looking for a home, and now that I have one, I don't want to let it go. Not yet, at least. I don't know what I want, to be honest, which means I should just carry on as I have been."

Dante nodded as he absorbed what she was saying. Richie walked over, distracted by his stock list, and took their order. They both ordered an espresso martini, returning to the silence.

"Jessie, it sounds like..." He sighed. "Are we..."

"I think we want different things. I can't string you along when I'm focused elsewhere." She risked a glance at him, afraid she'd find accusation in his steady gaze. "Maybe this moved too fast. I think you're fantastic. Wonderful... but... I... we..."

"Say no more." He slapped the bar with both hands before scanning the empty room. "I just remembered I have a thing. A newspaper thing. Cancel my drink, will you? I'll see..." Slipping off the stool, he glanced at her for a moment with a blank expression she'd never seen before. "See you around."

The door closed behind him, and Jessie rested her head on the bar. She groaned, wondering if she'd handled that well. She hadn't meant to break up with Dante when agreeing to the drink; she'd only wanted to talk, but it was the right decision, wasn't it? They *did* want different things.

"That bad?" Richie asked, sliding the espresso across the bar. "Whatever it is, it'll sort itself out."

"What it is, is over," she said, pushing back in the chair. Clenching her eyes, she said, "It was only a few days ago he was planning to meet my parents. I feel sick."

Richie pulled the extra martini to himself, nodding his understanding, his own gaze far away. "Ending things is rough work. But if your gut says it's not going anywhere, it's always better to do the right thing."

Despite herself, Jessie raised a brow at her friend. Richie rarely ventured into personal territory, but whatever relationship drama she had going on, he had something worse.

"Your turn," Jessie said, picking up her drink.

"Don't get too used to having the best espresso martinis you've ever tried on your doorstep for much longer," Richie said with an offhand shrug that didn't quite ring true. "Dad's closing the bar in the New Year. Last stop before the wrecking ball comes in to build a car park, or a skyscraper, or a great big gold statue carved in his image."

"Oh, mate. I'm sorry…"

"Bet it's his petty revenge because I gave those stallholders free drinks the other day." He downed half the drink in one gulp. "Not that he'd say that. Been giving me the silent treatment since. Notified me that the bar would be closing through a letter. A letter from my *own* father… can you believe it?"

"When it comes to Jacobscrooge, nothing surprises me anymore."

"*Ha*. Jacobscrooge." Richie tossed back the rest of the drink and slammed it on the bar. "I like it. Well, it was fun while it lasted, right?"

Glancing at the door, still able to see Dante storming out, Jessie sighed. "Yeah, fun while it lasted."

Richie scribbled something on a napkin before shoving it her way. It was a phone number with 'For emergency martinis' scrawled above it. "Or just if you want to hang out. You're the only friend I've made since moving to Peridale, so I've grown rather fond."

He winked before beckoning her in with a finger. "And as a friend, you should know I overheard Dad on the phone yesterday before the crash. The police are releasing the field back to him first thing tomorrow, so you know what that means."

"Changed my mind about the drink. How much do I owe you?"

Richie swapped it with his empty glass and slurped the foam off the top. "On me. Now, get out of here and get back to your café." Toasting the drink, he added, "Give Jacobscrooge hell, won't you? He deserves it."

Jessie returned the toast with a lift of the napkin before hurrying around the green and back to the café as she felt their window for change close to slamming shut on her fingers.

"Grab your thermal pants and thermos flasks," Jessie announced to the full café, meeting her mum's worried eyes behind the counter. "The digging resumes tomorrow, so spread the word because Base Camp Peridale goes up tonight. Our last stand begins *now*."

18

*B*arker's footsteps reverberated off the sterile floors as a guard escorted him through the maze of bright hallways. The corridors of a prison never ceased to unsettle him. Society's worst under one roof, and each wall had a story to tell. Today, only one story interested him, though he'd almost driven past the turnoff. An afternoon with Greg Morgan wasn't his idea of fun.

The guard ushered Barker inside the concrete chamber of the visiting room. Out of reach, a tiny window let in streams of winter sun through bars, and a metal table with two chairs occupied the room's centre. All twelve legs were bolted to the floor—only the best for their former elected official. He claimed the chair facing the door as the jangling keys moved closer.

Two guards escorted the dishevelled prisoner inside, his balance hampered by cuffs binding his wrists. In dingy joggers and a too-tight white t-shirt with several days of stubble, Greg Morgan had none of his usual slick political polish. Despite his unkempt nature, Greg's broad shoulders remained squared, his chest puffed.

Greg eased into the chair opposite Barker, a cocky smirk lifting his sagging cheeks. He appeared thinner, and a dark, glossy bruise encircled his swollen right eye. His gaze met Barker's with a flicker of recognition. Barker had witnessed the scene outside Wellington Heights when officers had dragged Greg from his penthouse hiding spot—a night neither man would forget in a hurry.

"Veronica's bloodhound finally comes sniffing," Greg said with the confident tone of a man not in chains. "How is my sister?"

"She'll be better when she knows the truth."

"Who am I kidding?" He scanned the room, taking in the concrete ceiling as if it were the Sistine Chapel. "What do I care?"

"You sent her a visiting order."

"Wanted to see her face when I delivered my

fantastic news." He tapped his nose. "She'll find out soon enough."

That's how they were going to play this? Barker knew these interviews well. Slippery on the outside, even slipperier on the inside.

"News?"

"Mind your business." He moved his cuffed hands from his lap to the table, metal rattling the steel. "So, to what do I owe the pleasure, Mr...?" His voice trailed, feigning ignorance.

"Barker Brown. Private investigator. I was the PI on the George Knight arson case that you were behind." Matching Greg, he clasped his hands on the cold steel. "*Correction*—the Cotswold Crew were behind burning the Knight family home down, on your orders."

"*Allegedly.*"

"And James was behind you. Wanted the Knight's road access to his little Howarth Estate patch, but just one of your many recent misdeeds. I refreshed my memory of your charges earlier." He parted his hands, arching his brows at Greg. "Not looking too good for you, is it? Several charges under the 2010 Bribery Act for unlawfully influencing the outcome of a planning committee. Even more charges under the 2015 Serious Crime Act for hiring gangs." He nodded at the bruised eye. "That shiner courtesy of the Cotswold Crew?

Local plods have caught most of them, so you must have quite a few familiar faces in your block?"

He fluttered his fingers. "*All* lies, I can assure you."

"You're looking at ten to fifteen years, and you've been denied bail. Doesn't seem like lies to me, Mr Morgan. You wouldn't be here if the prosecutor didn't think this case stood a good chance in court."

"They needed a scapegoat for all the recent... unrest." He shrugged as though he'd taken the fall for shoplifting some sweets for his mates. "My political dealings are not why you're here, Mr Brown. Perhaps you're researching your next novel? How are sales?"

Barker pushed back in the stiff chair, tilting his head at the smug prisoner; Greg had done his research. "You're right, I'm here for something much more serious than bribes and gangs."

"Pesky unpaid parking tickets?"

"Murder, Mr Morgan." The accusation brought no reaction. "I'm looking into your brother's case. Sebastian."

"She's still clinging to that fantasy after all these years? Veronica always thought she was the voice of truth, even when no one was listening, but I suppose she feels rather emboldened with that cushy little newspaper job. Hate to disappoint you, Mr Brown, but you've wasted your time coming here. No evidence *then*, no evidence *now*."

"So, you don't know what happened to your brother in 1979?"

"Thought he ran away."

"And you don't know how he ended up buried where the old market hall used to be?"

"Thought he ran away."

"And did you carry his body to that grave on your own, or did you have help?"

Greg smirked, leaning closer. "Thought he ran away."

"I see." Slippery. "And you weren't concerned?"

"You want to know the truth, Mr Brown? I didn't like my brother as far as I could throw him. Lazy good for nothing. Didn't understand the meaning of hard work. Discipline. Sacrifice."

"Is that what you did?" Barker said, lowering his voice. "Sacrificed Sebastian to fund your future?"

Greg's response this time was silence, his attention diverted to something under his nails. He picked at them as he let a fake-looking yawn flutter his lips.

"Okay," Barker said, palms flat on the table, sensing their allocated time slipping through his fingers. "Let's switch gears for a moment. I find your partnership with James Jacobson interesting. Quite the ambitious alliance. *He* pays *you*. *You* pull strings with all those contacts you have at the council. Used to work in the planning department, didn't you?" He paused, and Greg offered a measured nod. "You got your cousin, Martha, a job there organising the Christmas market."

"The previous organiser was a liability."

"Did you hear about what happened to her?"

"Tragic." He turned his hands over, still fascinated by his dirty nails. "She always was a reckless driver."

"So, you didn't have her brakes cut from in here? Didn't use your last remaining Cotswold Crew contact on the outside?"

Greg's eyes flicked up in an unblinking stare. "Quite the imagination you have there. I can see why you can't settle on one career. Hoping to make your name writing the tale of my downfall?"

"I have no interest in making a name. My writing comes from joy. You remember 'joy', don't you, Greg? You weren't always this cold, callous robot." He returned Greg's smile. "You were that boy who used to steal books for your big sister so she could read in secret. Your parents were pieces of work, weren't they?"

He glared from under his lashes.

No response, but Barker could hear the glass cracking.

"Martha came to visit you," he pushed. "What did she say? What did she discover that you didn't want people to know?" He paused for more silence.

"Martha's unconscious right now, but she won't be forever. She'll spill your secrets, eventually."

Nothing. Greg froze, staring at his hands in an unblinking stare, as if the robot had malfunctioned. In a sudden reboot, he inhaled a sharp breath, the smug smile returning.

"Let's circle back to your question about James," he said, clasping his hands again, metal scraping on metal. "He's a fantastic business man, you know? The term 'self-made' gets thrown around a lot, but like myself, James truly fits the mould. Grew up in poverty on that wretched Fern Moore hellhole, and still, he thrived."

"Like a winter rose."

"Let's not pretend the Fern Moore soil has any nutrition left in it," he said, his tone darkening with contempt. "James is the best of them, and he recognised my potential. When we first met at a gala, he saw someone eager to shake things up. He told me his grand plans to build a new estate of luxury houses, and I just so happened to know of some land the council was eager to unload; the rest is—as they say —*history*."

"Hmm," Barker grumbled his agreement. "It's a shame James has left you languishing in here, isn't it? Your cut of Howarth Estate won't help you much over the next ten to fifteen years."

"We'll see."

Greg's eye contact didn't waver, his grin growing with each passing second. Barker had seen that look many times—he had the eyes of a maniac bursting with confidence. Even in his current state, losing wasn't an option in Greg's mind. Barker wished he possessed even a drop of his optimism.

"So, you didn't kill Sebastian, but you still offloaded the farm to your... Uncle? Uncle Harold? Any regrets about that?"

"I didn't *want* the farm. Harold did. He always thought he should have been left it. Maybe he should have. My father did nothing with it except milking cows. It was an easy swap."

"Vincent Wellington's old architect said you tried to sell the farm to Vincent first."

He snorted a laugh. "Because I knew I could get more from Vincent than Harold. Turns out Harold borrowed the money from Vincent anyway, so I should have driven the price up. Funny, don't you think?"

The mania in his eyes grew, as did the upward stretching of the corners of his lips. Outside, keys rattled.

"What's funny?" Barker asked. "That you wish you'd charged your uncle more for the farm?"

The door creaked open and Greg launched across

the table, slapping his fingertips inches from Barker's. "Naturally... but that's not what I meant..."

Greg was back in his seat by the time the guard stepped in to announce their time was up. He rose to his feet before he needed to be dragged, flashing Barker a parting wink.

"Take the money and run like I did, Barker," Greg called over his shoulder. "Things are in motion you can't possibly stop. Best stand clear unless you want to get mowed down with the rest of them."

His laughter echoed around the corridor as the guard led him away.

"What's funny?" Barker called after him.

The laughter grew louder.

"What did you mean, Greg? What's funny?"

Twisting his head around the guard, Greg called, "That you've obviously let yourself get so distracted with that silly Vincent Wellington's nonstarter village plan. Good luck, Mr Brown."

Barker exited the prison, collecting his belongings with a growing sense of dismay and frustration. As he walked to his car, Greg's parting words taunted him. Barker typed out what he could remember from their interview before the details slipped away, but their implications eluded him.

Dropping into the passenger seat, Barker slammed his palms against the steering wheel, letting loose a short, sharp, aggravated cry. The horn blasted and glares of disapproval shot from around the car park.

Jabbing at the ignition button, Barker guided the car from the tight space, the questions he'd entered the prison with now multiplied. Whatever the truth, Greg's parting taunt confirmed the politician, whether by his own hand or through a conspiracy stretching across the decades, knew exactly what happened to Sebastian.

19

In the café's kitchen, Julia, Sue, and Katie unpacked boxes brimming with supplies for the upcoming camp-in. They sorted mountains of bottled water, portable lighting, fluffy socks and gloves and hats with bobbles, all amongst Julia's freshly baked mince pies and sugar-dusted Christmas biscuits—enough to fuel the volunteers over however many nights their rebellion lasted.

Sue paused her task of taking an inventory count, nibbling her lip. "Before I pitch my tent, James wants to meet with Neil and me to 'urgently discuss terms of our loan.'"

"What prompted that?" Julia asked, heaving a box of sleeping bags onto the island. "Does he know what we're up to?"

"Didn't mention it, but... Neil actually resigned from the library," she said, delivering the news with a smile that her eyes betrayed. "Got accepted for a little reception job at an accountant's in Riverswick."

"Oh, Sue. I'm sorry."

"A job is a job in this economy, right?"

"Having a job isn't so bad," Katie said, taking her time organising the sheet masks for the 'pamper parcels' she'd decided they needed. "Can be quite fun, actually."

"Spoken like someone who has only worked for a few years," Sue said.

"I used to model too, don't forget," she corrected, slapping on another 'Katie's Nails' sticker to seal the cardboard box usually reserved for takeaway cakes. "If Neil's feeling down, he can have a little pamper on me. I've never seen a man more in need of a chemical peel, and I just got my new qualification online for the extra strong stuff." She assessed them both. "I'll book you both in for next week."

Julia rested a supportive hand on Sue's shoulder, though a part of her was glad Katie's frivolity was there to lighten the mood. Even with their upcoming protest campsite being built on the field at that very moment, Julia wished she could summon the same hope as Katie that everything could be fixed by something as simple as a pamper day.

"All of these sheet masks must have cost a fortune," Sue said as she flicked through the box Katie had brought with her. She nodded at Julia, then the donation tin. "Thousands, I'd say?"

"*Coupons!*" Katie giggled. "And they're from South Korea. Not quite sure what the labels say…" She squinted as though she might be able to read Korean. "I'm sure they're fine. This one has a picture of a little snail on it. And he's smiling. I just wish I could have done more to help." Her bubbly demeanour deflated. "I still feel guilty for bringing James to the village with the manor sale."

"You've done plenty," Sue assured her. "*Plenty*. We'd have never been able to afford all this camping equipment if it wasn't for your generous donations."

Katie blinked in surprise. "Really? I didn't think I'd given nearly enough."

"It made all the difference," Sue assured her, hoisting a large box into her arms. "Now I'd better start getting these finished boxes out. I'd bet they've got the first tents up by now."

Sue left them alone, and Katie moved to the stack of tents Julia and Jessie had picked up from the camping supplies shop earlier.

"These had to be as cheap as my face masks," Katie muttered as she checked the labels. "My spare change really made *this* much of a difference? You must be more of a coupon queen than me, Julia."

Julia laughed, glad to let Katie think her few coins had turned the tide. Though Sue had suspected the sweet scent on the envelope stuffed with cash had belonged to Katie, Julia had been almost certain Katie wasn't their mystery donor. But if Katie hadn't donated the money, Julia wondered, who had?

But that question could wait. This brief moment alone with Katie presented the perfect opportunity to ask what Barker had wondered about.

"Speaking of donations and finances, has my husband spoken with you yet?"

"Not since he borrowed Father's diaries. Why?" She winced. "Is it about the brows? Because I know I took off more than I should have, but I just got carried away... and they were *so* bushy, and—"

"No, no, this isn't about Barker's beauty habits," she cut in, not admitting that she'd been so distracted that she hadn't noticed her husband's changing brow shape. "It's about that field out there and your ancestry." She lowered her voice, leaning in. "What do you know of Clarissa Wellington?"

"Clarissa?" Katie repeated, tasting the name. "I think she might be the one Father used to go on about. 'Don't end up like Clarissa!' he'd say. Can't remember why."

In hushed tones, Julia explained the situation she'd learned about from Arnold—how Clarissa had secretly borne an illegitimate child with none other than Duncan Howarth in the months before her premature death. A child Duncan knew nothing about until Earl Philip revealed the startling truth to the dying man.

"Oh, is that all?" Katie rolled her eyes. "The way Father would talk about her 'great shame,' you'd think she'd killed a man. *Several* men. *All* the men." She stuffed more masks into a pamper package and smacked on the label. "I know I shouldn't speak ill of the dead, but Father was a Grade A pig when he wanted to be."

Julia decided not to comment.

"That secret child, Katie—Edward—was *your* grandfather," Julia whispered, excitement making her words tumble out in a rush. "Your great-great-great-great-grandfather, if I've worked that out right. In his final days, Duncan made sure his son inherited his land before he died. Land he wanted to build his factories on before he changed his mind. Clarissa's brother sold it off before Edward was of age. Edward would have only been a little younger than Vinnie when he inherited."

Katie frowned, packing another box with more precision. She laid out a sheet mask, then a bottle of nail polish, before throwing in wrapped pink sweets along with the smallest bottle of champagne Julia had ever seen.

"Coupons?" Julia asked, peering into the box filled with more bottles.

"First-class flights and minibars," she whispered. "Used to be a little 'see how much free stuff we can fit in our hand luggage' game your father and I would play back when we could afford to jet set. Knew they'd come in handy one day." Adding a sticker to the box, her frown reappeared. "So, this Edward lost his land, and Father thought he deserved it? And all this was going on when I was a baby?"

"Seems that way."

"Okay." Katie nodded, spritzing the box with sweet candy-scented perfume before sliding it down to the growing pile. There were more pamper packages than tents, water bottles, and sleeping bags, and she still had enough sheet masks and 'free' champagne bottles for every house in Peridale, and maybe Riverswick too. "Maybe I'm just being... Katie-Brained, as your father calls it, but... I'm not quite sure why you're telling me this, Julia? Family history was always Father's game. I prefer the here and now, especially these days. I've never been happier, to tell you the truth."

"And I'm so glad to hear that." She clasped Katie's

hand. "But this is really important. You and Vinnie are Duncan Howarth's only living direct descendants."

"Right."

"Descendants to a man who was thought to have no descendants."

"Great?" Her smile wavered at the edges. "I *am* being Katie-Brained, aren't I? Spit it out. This is worse than watching *University Challenge*."

"As Duncan Howarth's direct descendant, you could still have a rightful claim to *that* land," Julia concluded, taking Katie's arms in hers. "I know it sounds mad, but this might be the only option we have. I thought we could win James at his game by playing our way, but I think we need to play his way. With paperwork, and applications, and an old ancestral claim to a patch of land that was illegally sold in the 1800s."

"Julia..." She pursed her pouty lips. "What do you think I'd do with a field? I don't know the first thing about farming!"

"You wouldn't have to farm anything. You could just leave it there. Just like it was. Just like it has been since the council cleared the market in 1979." Julia nibbled her lip. "It's the only weight we've had so far. I know it's a long shot, but will you at least think about it? You said you wanted to help us win against James, and this could really, *really* help."

Leaving Katie to ponder the implications of her buried ancestral links, Julia carried another bundle of tents out to the field. It had been worth a shot. Even if Katie wanted to go down the same well-trodden path her father had, it would be a slow, sticky process.

Out on the field, Dot, Ethel, and Percy had done a fine job organising the makeshift campsite to be their home until they were forced away; they had no plan beyond the morning.

Ten tents formed a horseshoe around the outskirts of the dig site, with Dot and Ethel bickering their way through the instructions for another tent. Percy tossed string lights around the diggers, adding a festive glow that made them almost as pretty as Katie's pamper packages. A few early arrivals—Evelyn, Shilpa, Amy—huddled together against the chill, bags resting at their feet as they awaited the cue to claim their plot. Jessie stretched to hang a banner across the 'PHASE ONE' sign with Brian and Neil's help, the bold lettering clear and concise:

'WE SHALL NOT, WE SHALL NOT BE MOVED!'

Julia surveyed their effort, a swell of pride fizzing in her chest. The odds were stacked high against them, but the willingness of her family and neighbours to dig in and fight filled her with hope. Even if they only bought one more day before the diggers ravaged the land, it would be worth it.

A lot could happen in a day.

She turned towards the narrow alley, where Sebastian Morgan had made a home under similar circumstances decades ago. Only a stone's throw from his forty-year resting place. He would have been in his seventies, fighting alongside them. Her mother, too. A fresh wave of determination coursed through Julia's veins; they could carry on Sebastian's legacy. She might not have solved his murder, and might never, but she could do this for him.

Beyond the alley, Richie's caught her eye, and Julia made a snap decision. Handing off the tent bundle to her gran, she told a white lie about going to check on Roxy at the cottage to see how she was getting on babysitting Olivia, but she marched straight for the bar's window.

The man she sought was absent, as were any customers, all except for Richie, scrolling on his phone behind the counter. She continued up the lane to the lavish bungalow where James resided. Her closest neighbour after Veronica, yet they couldn't have been further apart.

After struggling with the front gate's tricky latch, she steadied her nerves and approached the lion's den. She didn't know why it had to be now, but it did; she had to face the man who had inspired their fight.

One last attempt.

She knocked on the door, and it swung open to reveal a stunned James. From somewhere within came a male voice—James had company. He halfway closed the door to obscure the interior.

"Julia. What a... *surprise*. I was planning to come by yours tomorrow. I have some news I think you'll want to hear."

Despite his genial tone, Julia stood firm. "I'm glad I caught you first. Do you have a moment?"

"Of course, of course." He glanced over his shoulder. "Come on in, I just need to..."

"I'd prefer if we spoke out here."

He nodded and stepped outside, pulling the door shut.

"Before anything, I want to thank you again for what you did for Jessie. Pulling her from the road like that..." Julia shook her head. "That could have ended differently had you not been standing there."

"Anyone would have done the same."

"But it wasn't anyone. It was you. You put our differences aside in that moment. I won't forget it."

James rubbed at his jaw, bemused by her gratitude. "Well... you're welcome. And thank you for coming by. Have you given any more thought to my offer for the new café? I hope Sue showed you the plans."

"She did, and my answer remains the same as it

always has. No." She stiffened, strengthening her courage. "That's not why I'm here. I came here to appeal to you, James. To give you one last chance."

"Give me one last chance?" He laughed. "Oh, sweet Julia. You don't see the writing on the wall, do you? What do I need to do? Write it on the white cliffs of Dover?" Beckoning her in with a finger, he whispered, "You *cannot* possibly win this. It was amusing at first to watch you try, but now? It's all got a little *desperate*, don't you think?"

"Regardless, I need to remind you of the man I first met when you returned to Peridale. After your wife was shot at the garden party. When Barker and I cleared your name, despite the fact you were trying to destroy the library. We still helped you, because it was the right thing to do."

James shifted from one foot to the other, listening.

"And afterwards, you thanked us. You might still be in prison screaming of your innocence, if not for us. You said we might even be friends one day, and then you vanished. Retreated into the shadows, but before you left, the last time I saw you, do you remember what you told me, at Fern Moore?" Julia searched his face; he remembered. "You talked about that little boy raised there. Poor, overweight, neglected." She stepped closer, keeping her voice even. "Do you remember what you said you'd learned after that ordeal?"

Julia waited, and he shook his head.

"Don't wind up the locals." She flashed her eyes, her smile tight. "Your exact words, I think. Can you imagine that? That was only last summer, James. So, what changed?"

"I *was* suffering from a concussion..."

Was this all a joke to him?

"Why did you align with Greg?" she said, feeling a simmering within that could melt the snow under her feet. "Why did you try to gentrify Fern Moore into holiday flats through Benedict Langley? Intimidate the Knights into selling their land by having their house burned down? Bribe your way through committees?" Her volume elevated as months of frustration boiled over. "Why, James? I need to know —*why*? You have it *all*. Why are you trying to take more?"

He stared off, brow creased in contemplation. For a moment, Julia thought she glimpsed a flicker of remorse in his stony stare. Maybe her appeal had breached his hardened exterior to reach that lonely Fern Moore boy within.

But then he let out a slow, measured breath, rolling his head to meet her eyes. His stare burrowed into her.

"It's quite simple, Julia. *Why not*? What else is there to do?"

Was it really that simple?

Why not?

"All the collecting, the posturing, the dominance... You're just bored?"

She scrutinised him with fresh eyes, seeing not an opponent to be reasoned with, but something far more dangerous—a man inoculated to empathy, compassion, anything beyond self-interest. For James Jacobson, it was all a game to fill the hours. And he played to win at any cost.

How could she beat a man she'd never understand?

"Look around you," James whispered, gesturing at his luxurious home. "I won, Julia. I figured the game out, and I won, and I'll keep on winning." He leaned in, voice dropping to a whisper. "What's the point of all this fighting, eh? You want a house like this? A car like mine? Holidays for you and that kiddie of yours? Just nod your head. It's simple."

"Simple like it was for Sue and Neil, you mean?"

"And what about Katie and your father? They're doing amazing. Every coin has two sides." Laughing, he dug into his pocket for his phone. After a few taps, he tilted the screen and stood next to her. "Thought you might want to take your own stroll down memory lane. I was a little surprised to come across this during my research, but it's amazing what people upload to social media these days. I'd like to return the gift of reminding you of who you were last year."

Julia peered at the shaky footage, surprised as she recognised herself addressing a crowd on the village green. She vividly remembered that night—the aftermath of the ill-fated Cotswold Crowd Pleaser Festival held on the field at the centre of everything. When greedy music manager, Clive, held young Georgia hostage inside Julia's graffitied café. He'd just been outed for being behind electrocuting Jett, the lead singer of the headlining act, Electric Fury.

On the tiny screen, Clive flicked open a lighter, having just doused himself and the café in petrol. "You'll lose everything whether or not she dies. She's nothing to you."

Julia gulped as the video panned back to herself from the end of last summer. Standing on James' doorstep, she wished she felt as assured as her past self at that moment, even in the face of losing her café to a blaze. The camera wobbled on her smile, and Julia could remember exactly how she'd felt.

Fearless.

"I wouldn't lose everything," she said in the video. "Once upon a time, it would have been the end of my world. It was my sunshine when I needed it. I could have stayed there, soaking up that slice of sweetness forever, but I learned that there's more to life than what you do to make a living. It's too late for you either way, Clive. And you know it. If you want to burn my café to the ground, do it. It's just a building. I'll pull up a chair, get out the marshmallows, and start planning for the next one."

Clive's face contorted in rage as the camera person zoomed in on his reddened face, the flame from the lighter reflecting in his eyes. "It would kill you!"

On the tiny screen, Julia just shook her head, arms open wide. "You can't kill me that easily. Just let her go. She's a child. She's still—"

James cut off the video. "So, shall I bring the match? You bring the marshmallows?" Tucking the phone away, he ducked to meet her eyes. "Where's that woman, hmm? The one who knew that buildings were just buildings? Who was so willing to start over somewhere else? Take my offer. Let me buy your café and I'll build you the best café money can buy. I promise you'll never look back."

Julia turned to the faint twinkling of the lights dancing behind her café, seeing in her mind's eye the fledgling protest camp on the field. Should she give up when people were fighting so hard?

After all, the café was just a building. Hadn't she said as much in that clip? She had so much more now

—a husband, two daughters, family that supported her, friends who had her back.

But this fight wasn't solely about the café anymore. Phase *One*.

"No," Julia stated. "You think this is all about my livelihood, my 'bricks and mortar.' But I'm just the one standing in your way in this battle. And I understand why I need to hold out. Sebastian and my mother understood in 1979. The villagers who stood against Duncan Howarth back in the 1840s understood."

James heaved a weary sigh. "Oh, Julia. Why keep digging your heels in?"

She gave him a knowing tap on the nose. "Well, James... *why not*?" Any semblance of a smile dropped from his face, but Julia wasn't finished. "You may have been born and raised on the Fern Moore estate, but you spent too long away, James. Too long steeping in wealth and power. You've lost perspective on what matters." His eyes narrowed, but Julia pressed on, "For a fleeting moment after that business with your ex-wife's shooting, I thought *you* saw it. What's right under your nose? But then you forgot. You have a son, James. You *should* understand, too. It's a shame you forgot that lesson you learned." She stepped back off the doorstep. "You shouldn't have wound up the locals."

Julia walked down the garden path, feeling

strangely fearless. It wasn't the end, and maybe it hadn't made a difference, but now she knew there'd be no reasoning with James Jacobson. And he knew she couldn't be bought.

Not for all the cakes in Peridale.

As she reached the gate, James called after her, "Keep an eye out for the post tomorrow. I suspect you'll get a letter that changes your mind. When all of this is over, don't say I didn't try to be fair."

"Neighbour," she said, stepping through the gate, "I don't think you know the meaning of the—"

Through the window, she caught sight of the guest she'd heard when he'd answered the door. He didn't quite look like he used to, but when she realised who was staring at her through the glass, disbelief stole her breath away.

~

"You've been at this nonstop for two days," Jessie pleaded with Veronica in her dining room at the cottage up the lane. "Don't you think a break would do you good? A little one. Everyone's gathering down at the field for the camp-in. You could get some great shots for the paper."

Veronica shook her head, barely glancing up from the photocopied statement, so faded she was reading it with a handheld torch. "I appreciate the invitation, but I can't spare a moment. There are still stones unturned here. The answer's in these boxes. I *know* it."

"Any new leads since the last three times I asked?"

Veronica rifled through the heaps, selecting a file. "I'd forgotten about Sebastian's car. He drove an old Volvo. It was old even back then." Skimming the pages, she said, "1966. Inherited it from our grandmother. The thing barely ran before our uncle fixed it up. He drove it everywhere until..." She exhaled. "Until it vanished along with him."

"A car vanishing seems more unlikely than a person."

"Exactly!" Veronica dragged out the chair next to her, and, deciding to play along, Jessie sat. "The car's disappearance and Sebastian's are connected. We know he didn't run away to join a commune, so why aren't the police looking for his car now?"

Veronica stared at Jessie with an expectant look, and she realised her editor was awaiting an answer. "Oh, erm... because they're under-funded?"

"Nope."

"Lazy?"

"Try again."

"They hate vintage Volvos?" She tossed her hands up. "Especially the ones from 1966? Veronica... I don't know, and..." She paused to sniff and said, "...no offence, but when did you last shower?"

"There is *no* car." Veronica stared at Jessie with bloodshot pupils; she must have showered the last time she'd slept. "There *was* a car, and then there *wasn't* a car. The examination of Sebastian's..." She gulped, a line creasing between her brows as she rummaged through the hundreds of documents covering the table. "The autopsy report was *here*. It was..." Lifting one of the many coffee cups, she dragged out a page with bolder, fresher ink. "Arm and leg fractures? Skull fracture? Fractured ribs? I called the hospital, and Martha's injuries are uncannily similar."

"Martha fractured her skull?" Jessie winced. "I mean, she sort of did *my* head in, but I can't believe she did *hers* in too."

"She's alive, at least. And don't you see what I'm getting at? We know someone—probably Six—cut Martha's brakes to cause her crash." She lifted her gaze. "What if someone cut Sebastian's brakes, too? What if he swerved off the road to his death, and whoever cut the brakes cleared up the crash site, dismantled the car—that Volvo was only a tiny thing—and buried his body at the one place nobody would notice disturbed soil?" She stared, waiting for Jessie to speak, but she didn't know what to say. "Who am I kidding saying 'whoever', anyway? I *was* right all along. It *was* Greg. That was his modus operandi in 1979, and then again this week with Martha. And probably with Hugo Scott last year, and your brakes last month. Greg told Six to cut their brakes because that's how Greg killed Sebastian, and, until now, got away with it."

Jessie nodded, the information tumbling from Veronica making clearer sense. "But how can you prove it after all this time?"

"Maybe Barker got him to confess at the prison earlier?"

Jessie burst her bubble with a shake of her head. Barker had filled her in, and Greg had acted as he had every time Jessie had interviewed him; like a child playing a game.

Across the table, the open laptop announced a new email with a jingle. Eyes still on the papers, Veronica dragged the computer closer as someone knocked on the door.

"It's like Piccadilly Circus in here!" Veronica muttered, reluctant to tear her eyes away from the paperwork as she forced herself out of the chair. Taking the statement with her, she made her way to the front door, her age showing in her walk more than ever. "Have a look at that email, will you?"

Jessie double-clicked the notification, recognising

the corporate email address for Cotswold Media Group, the owners of *The Peridale Post*.

The preview alone knocked Jessie sideways:

Subject: Termination

Preview: We regret to inform you that effective immediately, your position as editor of *The Peridale Post* has been terminated due to your unprofessional...

She opened the email and scrolled down to the attached document cited as the 'unprofessional conduct', and Jessie couldn't argue with their assessment. The headline of the yet-to-be-published next issue of the paper leapt out: 'GREG MORGAN: MURDERER!'

How could Veronica torpedo her credibility like this, broadcasting accusations without proof? It went against everything she'd taught her. Back it up with facts. Facts over feelings. Facts are kings. Wherefore art thou facts? But here was Veronica's weak spot, on display, and after months working under her editor, Jessie now understood this was where it had always been leading.

Veronica had taken the job to bring down her

brother. Not because he was a sketchy politician or a corrupt clown with dodgy friends, but because—for forty long years—she'd held this single belief so tight, she couldn't see any other way. She couldn't wait for Barker's results, or the police to finish their investigation. She needed this to be true because if it wasn't, she'd been wrong all those years.

Jessie exhaled, pinching the bridge of her nose. This wasn't the time for blame. The damage had been done. Jessie's job was as good as dead, too. There was no way the next editor would inherit her with open arms; especially if they saw her drafts before Veronica got her hands on them. But she had the café to fall back on. Jessie would be fine, so now she needed to be there for her friend. She stood to join Veronica at the door, but a familiar voice drew her there quicker.

"*Mum*?" Jessie squinted into the dark. "If you're looking for me, I'll be back at the camp in a minute."

"I came to see Veronica," Julia said, exhaling.

Veronica had that faraway look in her eyes again, like she had the night she'd found out the bones had belonged to Sebastian. It was as though time had stopped.

"What's happened?" Jessie looked between them for an explanation. "Mum?"

"It's Greg," Julia whispered, glancing down the lane. "I just saw him."

"You visited him in prison?"

She shook her head. "He's at James' house. They've released him on bail."

The bad news got worse, and Veronica didn't even know she'd been fired yet.

"*Veronica*?" Jessie said, grabbing her unsteady former editor. "Say something, Veronica…"

20

1979

Veronica stepped off the bus outside the post office after the journey from Bristol. She adjusted the shoulder strap of her bag, straining to glimpse the hill concealing her old family farm through the swirling snow falling across the field.

"Finally moved the market debris," she said to herself.

The sight of a lopsided snowman guarding the village green market sparked fond memories. Whenever it snowed on the farm, Sebastian always made snowmen, no matter how old. She didn't doubt he'd made this one.

Huddling against the bitter wind, she glanced around for any familiar faces as the market wound down, but now that Christmas had come and gone, people seemed to be locked up in their cottages. Veronica didn't blame them. She'd still be in her warm flat in Bristol if Sebastian had bothered to call her.

It wasn't like him.

Following the alley between the post office and toy shop, she found the small snow-covered tent he'd told her about during their last phone call the day before Christmas Eve. Her brother was mad. Brilliant, brave, but mad. She couldn't believe he'd been camping out in protest for weeks without telling her, and she hoped he at least he had a warm sleeping bag. Crouching, she dusted off a layer of snow and found the zip.

"Sebastian, are you in there?" she called as she poked her head into the musky canvas shelter. She could still smell him. She chuckled at the sight of his brand-new portable Walkman that he hadn't shut up about during their last conversation. He'd said it was the only thing keeping him sane away from his vinyl records still at the farmhouse.

She pressed play on the tape inside, expecting it to be bursting with all his mopey singer-songwriters. But a faint, tinny chorus of some maudlin Christmas tune echoed from the headphones strung nearby. Only Sebastian would volunteer to spend winter in a tent choosing to listen to Christmas music; Veronica couldn't stand the stuff, but it tickled her that her older brother couldn't get enough. Strange that he'd leave his new favourite gadget in his tent.

A tap on her shoulder made Veronica spin around with a gasp.

"*Sebastian?*"

"You too?" A pretty young woman stared down at her from under a woolly hat, her sad smile full of apology. "Sorry, I didn't mean to startle you. I keep coming to check if he's snuck back too."

"Snuck back?"

"Yeah." The woman's eyes narrowed. "Pearl. Haven't seen you at any of the searches. How did you know Sebastian?"

"How did I *know* him?" Veronica stepped back from this strange woman. "That's not correct English. I *know* Sebastian. *Present* tense. I'm not some ex-girlfriend, he's my brother."

"*Oh*. Oh. I... I'm sorry... I... I assumed you knew. I..." Pearl's eyes fixed on the snow-covered cobbles. She wasn't Sebastian's usual type. Too much of an English rose. Too beautiful. Ordinary. His last girlfriend had a safety pin through her nose, and the one before was as bald as a just-plucked Christmas turkey. "I don't think I should be the one to tell you this, but—"

"Tell me *what*?"

"Sebastian is missing," she said. "Has been since Christmas Eve. We haven't stopped searching for him, but with all this snow... it's not been easy."

Pearl gestured towards the thread of torch beams sweeping through Howarth Forest behind the church.

"Is this some kind of joke?"

Pearl looked at her as though she had two heads and said, "Who would joke about something like that?"

"Did Greg put you up to this?"

"Veronica, I..."

"*Ha!*" She clicked her fingers. "I never told you my name."

Now she had three heads.

"Sebastian spoke of you," Pearl said, reaching out a hand to rest on Veronica's arm; the stranger's hand recoiled as Veronica shrugged. "I was helping with his protest. We were friends. I... I'm sorry you had to find out like this."

Veronica lost her balance as though the alley had tilted beneath her. Pearl caught her with a steadying grip, but gravity wouldn't stop pulling Veronica to the ground no matter how much she fought.

This was all a misunderstanding. This Pearl had got it wrong, but Sebastian *had* mentioned her on the phone, the unusual name ringing a bell now that Veronica had heard it a second time. And as Pearl struggled to keep Veronica on her feet, being this close, the ordinary English rose hadn't slept properly for days.

"I need to go," Veronica said, swallowing down hard as she used the wall of the toy shop to right herself. "I need to go to the farm. Maybe he's there."

"Veronica... the storm..." Pearl called after her. "It's not safe."

But nothing would stop Veronica as she charged across the field with her bags, knowing the direction to her home even through the thick snow. Shivering to the bone, she stumbled over the hill and ran down to the old farmhouse that hadn't changed.

In the barn usually filled with cattle, she found Uncle Harold working on a bike under the glow of a hanging builder's light, car parts where the cows used to be.

"*Veronica?*" Harold squinted, his moustache dancing around a cigarette. "That you? What are you doing here?"

"I could ask you the same."

"Fixing Martha's bike," he said, giving it a whack with a spanner. "Dizzy thing got it brand new for Christmas and crashed it into the creek by Boxing Day. Did Greg call you about..."

"About Sebastian?" She dragged open the barn gate and dumped her bags on the straw. "No, he didn't.

I just had to find out from some random lady in the village. Has there really been no trace since Christmas Eve?"

"Afraid not."

She pushed past her uncle and strode deeper into the barn, hands planted on her hips as she spun to face him.

"Why aren't you more worried? Your nephew is missing."

Harold scratched his brow and shrugged, not meeting her eyes. "You know Seb. Always been a bit odd, ain't he? Just swanned off somewhere without telling no one."

Veronica scanned the barn as she resisted correcting her uncle's grammar, taking in the stacks of old car parts and tools spread across the space where cows used to wander.

"Where are all the cows? You were supposed to be taking care of the herd."

"Yeah, well..." Harold rubbed his neck, leaving a smudge of grease across his skin. "Greg got rid of 'em. Sold the whole lot off just before Christmas. Your brother was too busy with his protest nonsense to help out. With no one left to tend 'em, Greg made the call."

Typical. Veronica had never been fond of the herd—milking at dawn, mucking out pens all afternoon—but without them, the farm had no income.

"What's all this then?" She nodded at the car parts. "Back on the rob, Uncle?"

"You're not too old for a smack, young lady. Just some old wrecks I'm fixing up. Greg's letting me use the barn for storage and such. It's good money."

Veronica saved her breath. The whole farm had gone mad without her even realising. She understood even less why her uncle seemed so nonchalant about his missing nephew.

"Better get on or Martha won't be happy," Harold said, giving his toolbox a pat. "Good to see you, even with the circumstances, and all. Maybe we can catch up proper later, yeah?"

Veronica left her uncle muttering over sprockets and chains, a knot in her stomach as she made her way up to the house.

Pushing open the back door, the wall of familiar scents hit Veronica first—cow manure with a hint of spilt gin and tobacco smoke. It hadn't changed one bit in six years; she could still see her mother and father at the table. Staring blankly in opposite directions after a hard day. Her mother, smoking with one hand, peeling a satsuma in the other while her father topped up his glass, barking orders long past sunset.

A door to a life she'd rather forget, still ajar.

She passed through the sitting room. All the sullen family pictures had been taken down, leaving only the shadows on the peeling wallpaper. A girl sat cross-legged by the fire, glued to a *Bagpuss* repeat on the small telly in the corner.

"Who are you?" the girl asked.

"Veronica?" she replied, recognising Martha's face somewhere in there; she must have been at least ten by now. "Your cousin?"

Martha shrugged, returning to the pink cat on the screen. The six years since Veronica's departure had whizzed by, but she couldn't blame her cousin; more than half her short life.

Upstairs, she paused by her old bedroom door and peered inside. It may as well have been a museum exhibit for how unchanged it was: her simple single bed, the beaten-up dresser—all leftovers from long before her birth. The shelf by the window held the small collection of Narnia books, all stolen from Mulberry Lane for her by Greg.

The sound of furious packing met her ears before she even reached Greg's room next door. She knocked against the open door and found Greg whipping clothes from his wardrobe into an overstuffed duffle bag.

"In a hurry?" Veronica asked.

Greg flinched at her voice but didn't turn.

"Veronica. You're home. I'm heading to Cambridge. I've saved up enough to get a flat near the university. Finally my time to get out of this dump."

"Bit early for term, isn't it?"

"September will be here before I know it. May as well get settled in properly over summer." He glanced at her over his shoulder. "What are you doing here? You didn't even come back for dad's funeral."

"I... I couldn't get the time off," she lied; it had been during half-term. "Where did you get the money for this flat?"

Greg continued stuffing clothes into his bag. "I've been saving for ages."

"Selling the herd, you mean?"

"Don't act like you care about the herd." He laughed, zipping up one bag before grabbing an old suitcase from under his bed. "I'm going into politics when I finish my degree. I'll be an MP in no time." He gave her a sly grin. "Maybe even Prime Minister someday. The sky is the limit for me."

Veronica resisted an eye roll at his grandiose dreams. "What are you doing about Sebastian?"

Greg shrugged. "He probably ran off with some hippie friends or joined the circus. You know how he is. Never could sit still or stick to anything normal. Who cares?"

The nonchalant dismissal of their missing brother

made Veronica bristle. "*I* care. Sebastian is our brother."

"Oh please, you only care about this family when it suits you."

The barbed words found their mark. Veronica crossed her arms. "And what about the farm? What happens now without the cows?"

"What about it?" Greg snapped. "I never wanted to run this dump anyway. Uncle Harold agreed to buy the place. Wants to sell cars or open some shop here or who knows what wild scheme he's got going this week. I honestly don't give a single damn as long as I'm shot of it."

Veronica let out a disbelieving laugh. "Uncle Harold? Buy the farm? He can barely afford his tobacco habit. He was always grovelling to Dad for hand-outs."

"A lot's changed since you flounced off, dear sister," he said as stacks of books went into the suitcase. "Our uncle has some powerful friends these days. You should try it sometime. It's not about *what* you know, it's about *who* you know."

Veronica took in her brother's expensive leather jacket and the new Rolex glinting on his wrist. Barely anything of the brother she'd left behind remained in this arrogant stranger.

"We just need a death certificate for Sebastian to

make the sale to Uncle Harold official," Greg stated, as if discussing the weather. "It's just a formality."

"Don't talk like that. Sebastian *isn't* dead."

He waved a dismissive hand, pushing past her to get to his drawers. "Yes, yes, but the farm legally must belong to *someone*. And Dad's will said only us male sons could inherit, and I'm not going to be lumbered with it." He dumped socks around the books before clamping the suitcase. "Now if you'll excuse me, I've got a train to catch."

Veronica blocked his path to the door. "You should stay for a few days. To help search for Sebastian."

Greg stopped and turned towards her, a cold, callous smile tugging at his lips. "Stick around like *you* did? Hopped on the first bus out when you turned eighteen and never looked back." He took a menacing step towards her. "I've waited long enough for my turn. You won't stop me, Veronica."

Veronica narrowed her eyes, a sick notion churning in her gut. "Did you have something to do with Sebastian's disappearance, Greggory?"

Greg's smile only widened, sending a chill down her spine. "I'd be very careful about accusations like that, dear sister. You might want to brush up on libel laws."

A wave of nausea swept over Veronica. She needed fresh air, needed to escape the madness pressing down inside the farmhouse walls. Whirling around, she shoved past Greg as he dragged his bags along the hallway, ran past Martha and *Bagpuss*, and burst outside into the snowy fields.

Thick flakes danced as Veronica gulped lungfuls of icy air. She searched the lonely rolling land she once called home, the childhood fields now blanketed, buried by winter's hold. An awful foreboding crept over her that she would never see her older brother again.

Sebastian had vanished just as she had years ago, but this time into a void from which he might never emerge...

21

*J*ulia wobbled on a slick patch of ice as she struggled to keep pace with Jessie. Further down the lane and almost at James' bungalow, Veronica forged ahead with a determined storm in her steps. Julia questioned if the revelation should have waited until morning.

The tricky latch on the gate finally slowed Veronica, her fingers clawing at the unyielding metal as Greg and James' laughter drifted out into the night.

"I can't decide who I want to strangle more!" Veronica seethed through gritted teeth as she shook the gate. "Greg for worming his way out, or James for lining his lawyers' pockets to make it happen."

"It's *temporary*," Jessie assured her, trying to pull

Veronica from the gate. "The trial's next year, and he won't get away with it. There's no way."

Veronica whirled to face her. "But we were so close to putting him away. For good. For Sebastian." She swiped at the tears streaking down her prickled cheeks. "This isn't justice. This is..."

"James Jacobson," Julia said. "Mr *Why Not*?" Stepping between them, she took their hands in her own. "As much as I want to see Greg get what he deserves, there's nothing more that can be done tonight. Can you hear that?"

Julia inclined her head, straining to catch the snatches of a tinkling piano singalong floating on the night breeze.

"*And so this is Christmas. For weak and for strong. For rich and for poor ones...*" Veronica sang along, her lips wobbling into a smile as her gaze drifted skyward. "Oh, Sebastian. You've never been too far away, have you?"

Clenching Veronica's hand tighter, Julia said, "There's no telling what they'll bring tomorrow, but the night still belongs to us."

"Mum's right," Jessie said. "You deserve the rest of the night off. We all do. Might even be a laugh."

Exhaling from deep within, Veronica squeezed Julia's hand in return. Arm in arm, they continued to the bottom of the lane, and when they reached the green, Julia couldn't believe her eyes. A line of bundled up campers with backpacks shuffled down the alley towards the piano music. Rather than squeeze around them, the trio snuck through the clear path of the café and into the kitchen.

"You're back!" Katie cried, still making her pamper kits. "It's a madhouse out there! Word got out and people started showing up with their own tents and food and blankets... it's a Christmas miracle!"

Sue emerged from the pantry, cradling tins of powered cocoa. "Gran reckons the whole village might turn up."

"Where are we needed?" Veronica asked, rubbing her hands together. "Do these boxes need to go out?"

With some of the cocoa tins bundled in her arms, Julia pushed through the gate, her steps faltering as she took in the sight before her. Where earlier that evening there had been only a handful of tents poking up from the frosty field, a vast village was emerging around the motionless diggers, their metal frames wrapped in twinkling fairy lights.

At the heart of the burgeoning campsite, Barker, Neil, and Brian tossed dry branches onto a crackling communal fire. The cheerful notes of the piano rang out while Amy tinkled at the keys. An enthralled audience crowded around her as their voices joined in a spirited rendition of 'Frosty the Snowman.' Dot's shrill warble soared above the rest, complemented by Ethel's throaty—and surprisingly deep—baritone, all while Percy conducted with a marshmallow-tipped stick. Shilpa sang along, handing out steaming samosas from a plate while Evelyn gave tarot readings cross-legged on a blanket.

"This is *insane*," Jessie marvelled, accepting a mug of cocoa from Denise, scooped from a large batch cooking on a small gas stove. "How has this happened at such short notice? We've barely had time to spread the word."

Sue hurried past, unfurling the cocoa tins next to where Julia had unloaded hers. "Gran and Percy haven't left their phone *all* afternoon, and Ethel went door to door round the whole village. I don't think people dared say no."

In all her years living in Peridale, Julia couldn't remember the last time she'd witnessed such an outstanding show of community spirit. After the disheartening trickle of the turnouts at their planning meetings, she'd been sure the rest of the village had given up.

But she'd underestimated her fellow villagers, and more were arriving with every passing minute, chatting and laughing as more tents popped up in the gaps around the diggers. Something resilient and powerful had awoken.

Julia felt a tap on her shoulder and turned to see Barker grinning at her. He pulled her into a warm hug.

"It's like a snowball effect," he said as they weaved through the tents towards the roaring fire. "Everyone's calling everyone, and word is spreading like wildfire. After what happened to Martha at the cancelled market, I think people are starting to connect the dots."

"And even if they aren't," Julia's father said, throwing a can of beer to Neil, "no one wants to miss out on being a part of this. People are going to be talking about this for years to come."

"*Decades*," Neil said, toasting his can after cracking it open. "The night Peridale fought back."

Barker took Julia by the arm and led her to a small red tent already kitted with plush sleeping bags and quilts. He pulled a thermos flask from the bundles and unscrewed the lid, and Julia's favourite peppermint and liquorice tea wafted out.

"Home sweet home," Barker said, pouring her a cup in the plastic lid. "I called Roxy, and she's happy to watch Olivia at the cottage tonight, and we can take turns after that. Otherwise, we're here as long as it takes to get our point across."

"Home," Julia agreed, toasting the tea as she

watched the tent village spreading around them. "Nowhere I'd rather be."

Maybe this wouldn't make any difference in the long run, but it was comforting to see the community band together. They had finally tapped into that elusive spirit of solidarity she'd been hoping to inspire for months. She wasn't sure what tomorrow would bring, but tonight, their little village had found its voice, and it would be heard.

After the arriving crowds started to thin, the carols stopped, and Percy and Ethel helped Dot climb atop the piano. She cleared her throat through the megaphone, silencing the crowd with a crackle.

"Thank you all for showing up to Base Camp Peridale," Dot cried, surveying the scene with a warm smile. "This might be our last stand against the forces that move to destroy us, and not for the first time. Our ancestors were lucky when Duncan Howarth had a change of heart in the 1800s. And too many of us—myself included—didn't fight hard enough in '79 against the late Vincent Wellington, but again, this village had a lucky escape. This time, luck isn't on our side." She looked off towards the bungalow. "Tomorrow, Mr Jacobson—*Jacobscrooge*—intends to continue digging up this field, and we aren't going to sit around and wait for another stroke of luck to slow him down." She waited, looking around the crowd. "I said... We aren't going to sit around and wait for luck, *are we*?"

A cheer rang through the crowd, and Julia lifted her sweet tea with a grin; her gran was born for this.

"Just look around!" Dot demanded, sweeping the megaphone across the crowd. "Family, friends, neighbours. We might not see eye to eye or agree about everything. We may annoy each other—" She smiled down at Ethel. "—some of us may even gossip a little too much, but you can't deny that we're a community. A *real* community. When it matters, *we* show up. This is what it's all about. *This* is what we're fighting for." Another cheer rippled through the crowd without prompting, and Dot allowed the clamour to swell for a moment. "So, grab some cocoa, wrap up tight, and join us for a little singsong, but first... has everyone got a drink? I'd like to propose a toast."

"*Pamper packs!*" Katie cried above the crowd. "The bubbly is on me!"

A mad flurry of digging commenced as people rifled through their packages, excitement fizzing upon discovering the surprise treat. When the noise died down, everyone looked back to Dot.

"What are we toasting to?" someone cried.

"*Julia?*" Dot called, waving her over to the piano. "I think the honour should be yours."

After an encouraging nudge from Barker, Julia made her way to the piano, and with Percy and Ethel's help, she joined her gran above the crowd. Dot's arm wrapped around her waist, holding her steady as she handed over the microphone.

There was so much Julia could say, but it had already been said on every flyer, at every meeting, in every article in the newspaper.

They all knew why they were there, and in the end, James Jacobson had said it best.

"Here's to not messing with the locals," she called, lifting her tiny bottle.

With a communal roar, a hundred mini champagne corks shot skyward. The victorious cry echoed into the night, loud enough that Julia hoped it carried all over the village. She looked off towards the bungalow, but she didn't get any further than the alley.

"And to Sebastian," she called, lifting the bottle again, she caught Veronica's eye in the crowd. "I'm sorry we still don't know what happened to him."

22

Barker awoke with a start, blinking into the dark tent. He glanced at the empty space beside him where Julia had fallen asleep nestled against his chest in her own sleeping bag. She'd rolled over in the night, and whoever had pitched their tent adjacent to theirs was snoring like they were sawing logs in half.

Even without the snoring, Barker knew he wouldn't fall back asleep. Not with the Sebastian Morgan case still weighing heavily, especially now that Greg Morgan had slipped out. And his parting words at the prison still echoed through Barker's mind—had he really let himself be distracted by Vincent Wellington's village plans from decades ago?

There was every chance that Veronica's forty-year hunch could be right, but if Greg was guilty, why hint at anything at all?

After kissing Julia on the patch of forehead poking out from under her hat, he unzipped the tent and emerged into the darkness. Most villagers still slept in their tents while a few early risers brewed tea over small camp stoves. Passing the smoking embers of the fire, he set off for his office to sift through the remainder of Vincent Wellington's diaries. He groaned when he remembered he'd taken the last few to the cottage for bedtime reading.

On his way home, he paused outside James' bungalow, contemplating knocking Greg awake to ask what he'd meant, but what would be the point? It was too early for more gloating and evading.

He continued up the lane, and all remained quiet within as he unlocked the front door with a held breath. The last thing he wanted was to wake Roxy. He peeked into the nursery, smiling at the sight of Olivia cocooned in her favourite knitted blanket, her nightlight still swirling.

He pulled the door shut, and without having a second to think, Barker ducked as a frying pan swung at his head, skimming the bobble of his hat.

"I thought you were a *burglar!*" Roxy exclaimed,

still yielding the frying pan like he still might be. "You're lucky I didn't grab a knife from the block!"

"Remind me never to get on your bad side," Barker said, nodding for her to lower the weapon. "I did try to be as quiet as I could."

"I was already awake." She nodded towards the master bedroom where someone was snoring louder than the racket that had awoken Barker. "And Laura's like this every night. I don't think I've slept in months. It's worse when the cases are like this one though."

Barker chuckled to himself at the thought of DI Moyes curled up in his bed with the cat, snoring the early hours away.

"I remember that feeling."

"I know. Julia used to complain to me about it." Roxy smiled, her panic at the intrusion easing. "What brings you back? I saw pictures online. Looks like everyone in the village is there. Protest over already?"

"No such luck." He gestured towards the small dining room. "Needed to collect some diaries. Couldn't sleep, and thought they might have more clues."

"Well, I'm awake now," Roxy said, spinning the frying pan in her hand. "I'll stick the kettle on."

They were soon seated across from each other at the table with coffee, and half of Vincent Wellington's remaining diaries divided between them.

"Got some news." Roxy slurped her coffee, opening her first volume. "Laura had to run off to the hospital when we were watching *Texas Chainsaw Massacre* last night."

"How... festive."

"Favourite Christmas film," Roxy said. "And Martha's awake. Or—she was for a while. Long enough for Laura to talk to her, but she doesn't remember much. Wasn't talking much sense either."

"Moyes mention anything useful?"

"Said she kept going on about a licence plate?" Roxy shrugged. "Mean anything?"

Barker repeated the words to himself. Had Martha caught sight of whoever sabotaged her vehicle before disaster struck? Why only recall the licence plate?

"Another puzzle piece I don't understand," he said.

"*Yet*," Roxy said with a wink. "Now, get reading. What am I looking for anyway? Can't believe I'm reading this old codger's diaries. He once ran over my sister's toes and blamed her for standing too close to his car."

"Sounds like Vincent. And anything juicy about Christmas Eve of 1979. Any mention of Sebastian or the party at the manor, but be warned, the man loved the sound of his own voice, even in the written form."

"Ugh, you're right," Roxy grumbled, flicking through. "Page after page of him prattling on about his ancestry and legal contingencies and other rubbish. You sure he says anything useful in these things?"

"Contingencies?" Barker asked, holding his hand out. "Grab another, I'll take that one. Could be important."

∽

After a toastier than expected night curled in her sleeping bag, Jessie emerged from her tent, working an ache out of her neck. All around the field, protesters crawled from their shelters looking similarly rumpled. Despite the chilly early hour, a sense of cheerful camaraderie filled the air as villagers clustered around camp stoves boiling water for tea and coffee. Dot, Percy, and Ethel were already rallying groups with hushed instructions.

She grabbed her toiletries bag and headed for the café where she joined the gang brushing teeth and freshening up at the sink, the kitchen as full as the café in a rare moment.

Julia and Sue were working at double speed, handing out steaming mugs and buttered toast to the protesters fuelling up for the day ahead.

Jessie bit down on her toothbrush as she spotted a familiar figure crossing the village green. Her heart gave an involuntary flutter at the sight of Dante. Spitting out the mouthful of frothy toothpaste, she smoothed her staticky hair and pushed through the beads as the bell above the front door rang.

"You came," she said, meeting him near the door.

Dante nodded, though his averted gaze held a guarded quality that pained her. "Yeah, well... wanted to show my support and all that." He scanned the corners of the café before looking at her chin. He bit back a smile and said, "You've got a bit of..."

"Left it there on purpose." She scrubbed at a glob of drying toothpaste "Did I...?"

"Almost." He reached out, hesitated, and wiped away the excess with a few brushes of his thumb. "Good as new."

They shared a soft chuckle, dispersing some of the uncomfortable tension she'd expected there'd be when she texted him before falling asleep. From Sebastian to Greg and James, and Howarth Estate, it was the outcome of her last meeting at Richie's that had kept her tossing and turning.

"Really glad you're here. It means a lot."

Dante hummed, gaze drifting over the swelling crowd crammed in the kitchen. Sensing they needed privacy for the conversation bound to follow, Jessie tilted her head towards the alley. Dante followed, and out of earshot from the protesters, Jessie turned to face him.

"About the other night, at Richie's..." She searched Dante's carefully neutral expression. "I'm sorry about how things went down. You caught me off-guard asking about travelling together, and safe to say, I could have handled that better."

Dante shrugged, scuffing a loose bit of gravel with the toe of his boot. "S'alright. Got the message loud and clear. You're not keen anymore. You needed a reason, and you took it."

"It wasn't like that..." She joined Dante in pebble scuffing. "Dante. I just..." She broke off with an agitated huff, gathering her thoughts. "I want you to live your dreams. Go on adventures. See the world. Nobody stood in my way, so I won't stand in yours, but I... I don't want to do that again."

She glimpsed a spark of hope flare in his eyes.

"You saying I should go?" He cocked his head, a teasing lilt entering his tone that eased her anxiety. "Want to get rid of me, eh?"

"I'm saying, go if you *want* to go. But for the record, pretty daft of you to think I went off you that quick. I was about to introduce you to my parents, you doughnut."

The last of the guardedness faded from Dante's

face as he smiled. Jessie's own lips lifted in return; felt good to see that smile again.

"Truth is," he said, his brows drifting up, "I was just thinking out loud. Wouldn't want to go without you, and if you don't want to go, neither do I."

"Dante... you're only young once. Don't waste that on me."

"*Waste*?" He laughed, nudging her arm. "Now who's acting like a doughnut?"

As Jessie's eyes drifted over Dante's shoulder, she spotted a small parade of familiar faces making their way past The Plough. Leading the group was Hilda Hayward from the Fern Moore food bank, with Billy right by her side.

"We heard the rallying cry!" Hilda called. "Gathered up as many as we could."

"A lot of people send their best wishes too," Billy said. "They're grateful for what your mum did for the food bank, but you know... the weather."

There were at least a dozen Fern Moore residents, which was a drop in the ocean compared to how many people lived on the estate, but an army considering the years of tension between the estate and the village.

"All numbers matter right now," Jessie said after giving Billy a quick hug. "Thank you. James and the builders could be turning up any minute now. And..."

She nodded down at her midsection. "Sorry about being weird about... I really am over the moon for you, Billy."

"You were weird?" He winked. "Didn't notice."

Jessie relaxed, pleased to avoid any tension given their history. She felt Dante step nearer behind her as Billy's easy grin ticked towards him.

"Reckon proper introductions are in order," Billy said, offering his hand. "Don't think we've met... Danny, isn't it?"

He extended his own hand to Billy's. "Dante. But close enough."

"Ah, sorry about that, mate. Afraid I've never met a Dante before."

As Hilda herded the group of Fern Moore residents towards the swelling crowd on the field, Billy lingered. His expression sobered as he met Dante's eye.

"Listen, do me a favour and look after our Jessie proper, yeah? She's one in a million. Treat her right." He threw an affectionate glance Jessie's way. "Reckon you're the luckiest lad in Peridale to have a diamond like her."

Despite herself, Jessie felt a flush creep into her cheeks. For all his faults, romance had never been one of them.

"Believe me, I know," Dante said. "Knew she was a

diamond the first moment I saw her giving Greg Morgan absolute hell at his library press conference. Not an ounce of fear."

"That's Jessie for you. So, you two are official then?"

Jessie traded a shy grin with Dante, both mumbling noncommittally. But the new lightness in Jessie's chest answered more clearly than words could, and she understood where her weirdness for Billy's baby news had come from.

Before she could stammer out a response, her dad's arrival provided a welcome diversion. His hair stuck up at odd angles and his eyes held the glazed look of someone who hadn't slept much; she'd noticed his tent was next to Shilpa's.

"Been up all night going over Vincent's diaries and I think I know what those contingencies are," he announced, flapping a diary in his hand. "I don't want to get too ahead, but... is your Mum around?"

"Glued to the coffee machine last I saw her. What contingencies?"

"I'll explain later," he said, pivoting to the door. "Oh, does 'licence plate' mean anything to you?"

"Licence plate?" she repeated. "Should it?"

"Martha seems to think so. She's awake."

Barker ventured into the café, leaving Dante and Jessie alone after Billy wandered to join Hilda on the field. The two of them mulled over 'licence plate' for a moment, but nothing.

"Veronica mentioned Sebastian's car last night," Jessie suggested. "Could go and find her? She might know what it meant."

As Jessie and Dante meandered through the rows of tents in search of Veronica's, Jessie slipped her hand around Dante's, leaning her head on his shoulder.

"You know, facing off with Greg at that press conference..." She peeked up at him. "I was scared stiff."

"Yeah, but you did it anyway, didn't you? That's the definition of courage, I'd say. Feeling the fear, and doing it anyway."

She smiled, nestling closer against him as they walked. She hadn't been jealous about Billy's impending fatherhood, she realised now. She'd been envious he was embarking on this new chapter with someone special while she'd mucked things up with Dante.

But clearly, that hadn't been the case at all.

They found Veronica cross-legged on a blanket in the opening of her tent while Evelyn waved crystals over her head, murmuring mystical incantations. Catching sight of Jessie and Dante's joined hands, Veronica shot Jessie a triumphant wink as if to say 'I told you so,' and Jessie was glad to see her looking well-rested for the first time in days.

"Some good news about your cousin," Jessie said. "Martha's awake. Dad said she mentioned a 'licence plate,' and we're hitting a wall with trying to—"

"*Wall!*" Dante cried, his hand clenching hers. "*Licence plate!* We saw it, Jessie. At the farmhouse. That wall…"

Jessie inhaled slowly as the connection dawned on her. "The wall…"

"There was a licence plate on the wall?" Veronica questioned, brushing Evelyn away to push herself to her feet.

"Not just one," Jessie answered. "A whole display of them. Looked like travelling souvenirs. Martha could have meant anything, though?"

"But she *lives* there," Dante pointed out. "Could be a clue."

"Worth a look," Veronica said, charging ahead across the field. "I can go on my own."

"Not a chance," Jessie said, catching up. "We're a team."

"Even though I've been fired?"

She'd read the email, then.

"If you've been fired, I quit," Jessie said, and she meant it. "I don't want to work for a paper who doesn't see that you're the best thing to happen to it. Their loss." Stiffening her spin, she said, "*Double* their loss. I was just getting good."

Eagerness propelling their steps, the three investigators hurried off in search of answers, the secret of Sebastian's fate possibly within touching distance. They reached the edge of the field, the campsite nothing more than dots in the distance as they scrambled up the hill.

At the top when the farmhouse and the ice cream barn came into view, Veronica paused and swayed on the spot. Jessie caught her elbow.

"You don't have to go any further."

"I'm fine," she said, pulling her arm way. "Haven't seen the place since the day I came back to the village to look for Sebastian. 'It is not in the stars to hold our destiny but in ourselves.'"

"Julius Caesar," Dante said. "Act One, Scene Two?"

"Glad one of my students paid attention," she said, casting a grin his way. "Good to see you again, Dante. You're looking well. Now, shall we push on? This is something I've needed to do for forty years."

Veronica tackled the hill like it was something she'd done hundreds of time—and might have—before marching towards the farmhouse. All was quiet inside, and at the ice cream barn, cars were already filling up the car park.

"This door was open last time," Jessie said as she tried the locked handle. "Do we kick it down?"

"It's solid wood," Dante said. "There must be another way in, and what if Harold is home?"

Veronica beat her fist down on the wood and waited. When no sound came from within, she fished a set of keys from her pocket and rifled through until she settled on an old brass one.

"Let's hope they didn't change the locks..." The lock mechanism crunched, and the catch released. "Would you look at that."

Stepping inside the kitchen with only the faintest sunlight peeking through the edges of the curtains, Veronica released a shaky breath as she took in her old home. Jessie rested a hand on her shoulder, but Veronica charged ahead.

"Where did you say this display was?"

"Sitting room," Jessie said, something on the kitchen table catching her eye. "Can't miss them."

She'd seen the same thick envelope in the bin at the café. Peeking inside, she found an ornate invitation to James Jacobson's upcoming Winter Gala at the village hall.

"Tonight," Dante read over her shoulder. "You think anyone will bother turning up?"

"You saw how many people went to his Halloween party," Jessie said, tossing the invitation back onto the kitchen table. "I suppose we'll have to wait and see."

Leaving the kitchen behind, Jessie and Dante traced the path Veronica had taken to the sitting room. Each taking a different way around the tartan sofa, they met Veronica as she stared at the wall of licence plates from all over the world, though the one dead centre was the only one that held her attention.

"RTD 234D," Veronica read aloud, as though each letter and number burned like acid in her throat. "I might not have remembered if I hadn't gone over the police paperwork, but that's it. That belonged to Sebastian's car."

"Then what is it doing there?" Dante asked.

Veronica sank onto the sofa, eyes fixed on her brother's licence plate. "You were right Jessie. Souvenirs... a *trophy*... a daily reminder that he'd got away with murder." She swiped sudden tears from her cheeks, turning away to look through the window towards the ice cream shop. "That night I came home and realised Sebastian was gone, Uncle Harold was in the barn. He was fixing a bicycle for Martha. A Christmas present she'd already crashed. Ironic, right?" She laughed, though the sound held no humour. "She'd have only been ten."

"What are you saying, Veronica?" Jessie pressed, sitting next to her as Dante took the other side.

"They'd sold the cows off," she continued. "Maybe that was part of their plan. Get rid of the cows to make the sale easier. The barn... it was filled with car parts. I didn't think anything of it. Uncle Harold was a mechanic. He was always tinkering with something, but..." She shook her head, piecing things together. "I'll bet anything those parts belonged to Sebastian's old missing Volvo. The one with this licence plate..."

23

Julia rapped her knuckles against Gwen's door, and after a few moments, the door creaked open a sliver, stopped short by the chain. Gwen peered through with a sigh.

"You again?" She huffed, the chain rattling as she moved to slam the door.

Julia wedged her boot in just in time. "Please, Gwen. Just five minutes."

With another exaggerated sigh, Gwen slid the chain free and opened the door wider, beckoning Julia inside with a bony finger. The pungent scent of hair dye filled the flat as she stepped over the threshold. Gwen's usually coiffed silver hair was slicked to her scalp, dark dye oozing at the roots. An evening gown sparkled on a hanger behind her, alongside a pair of red shoes with a baby kitten heel.

Gwen leaned on her swan-topped cane. "I won't offer you a seat. I'm rather pressed for time, as you can see. I'm off to a party later this evening, and every minute counts."

"Anywhere nice?"

"That Jacobson fella is hosting some posh gala at your village hall. Personally invited all us old cronies involved in the failed Wellington Village plans from back in the day." Gwen checked her darkening roots in the mirror before combing through some sections. "I thought a new dress and some colour might help me snag a wealthy widower. Maybe make up for lost time. In for my nails at noon, and makeup at three, so, you've only got about three minutes left."

Julia planted her feet on the threadbare rug. She wasn't leaving until she had some answers.

"The last few times we've spoken, I've had the sense that you haven't been telling me the whole truth," she started, making sure to look Gwen firm in the eye. "Of anyone, *you* said Harold Morgan was somehow involved in his nephew's disappearance. You said you had the most to lose, but Harold had the most to gain."

Gwen blinked. "Did I? At my age, the mind tends to wander..."

"You were right, though," Julia pressed. "Harold did gain, even without the development going ahead back then. Managed to get a loan from Vincent to buy his nephew's farm to start his own business. Judging by the queues my daughter saw at his ice cream shop this morning alone, Harold Morgan has crafted himself as one of the more successful businessmen around here. A tycoon, some might say."

At that, Gwen's composure flickered. Her gaze dropped to the floor as she worried a chipped fingernail.

"Yes, I suppose that's true." She hesitated. "Harold did gain a lot, and you're right, I did point you to him, and for good reason." Checking her roots again, she caught Julia watching her in the mirror, and sighed. "After Sebastian vanished and Vincent realised he wasn't going ahead with his precious village, he chopped me like deadwood. But Harold? He kept him in the inner circle for years. I'd heard whispers..."

She trailed off, shaking her head.

Julia leaned in. "Whispers of what?"

Gwen sighed, crossing the room with her cane to sink into her throne-like armchair; Julia chose to stay on her feet.

"Harold was a mechanic, but he wasn't the kind you'd want to take your car to unless you wanted it scavenging for parts. He ran a chop shop, if you like.

That's how Vincent met him. His old Land Rover was always breaking down, and he was too cheap to buy a new one, and Harold could always get him the parts he wanted. Must have seen some buried business acumen in him that I didn't see. And for his faults, Vincent could spot that. Like your daughter witnessed, lines out the door must mean Vincent saw correctly." She dropped her voice, as if afraid the very walls might hear. "When Sebastian vanished, Vincent gave Harold the money to buy that farm from young Greg. I always wondered…"

"Wondered what?"

"If that was Harold's payment for…" Gwen jerked her head sideways, as though the intention was obvious. "Payment for clearing the path. Vincent might have had a change of heart, but like you said, Harold still got what he wanted. A reward for getting rid of the thorn in Vincent's side?"

"And you've thought this for forty years?" A chill crept down Julia's spine. "Why didn't you say any of this before?"

Gwen rolled her eyes, stomping the cane on the rug. "And get dragged into more of Vincent's mess? That man bankrupted me, Julia. I've suffered quite enough at his hands, thanks very much, and Vincent Wellington wasn't a man you wanted as your enemy. So, I retreated. I got on with my life. My new life."

"You hid."

She hoisted herself up with the help of her cane in a flash. "And what of it? Who are you to judge me? I deserved to move on."

"And Veronica?"

"Well..." Gwen exhaled, staring down at the rug. "Yes, that is unfortunate. And I did consider going to the police to tell them my theory once Vincent popped his clogs, but I didn't want to kick up old dust. Until that digger dragged up the past, I hadn't heard so much as a whisper about Sebastian Morgan. He made the mistake of getting on people's nerves. Come the spring of 1980, very few people cared enough to keep looking for him." She shuffled to the front door, yanking it open. "Now, I really must wash this dye out if I want to make an entrance tonight. So if you don't mind, I really don't know anything else..."

Taking the hint, Julia stepped back out into the courtyard. Before Gwen could shut her out, Julia wedged her boot in the door for one last question.

"Do you really think Harold could have killed his own nephew?"

"Julia, when you've lived as long as I have, you stop being surprised by what men are willing to do for money and power."

The morning sun filtered through the window of the apartment at Oakwood Nursing Home, casting Barker's shadow across Arnold Jessop's breakfast tray. The architect sat in striped, blue pyjamas, using the edge of a toast soldier to scrape up the last remnants of a soft-boiled egg. His eyes remained glued to his miniature kingdom as the train whizzed around, acting as though Barker wasn't there as he had since the nurse had announced Arnold had a 'surprise' visitor.

"I know it's early," Barker began, taking the seat opposite without waiting for an invitation, "but I was hoping you could clarify a few more details about that land."

Jessop dabbed his top lip with a napkin. "Details, you say? Can't imagine there's much left to tell." His attention returned to the tiny railway engine traversing an icy pond. "Now, I'd prefer to focus on more pleasant diversions if you don't—"

Barker leaned over and yanked the plug from the wall socket. The train coasted to a halt halfway across a bridge. Jessop's bushy white brows gathered like storm clouds as he glared at Barker over his half-moon glasses.

"That wasn't very nice, was it?"

"What do you know about the contingencies attached to Duncan Howarth's land?" Barker asked, no more time to waste dancing around being polite. "I know you know more than you're letting on, Jessop. You were close to Vincent. He won't have kept what I read in his diaries secret from you."

The architect wiped egg yolk from his chin, seemingly weighing how much truth to reveal. When he replied at last, his tone held a hint of bitterness.

"The infamous contingencies that ruined my grand designs. You're aware the council purchased the pasture land from the owner's of the market once it burned down in 1969?" Jessop continued without waiting for confirmation. "They wanted to preserve it as a green public space for posterity. Admirable notion, but a lot changed over the next decade. Progress started to march on again after the post-war slump." He let out a raspy chuckle. "If only the bureaucratic buffoons had read the fine print in those old property deeds. You see, when a dying Duncan Howarth discovered his secret son stood to inherit that precious land, he was determined to protect that land after, as we all now know after that woman read that letter at the meeting, about Duncan Howarth's change of conscience."

"That woman was my wife."

"And a fine reading I heard it was." Jessop turned back to Barker, tapping his temple. "He wrote that letter in his final weeks, but Earl Philip visited his in his last days. Vincent thought the old Earl had a guilty conscience for locking Clarissa up in that manor, hiding her shame from the village. Duncan built that grand house to try and win her back—to get her attention, but Philip wasn't having it, and according to the letters Vincent read, he regretted keeping his daughter from the man she loved. Perhaps if she'd lived to see Edward's first birthday, Philip would have softened, but alas, fate had other ideas." He dabbed at the toast crumbs on his plate with his fingertip. "According to Philip's letters, Duncan was only furious with him for a moment. He wrote extensively of how much he smiled, even as consumption claimed his life. A part of him, and a part of Clarissa that could live after their deaths. A son who'd never known his real parents, raised to call his uncle his father. Duncan couldn't change that, but he could give his son security. Earl Philip was as fast and loose with his money as Vincent, and Vincent's daughter. Perhaps that is the Wellington curse."

"The contingencies, Jessop?"

"I'm getting there, lad," he said, staring at the train as though willing it to start moving. "According to Philip's letters, it was Duncan's final wish that his son take the land he'd bought for his failed factory empire, but only under the condition that the boy learned from the sins of his father. Duncan attached ironclad contingencies to the ownership papers—the land would forever remain for public use, and any development must be done with a unanimous vote from the villagers. Never to developed for private profit, no matter how many times it was sold. Quite forward-thinking of old Howarth, I daresay."

Barker nodded along, impatience rising. This was all information he'd already gathered from Wellington's detailed diaries during the small hours drinking coffee with Roxy. He needed more.

"But the contingencies weren't honoured?" Barker said. "Jonathan sold the land, and an indoor market stood there for a century."

Jessop held up a crooked finger. "Patience, Mr Brown. The train will arrive in the station, I assure you." He cleared his throat before continuing. "Since Edward was too young to manage his own affairs, that responsibility went to Jonathan, who—thanks to Earl Philip's meddling—was the boy's legal guardian. He hid the contingencies from the new owner's. It wasn't until Edward was an old man himself, and the market had stood for many years, that Jonathan confessed the truth when he was on his deathbed. Ironic that consumption came for Jonathan in the end too. Edward then handed the contingencies to the local government at the time, but the market was already there, so I suppose it was just filed away. That paperwork may have inspired the council's 1960s purchase, but by the time it came for Vincent to stake his claim, Duncan Howarth's original contingencies resurfaced." He gave a derisive snort. "After much back and forth, those blasted bureaucrats informed Vincent they would sell him the land at a steep discount—a token discount to right past wrongs of the land sale being approved in Edward's youth, they claimed."

"But the contingencies would remain unbreakable?" Barker guessed.

"Just so." Jessop nodded, looking off far through the window. "As you might imagine, dear Vincent cared not one whit about making historical reparations. He only wanted that prime land for his own grand plans. Once he learned profiteering potential would be severely limited, his fervour cooled considerably. And just like that, Wellington Village died. I tried to convince him to chase new pastures. There was always the Coleman farm, or the Farley's, and Harold looked to snag that dairy farm from his nephews, but the hurdle dampened his ambition. As did the arrival of Princess Katie, I might add. He dotted on her, but I can't say I'm surprised. He wanted to be a father as much as he wanted to built that village."

Barker shifted in his seat, thinking of the diary

he'd hidden away in his desk, but he wasn't here to talk about Katie's parentage.

Jessop settled back in his chair, bitterness creeping into his gravelly voice once more. "In the end, Vincent was nothing more than a pompous fraud. He let everyone believe he'd withdrawn his offer to respect Sebastian. To stop people suspecting him. But I saw the truth. His ego simply couldn't stomach admitting the council refused him. Men like Vincent Wellington don't take kindly to being told they can't have something, especially when it's something money cannot buy."

The pieces aligned in Barker's mind. He'd been correct in suspecting Greg's taunt about overlooking Wellington's old village scheme containing vital clues. Perhaps it had nothing to do with Sebastian Morgan's death, after all. His suspicions of Vincent Wellington being the culprit were fading with each new revelation. The news could help them fight against James, though.

"You say it was something money couldn't buy," Barker continued. "But development is due to start on that land. Do you know what became of Duncan Howarth's contingencies?"

Jessop gave a resigned sigh, shoulders slumping. "I've only kept up through *The Peridale Post,* but didn't Jacobson's ally, Greg, used to work for the council's planning department. I read in the exposé that Greg made the sale of the land possible and affordable for James. Can't imagine it was difficult for him to lose some pre-digital scraps of paper from the 1800s."

"No, I can't imagine it was difficult," Barker said, picturing them going head first into a shredder. "I appreciate you clarifying the real reasons Wellington withdrew his building proposals. Is there anything else about this business you've kept to yourself over the years?"

He hoped against hope for a breakthrough lead. But the aged architect merely gazed at his breakfast plate, seemingly debating how much more truth to reveal.

When Jessop replied at last, regret tainted his words. "Perhaps it would feel good to get this off my chest, after all."

"Oh?"

"There is one further detail," Jessop began, his voice deepening a shade as he peered over his half-moons. "This is only speculation, mind you. A gut instinct. But on the night of that blasted Christmas Eve party at the manor... I witnessed Harold Morgan tinkering under the bonnet of Sebastian's car shortly before leaving Wellington Manor." He exhaled heavily. "At the time, I assumed Sebastian's uncle merely fixed a mechanical issue. He was always tinkering with Vincent's Land Rover when it broke down every other week. But given how events transpired..." Jessop raised his eyes to meet Barker's. "Now I wonder if Harold tampered with the vehicle's workings?"

Baker absorbed this new information, thoughts churning. Is that what Martha had been referring when she'd said 'licence plate' after waking up from her own sabotaged accident—had foul play sent Sebastian's vintage Volvo veering off the road that fateful night?

"Intriguing theory," Barker remarked. "But I never mentioned anything about a car, and yet you're talking as though it's a sure thing. I'm going to need you to keep elaborating, Jessop."

The elderly architect removed his spectacles with a weary sigh. He seemed to age a decade as he rubbed the lenses with a monogrammed handkerchief pulled from his pyjama pocket.

"That part pains me most to admit, but I suppose you deserve the whole truth." Jessop's voice dropped to a hoarse whisper. "A few days after Christmas, when the village was searching for the missing hippie, I witnessed Vincent Wellington himself ordering groundskeepers to remove an old oak from his property soon after Sebastian's disappearance. Right on the corner where the road meets the driveway. He refused to explain why... but I was sure I saw tyre marks on the road, leading right to that tree."

Comprehension crashed over Barker with the weight of an uprooted tree. Jessop's decades of silence suggested a crash cover up.

"You believe Sebastian died in a car accident that Wellington concealed?"

The architect nodded, shame clouding his eyes. "And for my silence over the years, Vincent rewarded me handsomely. He never said it was for that, but I knew he suspected I knew the truth. And I exploited that. I convinced myself the truth would only destroy more lives... I took the money... I made myself comfortable... I... I..."

Jessop gazed around at his lavish apartment and intricate train set kingdom—a gilded cage purchased with blood money. When he met Barker's gaze once more, resignation etched the wrinkles deeper around his mouth.

"I thought myself a practical man for looking the other way while pocketing Vincent's hush payments. But now I fear the true cost may have been my conscience." Gripping the arms of his wheelchair, he rolled himself back from the table and leaned down to scoop up the detached plug. "Now, I believe our business has concluded. You'll have to excuse this old fool to the solitude he deserves."

Barker studied Jessop's slumped form but sensed further argument would prove fruitless. The train resumed its journey, and Arnold Jessop once against lost himself in the miniature world he ruled over. Sighing, Barker wondered what could have become of the man if he hadn't spent a lifetime regretting how he'd made his fortune. As he turned to exit, a familiar envelope on the desk caught his eye. Jessop had received an invitation to James Jacobson's upcoming Winter Gala.

"I shan't go," Jessop called once Barker was at the door. "Jacobson came to invite me personally, and I saw far too much of Vincent in him. If I didn't know Vincent was incapable of spawning his own heirs, I would have been sure James was of his flesh."

~

After leaving Gwen's flat, Julia rushed back to the village as urgent questions swirled through her mind. Had Harold Morgan really accepted payment to sabotage his own nephew's vehicle all those years ago? And if so, how to prove it after all this time?

As she neared the village green, raised voices echoed from the direction of the protest camp. She picked up her pace, nearly colliding with Barker and Jessie approaching from their own missions. One glance at their tense expressions told Julia they too had important news to share. But before any of them could speak, shouts and chanting erupted from the field.

They broke into a run, arriving to find the police advancing on the protesters. Dot, Percy, and Ethel struggled against the officers grabbing at their coats, trying to hold the line blocking the diggers. Behind the police, James Jacobson stood with smug command, directing the officers' actions through a battering ram of insults.

"Fools!" James cried. "I ordered you removed from my property this morning."

"We shall not, we shall not—"

James snatched the megaphone from Dot's hands and smashed it to smithereens on the cobbles, the harsh crack echoing around the walls of the alley. While the police turned a blind eye to James' outburst, they continued wrestling with Dot, Percy, and Ethel.

Jessie turned to Julia. "What do we do?"

Spying the protesters' linked hands as they retreated from the police, inspiration struck Julia. "Form a circle!" she cried. "Around the tents and equipment! Join hands."

Julia charged through the café and out through the back, running around the advancing officers as a human barricade took shape. More villagers rushed to add their own hands, the chain soon spanning what had to be at least one hundred people ringing the idle diggers. James gaped at the scene, stomping his foot like a thwarted child.

"This is *ridiculous*! *Arrest* them. Arrest them *all*!"

But Julia noted the hesitance in the officers' postures to start grabbing people. Such a mass arrest wasn't feasible, and they knew it, and they weren't strangers. Peridale was only so big. The officers would be looking at their next-door neighbours, their aunties and uncles, their school friends.

Before the standoff could escalate further, DI Moyes arrived on the scene, with Roxy pushing Olivia in her pram alongside. Moyes pushed through the officers, taking in the scene with the same confusion Julia had felt when arriving. Barker and Jessie held tight either side of her as the circle continued to grow.

"Puglisi! Whose orders are you operating on here?"

The policeman shifted his weight. "Uh…"

"*I* called the superintendent!" James barked, tossing his hand at the field. "This is trespassing. This field is *mine*, and my builders are waiting to start the work they're being paid for. Work that has already been delayed beyond reason."

Moyes considered James a long moment, exhaling

a stream of vape smoke as she scanned the scene. She paused at Julia, and they shared a nod.

"Stand down, Puglisi," she called. "All of you, stand down."

"I'll have your job for this," James shouted, spittle flying from his lips. "I'll have all of your jobs..."

Moyes turned her back on him, facing her officers. "You heard me, lads. Pull back." Once they started, she pinned James with a warning glare. "One more outburst from you and I'll have you arrested for disturbing the peace and aggressive behaviour. Are we clear?"

James scowled but held his tongue as the police withdrew. Julia felt the circle around her loosen its grip, a ripple spreading. Richie Jacobson emerged from his bar. He joined his father's side before shaking his head and walking towards the circle.

"Richie, I'm warning you..." James cried, more desperate than Julia had ever heard him. "Don't you—"

"*Dare*?" He parted the circle between Dante and Veronica on Jessie's other side and joined hands. "You've gone too far this time, Dad. This isn't a game to them. Open your eyes."

Julia inhaled as a familiar scent drifted down the line on the morning breeze. The donations... they *had* come from James' pockets, after all, not that he'd known about it. It hadn't been the richest man in the village, it had been the Richie-st. For now, Julia held her tongue, leaning forward to wink her thanks at him. His pale cheeks flushed as he turned back to glare at his father.

Outmanoeuvred, James backed away before pivoting on his heel and storming off. A cheer went up amongst the protesters as DI Moyes sent her officers back to the station with their tails between their legs.

"When one megaphone dies..." Dot said, digging in one of the many supplies boxes stacked by the post office to pull out another wrapped in plastic. Through the new one, she called, "Well done, everyone."

In the celebratory chaos, Julia spotted Barker and Jessie waiting by her yard gate. She hurried over to join them, anticipation rising.

"I know who killed Sebastian," she told them breathlessly.

Barker nodded. "Me too, and I know why. Jessie, Veronica isn't going to be happy, but—"

"She knows it wasn't Greg, and we know how," Jessie chimed in, pulling out her phone. "We found proof. This is the licence plate Martha was talking about. After all these years, I think she connected the dots and confronted Greg about it in prison. He must know the truth."

"Oh, he knows," Barker confirmed. "So, what now?"

Julia looked out at the swelling piano-led celebration spreading across the field as a fresh fire ignited. "I think we see who shows their face at that gala tonight. Turns out, it's not a party to be missed."

24

Rather than glittering chandeliers, James' lavish Winter Gala was illuminated by the harsh overheads usually reserved for community meetings and jumble sales. The handful of guests mingling by the lonely buffet table only emphasised the cavernous space and conspicuous absences. Given how little he'd decorated the hall for the occasion, James must have suspected his gala didn't stand a shot against the tent village on his land. When Julia had left the camp to nip home to change with Barker, they'd been dancing around the campfire thanks to guitars joining Amy's piano.

"Have I mentioned how beautiful you look tonight?" Barker whispered, kissing Julia's neck, inches from the swooping sweetheart neckline of one of her favourite red velvet vintage dresses. "And you smell incredible. New perfume?"

"I think that's called 'washing after spending the night in a tent,'" she said, taking in her husband's crisp white shirt and black tie. "But you look pretty handsome yourself."

"Rubbish turn out," Jessie said, handing them both champagne. "No Greg yet either. He'll come, right?"

"And miss his grand release?" Veronica forced a laugh, downing her champagne in one. "Unlikely. He wouldn't miss this for the world."

Jessie fingers tapped on her phone, no doubt sending updates to Dante now that they were seemingly back on. Julia hoped that when the dust settled, she'd get to properly meet the lad who'd been making Jessie smile so much lately. When she'd seen them together at the camp-in earlier, they'd look at ease in each other's company.

Someone who didn't look at ease was James as he spoke with Katie in the shadow of the stage. A band had been hired, but they weren't putting much gusto into their run-down of the Christmas standards for the twenty or so people milling about the hall.

"What do you think they're talking about?" Barker asked, joining Julia in watching Katie holding her ground against James. "Did you tell her about Duncan?"

"I did."

"And did you ask about her mother?"

Eyeing her husband, she shook her head. "You told me not to. What's that about, Barker?"

"Nothing to do with any of this," he assured her before sipping his champagne. "It can wait."

Before Julia could push why Barker was being so secretive about what he knew about Katie's mysterious mother, the burst open of the double doors seized her focus. Arnold Jessop rolled himself inside, dapper in a three-piece suit and scarlet cravat. His entrance stirred life into the morose atmosphere for a moment as he steered towards an empty table near where Harold Morgan slouched alone, a half-finished pint clutched in one meaty fist.

Harold's hooded eyes tracked the architect's progress. When Arnold reached his table, Harold shoved back his chair and moved to another. Gwen, who'd been lingering by the edge, took a seat next to Arnold. Her freshly dyed hair stood tall, her silver party dress sparkling, and her professional make-up knocked back the clock a few years than when Julia had seen her that morning. She strained to overhear their exchange as Jessop captured Gwen's hand and brought it to his whiskery lips.

The doors opened again, and laughter erupted from behind as Ethel and Dot joined the party, fluffy in their fur coats. They went straight for the buffet table, pulling carrier bags out of their coats to stock up.

"Music could be worse," Jessie conceded as the pianist struck up *Winter Wonderland*. "Hardly the extravagant night James promised, though."

"Seems he can't help not living up to his own hype."

Julia watched as James stormed away from Katie to weave around vacant tables towards the exit, but before he could leave, the doors opened and a large figure filled the doorway. Julia's breath halted in surprise to see the all-too-familiar figure of Six leaning, hands stuffed into the pockets of his suit. The final known member of Greg Morgan's bruised Cotswold Crew gang scanned the room with detached interest until his gaze fixed on Jessie. He inclined his head in greeting before moving to the bar.

"What's he doing here?" Julia whispered.

"I invited him," Jessie said, draining her champagne before snatching Julia's. "I'll get us a top-up."

Julia didn't have long to ponder why the notorious enforcer was at the gala or how Jessie could have invited him. A hush swept the hall in the silence between songs. All eyes turned to Greg Morgan as he strutted in wearing a tailored suit. Even in a suit, he still managed to exude an air of menacing dishevelment. Stubble clouded his jaw and the remanets of a black eye shadowed his right side.

He strode straight to James with arms extended as if expecting an embrace between friends. James stiffened, patting Greg on the back before directing him to the bar.

"The guest of honour arrives," Veronica muttered. "The stage is set. When do we—"

The clink of a fork against a glass silenced the room, and the band faded out one instrument at a time. "I'd like to propose a toast, everyone. As some of you may know, I was recently held in—"

"Is *now* the time?" James cut in.

"Now is the *perfect* time!" Greg insisted, thrusting his champagne in the air. "To new beginnings. To second chances and fresh starts..." He scanned the room. When he noted Veronica's presence, his smarmy smile turned venomous. He toasted the glass in her direction, but he wasn't finished with his toasts. "And to absent family, and to my dear brother, Sebastian, snatched from us far too soon by this terribly cruel world..." He placed a hand over his heart, miming overcome emotion. "Here's to harsh realities, ugly truths, and necessary sacrifices—"

"Are these toasts going to go on all night?" Dot cried, making no attempt to hide the tray of sandwiches as she tipped them into the bag.

"You have a point, Dorothy," Ethel said, fanning a yawn as a bottle of champagne disappeared into her fur. "I much prefer our party. Far less talking…"

Dot and Ethel scuttled out, leaving the room sitting in wary silence. Jessie touched Veronica's rigid back while Julia took her turn to throw back some champagne. The wheels were already in motion, and the night was about to turn.

To Julia's horror, Veronica crossed the room and didn't stop until she was toe-to-toe with her brother; this wasn't part of the plan. Julia, Jessie, and Barker hurried to catch up.

"What a *thoughtful* toast, Gregory," she remarked, subdued fury simmering beneath her even tone. "Which one of your speechwriters wrote that for you? If you have any left now that you've resigned."

"Soon to be reinstated, I'm sure."

"I'm sure." She rose her glass to him. "And since we're reminiscing about absent family, please allow me to return the sentiment…"

Veronica swivelled to face the room. "Another toast to my dear brother, Sebastian Morgan. A caring, principled man struck down too soon by unconscionable cruelty…" As rattled guests lifted their glasses, Veronica speared Harold with a molten glare. "To greed's innocent victim, felled by the hands of..." With poisonous precision, she adjusted her aim, glass held aloft. "...*You*, Uncle, dearest."

Confusion and disbelief rippled around the room as all eyes swung Harold's way. The bulky man tugged at his collar, sweat beading his ruddy forehead. His moustache danced as he buried his face behind his pint.

"This is meant to be a party, isn't it? Band, whip up a song?" A nervous chuckle escaped his lips, but the band remained silent. "Had one too many of glasses of champagne, I'd say."

Jessie stepped forward, reaching into her leather jacket. She pulled out a metal licence plate and tossed it at Harold's feet. By the time it clattered to a stop, Harold had finished his pint.

"The licence plate for Sebastian's car," Veronica said.

"Found on your wall," Jessie added. "Displayed like a trophy."

"You were seen 'fixing' his car the night Sebastian vanished," Barker called, looking back at Arnold, hiding behind his champagne.

"Did Vincent pay you to eliminate the threat to his precious Wellington Village plans?" Julia asked, taking her turn to glance at Gwen, busy with her freshly manicured nails. "Or did you not need the order? You wanted that farmland from Sebastian, so you had somewhere to start your business. But Sebastian wouldn't sell to you."

"Greg, on the other hand," Veronica picked back up, toasting at her brother again. "Greg would have sold anything if it gave him the money to get him off that farm. To anyone. Just so happened that you really wanted that farm, Uncle. Always did resent grandad for leaving it to the younger brother, didn't you?"

Harold said nothing, staring at one spot on the floor.

"That's why Martha is currently in intensive care, isn't it?" Jessie accused. "After all these years, she figured it out. She saw that licence plate on the wall, and she put the pieces together. Her father killed Sebastian, but rather than go to the police, she made the mistake of going to the one man she blindly trusted..." Jessie joined Veronica in staring at Greg. "She went to see her dear cousin, who she grew up with, who couldn't possibly do any wrong. And she told you her theory, and what did you do? You set your Pitbull on her."

Greg turned, his eyes widening as he noticed Six leaning against the bar for the first time. The man's expression didn't change, but Greg took several steps away.

"What *utter* nonsense!" Harold erupted, pleading with the sparse room. "My daughter crashed because she wasn't a great driver. And I'll hear no more foolishness about Seb or that old car of his. Why speak ill of the dead, eh?" He attempted an extravagant bow towards Veronica. "My dearest niece, shouldn't this be a night of celebration? Leave the past well enough alone, eh?"

"But it's true, Uncle," Veronica said. "That night when you were fixing Martha's bike, you looked me in the eye and told me you didn't know where Seb was, the parts of his car scattered all around."

Gwen rose from her chair, nodding with a wagging finger. "Don't think I've forgotten your mechanic's chop shop. Stripping cars and selling them for parts was what you were best known for before Vincent legitimised you."

"Admit it, Harold," Julia said. "You cut your nephew's brakes outside Wellington Manor, and then you waited for him to crash."

"And Vincent had the tree removed to hide the evidence," Arnold spoke up for the first time. "And I wish I hadn't stood by and watched. It *was* you, Harold. I've known it for forty years."

"Me too," Gwen confirmed.

"I only wish *I* had," Veronica said, glaring at her uncle with a tilted head. "I should have known. Greg ran off, but you? You didn't even join the searches, you just got on with taking over the farm, knowing you'd got away with murder."

Harold shook his head in frantic denial against the circle of accusations. When he replied at last, his voice was scarcely a whisper. "It was never meant to end that way. Just wanted to give him a scare... make him think Vincent was out to get him for real... I thought if I..." Harold lifted pleading hands. "If I'd known the road was as icy as it was that night, I would never... I didn't think he'd die. I was going to make him the offer to sell to me once he recovered. He didn't *want* that farm. He didn't care about using it..."

He sank to his knees, hands clasped towards Veronica. "You had a good life, Veronica. You were a teacher, and now an editor. And Greg went into politics. Sebastian was... he was a waster... I..." His gaze swung Greg's way, seeking approval that wasn't granted. Greg had watched the scene unfold with detached disinterest, staring into his champagne. "I was the eldest. That farm should have gone to me. Your father knew it. Sebastian knew it..."

The doors opened and DI Moyes made her entrance with an entourage of officers, and Julia couldn't wait to see the cuffs around Harold's wrists. His excuses fell on deaf ear, forty years of rationalisations only making the pain in Veronica's eyes grow more.

"This isn't right," Harold bemoaned as he was pinned to the cleared buffet table. "It's been forty years."

"Justice, no matter how late," Julia found herself saying. "Now Sebastian can rest."

"Like *heck* he can!" Harold cried as they pulled him to his feet. "If I go down, I'm not letting you get away with this, Greggory." He swivelled to impale Veronica with a triumphant sneer. "All these years, you might not have suspected me, but you were right to suspect Greggory. Go on then, lad. Tell them. Tell your sister how I didn't bury that body alone."

All eyes swung Greg's way in dawning horror as the depth of his deception sank in. But Greg merely arched an indulgent brow, shaking his head as if resigned to weathering the outlandish imaginations of misguided souls.

When DI Moyes stepped forward warily, Greg sighed. "Honestly now, this has gone too far. I was released from prison. You're not going to believe the ramblings of a deranged man, are you?"

Jessie folded her arms. "Did you help bury the body?"

Greg emitted a long-suffering sigh. But his nonchalance slipped when Veronica strode right up to him until they were nearly nose-to-nose again. DI Moyes hovered by, holding up a hand to stop her officers swooping in.

"Tell me the truth, Greg," she muttered, barely above a whisper. "If there's a shred of that boy who used to wrap up Narnia books in old scraps of newspaper and make bows out of old bits of string, for once in your life, tell the truth."

Greg held her fiery stare. Something unspoken passed between them—a confirmation from grim memory only they shared—but no confirmation or denial came.

"Well, I believe that's quite enough excitement for one evening..." he announced, straightening his lapels. He turned on his heel and made for the exit while all eyes followed in stunned disbelief.

But Barker and Jessie moved to block his path, and Gwen staggered over on her swan cane too. Greg halted, scanning for an alternative escape route, but Julia stepped in his path, as did Veronica, and she heard Arnold wheel up behind her. James stayed off to the side, watching proceedings like he'd given up entirely.

Outnumbered and outwitted, Greg's composure finally cracked.

"Arrest him," DI Moyes called, clicking her fingers. "Game's over, Greg."

"Arrest me?" he cried, backing towards the buffet, shaking his head. "On what grounds? You have no evidence! You can't prove I dug that grave. You can't—"

"Harold didn't mention that you *dug* the grave," Veronica interrupted.

Greg's jaw flapped as he searched for the right comeback, the right phrases, the right lie... but nothing sprung forward.

"Even if you hadn't just slipped up in front of all of these witnesses," Moyes said, beckoning her officers to get closer. "I had a very enlightening chat with your pal, Six, earlier today. And not just a chat. A signed statement, detailing every pathetic, manipulative, scheming job you employed the Cotswold Crew for, including having Six cut Martha's brakes."

"I... He..." Greg sputtered.

Veronica let out a slow, cold laugh, dropping her head. "Oh, Greg. That's why you go straight to cutting brakes, isn't it? You saw Uncle Harold pull it off so flawlessly... he inspired you to become his little copycat. Your political rival, I can understand, but our own cousin?" She lifted her head with a snarl. "Martha idolised you. How could you?"

With a snarl of rage, he whirled and seized Veronica's shoulders, grappling her back against his chest. She gasped as he yanked a concealed gun from his jacket and pressed the muzzle to her temple. Several guests shrieked and recoiled in terror as Julia's heart stopped all together.

The gun Jessie had found, here in the flesh.

"Tell your officers to stand down!" Greg barked through clenched teeth. "Let me pass, or she dies. I won't go back to prison... you can't make me..."

"Greg..." Julia cried, hands raised as she edged nearer. "Take it easy. This won't help anything..."

"*Shut it!*" Greg snarled, dragging Veronica with him as he edged sideways along the wall. "You have no idea what I'm capable of." His wild stare alighted on Jessie and he beckoned sharply. "You. Veronica's pet... Fetch me your car, there's a good girl. And no tricks."

When Jessie didn't instantly move to obey, Greg jammed the pistol barrel harder against Veronica's skin. Even with her glasses askew, Veronica took deep, slow breaths, eyes already closed.

"Want to test how serious I am?" Greg sneered at Jessie. "Tick tock..."

Exchanging an agonized look with Julia and Barker, Jessie backed away with hands lifted in surrender. Moyes gave her the nod, and Jessie slipped outside, letting in the whispering of the crowd that had formed. Greg resumed edging Veronica towards the exit, his harsh breaths rattling loud in the dead silence. But a few feet from freedom, James planted himself firmly between Greg and the door.

Though James said nothing, his cold stare spoke volumes.

Greg choked a strangled laugh. "Oh my... to think you and I shared a drink only last evening, Jacobson. Can this truly be happening?"

When James still didn't budge, Greg's amusement morphed to impatience.

"She ruined my life, James." His voice dropped to a whisper. "She tried so hard in 1979, and yet I rose. She could have left me alone, but all those articles about me this past year. All those articles about you... all the protests, and the fighting. She's made both of our lives hell with all of her lies."

James exhaled, and still he didn't budge. Outside, a car door slammed, and Greg's impatience grew as he tried to step around James. He moved with him, and Julia couldn't believe what she was witnessing.

"I don't think she ever printed a word that wasn't true, Greg," James said in a calm, measured tone, "and as much as you can convince yourself better than anyone I've ever met, you know deep down she's right about you."

"Suddenly *you're* better than *me*?"

"I never wanted anyone to get hurt, I just..." He looked around the room, though his eyes didn't reach anyone particular. "I just did what I always do. Greg... you *cut* your cousin's brakes... you *buried* your brother..."

With a grand flourish, he spun Veronica away and she landed in a heap on the floor. He aimed the pistol at James instead, finger tightening on the trigger.

"Last warning, Jacobson."

The door opened behind James and Jessie stepped inside. Greg's gun pivoted, freezing Jessie in the doorframe. Julia set off at a run, but firm hands gripped her in place, no idea who they belonged to or why they were trying to stop her.

"Have it your way," Greg said through a snarl.

A deafening shot blasted through the village hall, and with it, Julia's world. The hands sprung free of her and bodies moved in to tackle Greg to the floor. She met Jessie's eyes through her tears, and Jessie looked down as James dropped to the floor in a heap at her feet.

A puddle of crimson pooled around him on the shiny floorboards as time seemed to contract and shrink around Julia. Jessie ran at her, the force of her body crashing into her knocking her back into the present, the blast still ringing through her ears.

Over Jessie's shoulder, she watched dumbfounded as Barker wrenched the gun away while uniformed officers wrestled Greg to the floor.

The crowd outside spilled in, stopping at James' unattended shape, the blood going further and wider as he stared up at the ceiling, gasping with his fingers at his midsection. Sue burst from the crowd and dropped to her knees, barking orders that Julia couldn't quite understand through her ringing ears.

The police dragged Greg away, his mad laugh echoing around the hall as he looked down at his final act of devastation.

It was over, but at what cost?

25

The harsh fluorescent lights of the hospital corridor pierced through Julia's bleary vision as she startled awake. Her neck and shoulders ached, cramped from a night spent slumped in the hard plastic chair outside the intensive care unit. As she blinked away remnants of uneasy dreams of guns and never-ending pools of blood, Barker appeared before her, extending a steaming paper cup.

"Thought you could use this. Vending machine coffee, so you've been warned."

She managed a wispy smile, accepting the coffee. The hot cardboard soothed her palms. "You're a lifesaver. What time is it?"

"Half-six. Will be light in a few hour." He nodded towards the wall of windows giving a muted view of the dark rolling Cotswold fields. The glass held more of Julia's haggard reflection than any glimpse of sky, but the world beyond was brighter than the restless night before.

She gulped half the contents of the cup, and even terrible coffee tasted like heaven after the harrowing events of the endless evening behind them. The gala, Greg's unveiling, that awful confrontation, Veronica held at gunpoint...

Julia shuddered. "Where's Jessie? Was she here all night too?"

"Popped out an hour or so ago to see Dante," he said. "After the police took her very long statement, the last place she wanted to be was a hospital."

Julia exhaled in relief. "You think she'll be alright?"

"Our Jessie is a tough cookie." Barker gave her arm a supportive squeeze. "The worst behind us now. Greg and Harold are in custody for Sebastian's murder, regardless of who cut the brakes. And even if James beats his injury..." His hand gestures conveyed dubious prospects. "Well, I doubt he'll be the same man again."

"Oh, Barker." Julia rubbed her eyes, yesterday's mascara from the party crusting her lashes. "What a night..."

"What a night indeed, my love." He pulled her

close. "We're all okay."

She peered through the small window of the door separating them from the intensive care unit. Various monitors issued muted beeps and pings marking James' tenuous hold on life after Greg's enraged bullet ripped through his abdomen. By some miracle, the surgeons had managed to remove the bullet.

Barker nudged her arm, interrupting her grim study of the ailing man who'd caused their village such grief and yet had sacrificed himself in the final moments. Hurried footsteps echoed from around the far corner and Richie Jacobson hurried towards them.

"Hospital just called me," he rasped. He sucked in an uneven breath, raking a hand through his dishevelled hair. "Said Dad's conscious again. Said he asked for me... I... Was it as bad as people are saying?" He searched Julia's face. "The wound? The blood..."

"No," Julia heard the lie in her voice, and so did Richie, given the pursing of his lips. "Yes, it was. He stepped in front the gun. He stopped my daughter from being killed by that madman. That's why I'm here. I can't leave until I've thanked him."

"Will you come with me?" Richie asked, staring at the door. "I don't think I can do this on my own."

Julia handed her coffee to Barker and pushed herself up. Holding the door open for Richie, she nodded in with a smile before following him. The door closed behind them, the hospital becoming even quieter.

"You know, when Mum was shot last summer, that was the best thing to happen to her," he whispered. "Said it reset her whole mindset, being that close to death. But knowing Dad…" His mouth twisted into a strained laugh. "Reckon this might just make him more unbearable."

"I think it'll change him," Julia said. "Doesn't have to be for the worse. The world acts in mysterious ways." She inhaled, picking up the faintest whiff of that sweet scent again. "And so do people. Thank you for those donations, Richie. We couldn't have fought half as hard without them."

"Oh, I didn't—"

"Your aftershave made it onto an envelope," she said, digging into her pocket to pull out a napkin. "And Jessie gave me this. 'For emergency martinis.'" From the other pocket, one of the envelopes. "'For the cause.' 'For' is the same both times, see?"

Richie's cheeks flushed pink.

"Busted," he admitted, rubbing the back of his neck. "Couldn't stand by and do nothing, you know? And I had more of my dad's 'sorry I missed your birthday again' jewellery than I knew what to do with, and he has expensive taste. Only had to sell a few bits."

"It made all the difference."

He exhaled heavily, like a weight lifting from his shoulders. "I've fallen in love with this village. The people, the charm... it's so warm and welcoming. Even when people were boycotting my bar, they were always so polite about it."

"Even my gran and Ethel?"

"Okay, maybe not *them*." He laughed. "Makes me wonder if I could ever find somewhere so nice again. Who'll want me sticking around after all Dad's done? Can't imagine anyone would be too keen to have a Jacobson lurking about."

Julia touched his arm gently. "In my experience, Richie, Peridale is the perfect place for second chances. Don't pack your bags just yet."

Richie's lips quirked in a ghost of a smile as they reached the door to his father's private room. Julia nudged him towards the door, and after a moment to compose himself with a breath, Richie disappeared inside. Julia sunk into another chair, giving father and son their privacy.

She didn't mean to, but her heavy lids clamped shut once more. Richie shook her awake, and nodded that it was her turn. She pushed into the room, not knowing what to expect.

Propped up in bed, James eyes remained closed, though constant wincing exposed his excruciating discomfort. Various tubes and wires tangled the bedrails like metallic cobwebs. Even ventilated and immobilized, the man inflicted apprehension within her. His exploits had very nearly cost innocent lives. Perhaps even her family's entire future.

And yet by taking Greg's bullet, he had saved Jessie's life. Who knew how many others might have been caught in the crosshairs during Greg's crazed escape?

"How are you feeling?" she asked, hovering at his bedside.

James parted cracked lips. "Spectacular."

His raw tone belied the sarcastic quip, but gallows humour seemed fitting from him. Julia clasped his hand where it lay limp atop the sheets. His usual domineering grip was absent.

"I want to thank you again for what you did. Pulling Jessie from the road, and then stepping in front of that bullet..." Julia shook her head. "You didn't hesitate either time."

He blinked slowly, rather harmless without his usual imposing stare. "What anyone would do."

Julia gave his hand a light, significant clasp. "Like I said last time, it wasn't anyone. It was *you*. So truly, thank you."

James regarded her a long moment, and when he replied at last, his hushed tone resonated with poignant sincerity she hadn't conceived possible of him.

"When I saw Greg grab Veronica, it was like a spell broke. How detached from reality I was." He swallowed thickly. "I knew he wasn't a good guy, but I knew I wasn't either. But at the end, it felt like I was staring at a stranger wearing Greg's face."

"I think you saw the real Greg," she said. "And I saw the real James."

Silence hung for a moment before he continued. "Reckon I got rather caught up in rewriting my personal history. Trying to seize the control, the influence. Everything I never had in those tiny flats when I was kid." His lips twisted. "Wanted to leave my mark on the village I grew up in the shadow of. Prove I wasn't just lucky. Keeping winning, again, and again, and again…" His burning enthusiasm gave way to remorse as his eyes found Julia's. "I'm sorry, Julia. I know it changes nothing, but I needed you to hear it."

Julia's throat tightened. "Thank you, James, but you're right. It changes nothing, and it's not an apology I can accept for the whole village. Words only go so far, especially when your actions have done so much harm."

Exhaustion seemed to overtake him then. His eyes sagged shut as laboured breaths hissed through parted lips.

"What do I have to do?"

Julia regarded him seriously. "Take your own advice. Stop winding up the locals." She paused, glad to see something of a smile on his sagging face. "Call off the diggers and let the Howarth Estate become yet another failed development project lost on the winds of time. If you truly want Peridale to become your home, then leave it be. Leave the village in peace, and the people will do the same to you."

"That simple?"

"Always was." She exhaled, feeling the weight of months of tensions easing. "People have short memories, even if they pretend otherwise."

James nodded weakly, seeming to accept her words despite their binding finality.

"What will you do with that field now?" Julia asked.

"Turns out it might not *technically* be mine after all." He let out a dry chuckle. "Reckon your stepmother could be receiving a visit from my lawyers soon enough about that. She was very insistent at the party that she was a descendant of Duncan Howarth?"

"Seems that way."

"She's the last person I'd have expected," he said, before adding, "No offence."

His attempt at humour landed flat in the stark hospital room, but Julia appreciated the sentiment behind it. Extending such an olive branch would have been unthinkable days ago. James' lids started to close and she let go of his hand. She shifted to leave but James stirred once more, cracking his eyes with visible effort.

"The post." Fresh tension mingled with pain washed across his face. "Was there that letter I warned you about?"

"I've not been back to the café since."

"You'll know it when you see it." He grimaced, breaths accelerating as some fresh wave of torment seized him. Julia leaned closer, straining to catch his fading words. "Don't even open it. Just throw it away... not important now."

His lids fell shut, chest heaving with pained effort. She hesitated, wondering if she should summon someone. But the monitors showed no fresh alarms, so she waited quietly until James' ragged breathing eased.

When she felt certain he'd drifted back to much needed rest, she stepped away. Her own exhaustion infused every muscle and joint, but first, a return to the café was in order.

After dropping Barker off at their cottage to relieve Roxy of babysitting duty, Julia walked down to the café as the morning winter sun cast golden rays across Peridale. In the field, Dot, Ethel, and Percy, were commanding their army of volunteers to take their makeshift campsite down tent by tent.

It had bought them a day, and as Julia had suspected, a lot could change in a day.

In the empty café, Julia rifled through the mail. Bills, adverts... and there it was. Just as James predicted. Her fingers tensed, poised to rip the wretched thing to shreds unread. But curiosity steadied her hand. She had to know what James' final scheme entailed before she consigned it to oblivion.

She ripped it open, and after a tense moment, she pulled the contents out. No donation or invite to a glamorous party. The letter detailed plans for a compulsory purchase order for her café directly from Westminster. In the end, all the protests in the world wouldn't have made a difference.

Unlike James, they'd dodged a bullet.

She screwed the letter into a tight ball and flung it into the blender. She pressed the button with relish, watching James' last scheme disintegrate into worthless scraps of pulp. Let him try again if he dared, but she knew he didn't dare.

Peridale had won, and the village would endure—and she pitied the next deep pocketed developer who tried to change that. As she tipped the letter confetti into the bin, she hoped she'd be around to show the next generation a trick or two.

26

The scent of roast turkey and stuffing filled Dot's dining room as the family gathered around the heaped table on Christmas day. Golden fairy lights twinkled amidst fragrant fir garlands decking the mantlepiece and windows. This year, they had more to celebrate than good food and even better company.

Julia settled into her chair with a contented sigh, comforted by the chatter and laughter swirling around her. Jessie recounted the dramatic showdown at the village hall with more humour than the evening held, while Barker and Percy argued good-naturedly about which actor played Poirot best. Even Ethel seemed in high spirits, cackling over a replenished glass of sherry at some story Sue was whispering to her. Veronica gazed out at the swirling snow, a faraway smile touching her lips, though even she seemed the lightest Julia had ever seen her. Dot hurried about refilling drinks, while Brian, Katie, and Neil entertained the kids with their mountain of new toys.

"I still can't believe that field's mine now," Katie said, shaking her head with a giggle. "Me a landowner... again!"

"Typical of a Wellington to land on their feet," Dot said with a roll of her eyes. "But well done, dear. Or is it Howarth now? Oh, I can't keep up."

"Katie Wellington-South-Howarth? It's got a little ring to it."

"Mother, why'd you have to put that idea in her head?" Brian cried as an electronic toy beeped and flashed in his hands, more interested than Vinnie. "What's wrong with Katie South, eh?"

"My names are my story," Katie said.

"Almost wise," Jessie said, raising her glass to Katie. "Triple barrelled? Why not?"

"Why not," Julia agreed. "And I can't think of anyone better suited. You've seen life from every angle. Rich, poor, somewhere in the middle... I think that field is in safe hands."

"I think you're right. My own father..." Katie trailed off, conflict shadowing her face. She worried her lower lip with her teeth. "I want to do proper by

Mr Howarth's legacy. But I haven't the foggiest idea where to start. All my instincts are so very Wellington, and something tells me that's the last thing I should do."

"Why not let the village decide?" Jessie suggested. "Hold a vote? A fair vote. Really make it a community effort?"

Murmurs of agreement circled the table.

"A public garden would be lovely," Percy suggested wistfully. "Somewhere to walk the dogs. Maybe even a little stage for outdoor events."

"I think a market," Dot said. "A nice outdoor market. Nothing too big… just somewhere like the Christmas market, but all year around. Would bring in a good number of tourists, and I know the locals would love it."

"Hasn't been the same since the indoor one burned down in 1969," Ethel agreed. "Perhaps it should be left alone, though? It's a fine field."

"As long as it honours Duncan's final wishes," Barker called above the noise. "Whatever Katie does with it, it should be for the people of Peridale, which is why I vote that you hold a vote. After everything, I think people deserve to have their say."

"Well said!" Neil agreed. "We can hold it at the library, if you want? We hold the local elections sometimes." He quickly added, "I suppose this is a good time to mention that James let me un-resign. He's promised to go back to taking a backseat."

"We'll see how long that lasts," Dot grumbled.

"Not just that," Sue said, pushing her plate away as she dabbed at her mouth. "The money fairy came for us in the end. He's agreed to wipe the loan. Said it was pocket money to him, and as quick as he got us into the mess..." She clicked her fingers. "He got us out of it."

"Oh, to be that rich," Ethel sighed.

"Trust me, you don't want it," Katie said, shaking her head.

As the chatter continued, Julia found herself tuning out as she stared at the portrait of Duncan Howarth still hanging over the fireplace. The wait was over—his dying wishes would finally carry forth into Peridale's future now, only a few generations delayed. She raised her bubbling glass of buck's fizz, and Dot tapped her fork on her glass, directing everyone to Julia.

"To Duncan Howarth," she said. "And new beginnings in Peridale."

"Some peace and quiet too," Dot agreed, raising her glass.

"And new friends," Ethel added, toasting to Dot, Percy, and Veronica.

"To Veronica and I getting our jobs back at the

paper," Jessie announced to gasps, though she'd told Julia two days ago. "And to the increased budget we negotiated for being right all along." She sipped her fizz, and added, "And Dante I making it official."

A chorus of 'aww' rang around the room, darkening Jessie's cheeks a shade, and Julia couldn't have been happier for her daughter, though they still hadn't had the official 'meeting the parents' date yet.

"To my new book finally having a title and *almost* a finished first chapter," Barker said, continuing the toasts. "And Julia and I's third wedding anniversary."

"And what would have been your mother's sixty-eighth birthday," Brain said, sniffing back tears. "Still think about you every day."

"To Pearl," Katie agreed with her glass. "And to the twins, four today also."

"The twins," Sue and Neil chorused.

Veronica cleared her throat as she raised her glass. "To Sebastian. At peace at last." They all echoed the toast, and Veronica's face broke into a wide grin. "And what Jessie said. To us getting our jobs back. We did a bloody *fantastic* job."

Julia couldn't argue, and the latest headline 'PEACE IN PERIDALE AT LEAST' had joined the wall of framed pictures in her café. She toasted to Veronica, and the two women shared a smile. Peace, at last, not just for Sebastian, but for Veronica too. The woman who waited forty years, not just for answers, but for family, and Julia was more than happy to welcome Veronica into the clan with open arms.

∼

The glow from the desk lamp cast long shadows across the basement office, creating a soft halo of light around Barker as he leaned back in his chair on Christmas night. Before him, his laptop screen glowed with the beginnings of a new tale, *The Man in the Field*, a story inspired by the tragic threads of Sebastian's life and untimely death.

His fingers hovered over the keyboard, the characters, and their secrets ready to spill forth, when a soft knock at the door pulled him from the ending of his first chapter. He glanced up to find Katie peering around the unlocked door, an unusual nervousness about her.

"Do you have a minute?" Katie's voice held a tremble, betraying her usual composure. "I promise, I don't have any wax strips this time."

Barker laughed, though his own nerves betrayed him. "Of course, Katie. Come in." He gestured to the chair across from him, closing the laptop with a soft click. "What's on your mind?"

Katie took a seat, her hands fidgeting in her lap.

"It's all this talk of family trees and legacies... and finding out that I'm related to Duncan Howarth. I haven't thought this much about the past in ages, and it's got me thinking about the future too. Not just my future, but Vinnie's... and... I've been thinking..." Her voice dawdled off as she gathered her thoughts. "I don't really know where I come from."

Barker leaned forward, his brow furrowing with concern. "What do you mean?"

"Well, you don't know who your dad is, do you?"

He shifted, shaking his head as he glanced at the picture of his mother in amongst the frames on his desk. Even on her deathbed, she'd made him promise not to go looking for his father.

"I don't," he said.

"Well, I know my father, and that I was born at the manor, but... my birth certificate..." she said, a flush creeping up her neck. "It just lists a 'Mrs Wellington' as my mother, but there's nothing about her—no first name, no records. It's as if she never existed beyond that title. I don't know who she is, and Father would get so angry if I dared ask."

A heavy silence settled between them, filled with the weight of unasked questions and unspoken histories, and Barker's mind went straight to the diary still hidden in the drawer to his left.

"How about this?" she said with a girlish lightness

all of a sudden. "You help me find my mum, and I'll help you find your dad? I know you're a PI and better at this stuff, but I can... help?"

The request hit Barker like a physical blow, stirring up the promise he'd made to his mother—a promise to let sleeping dogs lie. But seeing Katie's hopeful expression, her yearning for a connection, for a family, he found himself nodding despite the guilt that gnawed at his conscience.

"I'll help you, Katie," he said, his voice firm with newfound resolve. "We'll find out where you came from."

A bright smile broke through Katie's apprehension, a spark of excitement at the prospect of finding a living parent, perhaps even a grandmother for little Vinnie. She rose, thanking Barker before slipping out of the office.

Once alone, Barker's hand drifted to the bottom drawer of his desk, pulling it open to reveal the diary of Vincent Wellington that he'd hidden as soon as he'd read the first entry in the office above the salon.

He'd wondered if she'd known the truth, but after her unwitting challenge, he felt the weight of responsibility settle on his shoulders. He opened the diary to the marked page, the words blurring as the implication of what he had to do next sank in.

Katie Wellington wasn't really Katie *Wellington*.

The revelation had rocked him on the first read, but how could he tell her? They weren't just searching for one of her missing parents; they were searching for two.

"'Today is the day that my darling daughter Katie joins the Wellington family,'" Barker read aloud the words of the late Vincent Wellington. "'The adoption process was long and difficult, but at least, it is over...'"

Barker rubbed his temples, the diary lying open like an accusation. He would have to tell her, but the timing and the words escaped him. For now, the diary would stay hidden, the secret safe within these walls until he could find a way to ease Katie into her past.

With a heavy heart, Barker pushed the drawer closed, the click of the latch sounding unusually final. He glanced back at his laptop, the characters in his book paused mid-drama, suspended in a fictional world where he controlled the outcomes. If only real life were so simple.

For now, the mystery of Katie's mother would join the ranks of stories waiting to be told in the quiet of the basement office. And he doubted they'd find his father along the way. It wasn't like he hadn't tried before, but maybe this time...

27

1979

*I*n the small kitchen of the her mother-in-law's cottage, Pearl found solace in writing down her mince pie recipe in her new recipe book, also a gift from her mother-in-law. Dorothy could be sweet when she wanted to be, and the blank book had warmed Pearl's heart more than the flashy jewellery Brian insisted on lavishing upon her. The oven's warmth caressed her face as she opened it to check on the Victoria Sponge cake—a sweet thank you for Dorothy, not just for the recipe book, but for letting them live with her for as long as they had.

As the cake rose, so did Pearl's spirits, lifted by the scent of sugar and vanilla. The kitchen was her sanctuary, a place where worries about Sebastian's whereabouts were exchanged for the certainty of recipes perfected over time.

"Be happy, wherever you are," she murmured, a mantra for her missing friend that she allowed herself to repeat only in these solitary moments.

Once the cake was golden and ready, Pearl snuggled Julia into her pram, and ventured out into the thawing landscape. Their path took them to the playpark beside the police station—mostly empty, save for Vincent Wellington. He was an unlikely figure against the backdrop of swings and slides, his attention tethered to the pages of a small journal he was scribbling in.

Katie, with her tufts of blonde hair peeking out from under a knitted cap, was propped in a stroller, her eyes wide with the newness of the world. Hilary, the housekeeper, hovered nearby, a watchful guardian content with her role.

Pearl drew near, the pram leaving trails in the snow' crust. Vincent's presence, once intimidating, now struck her as oddly vulnerable. She cleared her throat, breaking the silence between them.

"Must be the same age as my little one," she said, nodding towards Katie.

Vincent glanced up, his eyes softening at the sight of his daughter before they shuttered again.

"Hmm," he grumbled, eyes still on his book. "If

you're here to ask about Sebastian again, I—"

"Just wanted to know if you'd changed your mind," she said, nodding at the field by the toy shop.

"Wellington Village is off the cards. Turns out, being a family man requires... adjustments."

A smile tugged at the corner of Pearl's lips, one that carried a sense of shared understanding between two parents in the quiet park.

"Sebastian would have been glad to hear that," she said, allowing herself the brief indulgence of imagining him off on a beach somewhere, protesting something new. "Wherever he is."

Vincent grunted, a dismissal of the topic along with the man it concerned. He scribbled something else in his notebook, then snapped it shut, his face once again an unreadable mask.

"Well, have a nice afternoon," he said, pushing himself up. "Hilary, take Katie back to the manor, I have business to attend to. And draw me a bath, will you? I'm frozen to the bone."

The housekeeper grumbled under her breath as she pushed Katie away, leaving Pearl to wonder what would become of the little girl raised by the housekeeper. Stroking Julia's cheek, she offered a silent promise to always be there.

Leaving the park, she strolled across the village and approached the threshold of their new home, the creak of the gate and the crunch of snow underfoot announcing her return. She paused, smiling at the sight before her.

Brian was locked in a comical battle with an antique wardrobe that seemed to have a personality as stubborn as its new owner. The wardrobe wobbled, its legs flailing in the air like an upturned beetle as Brian grunted and heaved with a theatrically pained expression.

"Need a hand there, or are you just practicing for the village pantomime?" Pearl called out.

Brian stopped mid-shove, looking over the bulky furniture to shoot her a grin. "Ah, my dear, this beastly cupboard is merely receiving the Brian South special treatment," he declared, puffing out his chest with mock bravado. "Rest assured, it shall soon learn its place."

Pearl laughed, shaking her head as she wedged the pram past the chaos and into the kitchen. It was small, but it had counter space, an oven, and would suit her just fine. And Julia liked it, if her peaceful-looking nap was anything to judge.

Returning to her husband, Pearl leaned against the doorframe, arms folded, watching as he resumed his wrestling match. "You do realise that if you break it, we'll have nowhere to store our clothes."

With a dramatic groan, Brian gave one last heave,

and with a thud that shook the tiny cottage, the wardrobe settled into place. He stood back, hands on hips, admiring his handiwork.

"There," he said, turning to Pearl with that boyish, cheeky smile that had first caught her attention. "You doubt my skills, my love. But I am a man of many talents."

"And modesty is clearly not one of them," she said as she ran her hand along the wood grain, admiring the craftsmanship. "It's beautiful, though. Will look lovely in our bedroom, when you manage to wrestle it upstairs."

Brian wrapped his arms around her from behind, resting his chin on her shoulder. "Not as beautiful as you," he murmured, his voice that soft tone she only heard when nobody else was around—*her* Brain. "This is just the start, Pearl. I'll fill this house with everything you've ever wanted."

Pearl leaned back into his embrace, her heart swelling. "You've already given me everything I want," she whispered, turning to face him. "You and Julia are my everything."

Brian's eyes sparkled with mischief. "Everything, huh?" he asked before his expression turned more serious, tender. "How about we add a little more love to this home? Maybe a little brother for Julia?"

Pearl bit her lip, a mixture of anticipation and

nerves fluttering in her stomach. "Let's just settle in first, shall we? Get a few more pieces of furniture, maybe a rug..." She trailed off, meeting his gaze, which was filled with dreams and possibilities. "But maybe... another girl?"

Brian's laughter filled the room, echoing off the bare walls and making the space feel lived in, loved in. "Another girl will be fine by me. But let's make a deal —we fill this house up, with love, with laughter, with children, with memories."

"House?" Pearl shook her head. "*Home.*"

As they stood together in the half-furnished room, the future seemed bright, a blank canvas ready for the vibrant shades of their life together.

28

*I*n the café on the first day of the new year, Julia turned to the wall adorned with photographs. Carefully, she added two more. The first, a black and white image of her mother, Pearl, young and fierce, standing beside Sebastian with signs of protest in their hands. The second, a colourful one, showed Julia herself, side by side with Dot and the others taken at Base Camp Peridale by Jessie for the paper.

As Sue and Jessie stepped into the café, their laughter spilled into the space, a joyful counterpoint to the quiet that had preceded them. They greeted Julia, each with a bright "Happy New Year," the café seemed to breathe a sigh of relief that they'd made it.

Together, they prepared for the day ahead, each

task performed with a lightness borne of the knowledge that they were stepping into a time of peace, however temporary it might be. They chatted about the mundane, the ordinary, the beautifully banal moments of life that Julia had missed amid the clamour of their fight.

As the regulars began to filter in, craving the comfort of their daily routines, Julia took a moment to look around her. The café was more than a business; it was a haven, a community hub, a witness to the lives that intertwined within its walls.

"We've earned this," Julia said to Sue and Jessie when they were behind the counter.

Julia looked at the new photographs again, her resolve solidifying. The people of Peridale might one day forget the details of their struggle, but she would carry the story with her. It would live in every poured coffee, in every slice of cake, in every welcoming smile she offered. It was their legacy, written in the very fabric of the café, indelible and enduring.

And as they served their customers, chatting and laughing in the warm glow of the café, Julia felt the true weight of victory. Not in battles won or lost, but in the normalcy, they had fought to preserve. This, she realised, was the most normal day they'd ever had—and it was perfect.

James Jacobson had stood down.

Greg Morgan was behind bars.

And Peridale could breathe a sigh of relief, finally.

At noon, that calm vanished when her gran breezed through the door, a flurry of excitement in her wake, waving an envelope.

"I've got a surprise, straight from sunny Spain!"

Julia, wiping her hands on her apron, glanced up with a smile, her eyes following Dot as she approached the counter. "What's got you all animated this frosty morning?"

"Oh, it's not just the morning frost that's thawing today!" Dot exclaimed, presenting the envelope with a flourish. "Your dear Great-Auntie Minnie has invited us back to her hotel. Some big relaunch, or so she says. And guess what? She's sent us a *thirteen* tickets!"

"Count me in, and Barker too," Julia said, not even needing to think about it. "A holiday is just what we need."

"Me, Neil, and the twins makes three."

"Of course," Dot replied, making a note "Olivia will need a ticket too."

Ethel, who'd been peering over the rim of her newspaper with an arched eyebrow, finally spoke up, "And what about me? Or am I to be forgotten now that the Greg and James saga has concluded?"

Dot turned to her with a huff of mock indignation. "Forget you? *Never*! I wish..." She winked. "You're part of the gang, Ethel. You're coming, whether you like it or not."

With a satisfied nod, Ethel marked the spot in her newspaper and folded it.

"Um, can I bring my boyfriend?" Jessie asked. "Next best thing to travelling is a holiday, right?"

Dot clapped her hands once, like a conductor calling for attention. "Right, everyone, mark it in your calendars! March will be upon us in no time, and we all *deserve* this holiday. A grand Spanish adventure awaits!"

As the news settled around them, the café seemed to glow a little brighter, the promise of shared laughter and memories-to-be knitting them even closer.

As the door jingled with the arrival of more customers, Julia's gaze swept over her friends and family, her heart full. They had weathered the storm together, and now they would bask in the sun as one.

"So, it's settled then," Julia declared, her voice lifting above the chatter. "We're all going on a holiday, and not a moment too soon!"

And in the cosy café, amidst the clinks of cups and the soft laughter, a sense of anticipation took root, promising new adventures on the horizon.

Thank you for reading, and don't forget to
RATE/REVIEW!

PRE-ORDER Sangria and Secrets! Join Julia and the gang for their return to Spain (a sequel to Cocktails and Cowardice, the 20th book in the series) coming Spring 2024!

Thank you for reading!

DON'T FORGET TO RATE AND REVIEW ON AMAZON

Reviews are more important than ever, so show your support for the series by rating and reviewing the book on Amazon! Reviews are **CRUCIAL** for the longevity of any series, and they're the best way to let authors know you want more! They help us reach more people! I appreciate any feedback, no matter how long or short. It's a great way of letting other cozy mystery fans know what you thought about the book.

Being an independent author means this is my livelihood, and *every review* really does make a **huge difference**. Reviews are the best way to support me so I can continue doing what I love, which is bringing you, the readers, more fun cozy adventures!

WANT TO BE KEPT UP TO DATE WITH AGATHA FROST RELEASES? *SIGN UP THE FREE NEWSLETTER!*

www.AgathaFrost.com

You can also follow **Agatha Frost** across social media. Search 'Agatha Frost' on:

Facebook
Twitter
Goodreads
Instagram

ALSO BY AGATHA FROST

Peridale Cafe

30. Mince Pies and Madness

29. Pumpkins and Peril

28. Eton Mess and Enemies

27. Banana Bread and Betrayal

26. Carrot Cake and Concern

25. Marshmallows and Memories

24. Popcorn and Panic

23. Raspberry Lemonade and Ruin

22. Scones and Scandal

21. Profiteroles and Poison

20. Cocktails and Cowardice

19. Brownies and Bloodshed

18. Cheesecake and Confusion

17. Vegetables and Vengeance

16. Red Velvet and Revenge

15. Wedding Cake and Woes

14. Champagne and Catastrophes

13. Ice Cream and Incidents

12. Blueberry Muffins and Misfortune

11. Cupcakes and Casualties

10. Gingerbread and Ghosts

9. Birthday Cake and Bodies

8. Fruit Cake and Fear

7. Macarons and Mayhem

6. Espresso and Evil

5. Shortbread and Sorrow

4. Chocolate Cake and Chaos

3. Doughnuts and Deception

2. Lemonade and Lies

1. Pancakes and Corpses

Claire's Candles

1. Vanilla Bean Vengeance

2. Black Cherry Betrayal

3. Coconut Milk Casualty

4. Rose Petal Revenge

5. Fresh Linen Fraud

6. Toffee Apple Torment

7. Candy Cane Conspiracies

8. Wildflower Worries

9. Frosted Plum Fears

Other

The Agatha Frost Winter Anthology

Peridale Cafe Book 1-10

Peridale Cafe Book 11-20

Claire's Candles Book 1-3

Printed in Great Britain
by Amazon